The Shade
of My Own Tree

The Shade
of My Own Tree

Sheila Williams

ONE WORLD

BALLANTINE BOOKS • NEW YORK

A One World Book
Published by The Random House Publishing Group

Copyright © 2003 by Sheila Williams

www.ballantinebooks.com/one/

Library of Congress Cataloging-in-Publication Data

Williams, Sheila.
The shade of my own tree / Sheila Williams.—1st ed.
p. cm.
A One World book.
ISBN 0-345-46517-2
1. Women—Appalachian Region—Fiction. 2. Appalachian Region—
Fiction. I. Title.

PS3623.I563S48 2003
813'.6—dc21
2002043652

Cover design by Dreu Pennington-McNeil
Cover illustration by Christopher B. Clarke

Text design by Susan Turner

First Edition: September 2003

147429898

. . . At last I am a woman free!
No more tied to the kitchen . . .
No more bound to the husband
Who thought me less
Than the shade he wove with his hands
No more anger, no more hunger,
I sit now in the shade of my own tree.
Meditating thus, I am happy, I am serene.

SUMANGALAMATA
(6th century B.C.E.)

• • •

. . . if you don't have dreams, you don't have anything.
And I wasn't willing to give mine up and become
poor in spirit.

THE SHADE OF MY OWN TREE

ACKNOWLEDGMENTS

I am learning to sit under the shade of my own tree, but I'll let you in on a secret: I do not sit there alone.

Thanks, as always, to my dedicated agent, Alison Picard, and to my wonderful editor, Shauna Summers. Shauna, good luck to you.

I appreciate the assistance of the dedicated staff of the Kentucky Domestic Violence Association in Frankfort, especially Keely Bradley and Christy Burch, for listening to my questions on this disturbing issue and gently but firmly correcting some of my own misconceptions. My words in this book are inadequate in describing the tenuous nature of the lives of domestic violence survivors, their bravery and strength. These women deserve medals.

Thanks also to Joseph D. Ketner, director of the Rose Museum at Brandeis University, for providing a historical framework for the phenomenal African American artist, Robert S. Duncanson (1821–1872), a man whose work and influence have been largely forgotten in our own time. Joe was kind enough to listen to my hypotheses and provide insights into the times during which Duncanson lived, and into his life and the impact of his work.

Not all guardian angels have wings. Many, many thanks to Lori Bryant-Woolridge for her friendship, patience, and guidance (and willingness to share long-distance telephone costs!) over these past few months—I couldn't have done it without you—and to Silas House, who has been so generous with his support, advice, and encouragement.

Special thanks to my high-school classmate, Claudia Cook Ellington, a talented painter whose "kitchen" studio was the model for Opal's, and to Gayle Harden-Renfro, an inspired fiber artist, who was kind enough to allow me to observe her at work as well as share her observations on her art and work process.

Last, but not least, many thanks to my mother, Myrtle Jones Humphrey, my children, Bethany Smith and Kevin Smith, my sister, Claire Williams, and my husband, Bruce Smith.

The Shade
of My Own Tree

Prologue

I live in a small river town that is nestled in a valley at the northern edge of the Appalachians. It is a place where big-city hustle and provincial gentility are constantly at war. The town is quaint and small but only on the surface. It is a river town. Over the thousands of years these dark waters have flowed past, they have brought pretty much everything in the world with them. The town has seen it all, so it's not surprised by much. And the things that don't quite add up don't have to. The town's charter reveals that it was established in 1792—but its sensibilities are years older than that.

The midwestern temperament ruled where I grew up, which means there wasn't much of a temper at all. *Eccentricity* was just a word in the dictionary. The dispositions, language, food, and, especially, the landscape were even and plain. No hills, no valleys. Even the waterways weren't that deep.

Not like here. There are valleys and gently rolling hills. And those hills turn into mysterious-looking craggy peaks farther south and east in coal country. When the weather changes, the fogs and mists roll in. Rocks and fertile river bottom land, hills and marshes. You can't see around the next bend in the road.

And then, there is the river.

This river is old, deep, wide, and dark. The river has presence. People have lived along its banks for thousands of years, but they still don't really know it. It has a history and is content to keep its own secrets.

Some time ago, a bridge fell and many people died. The divers brought in from the city to retrieve the bodies still have nightmares. They say that there were catfish on the river bottom that were as big as a full-grown man. The old-timers weren't surprised.

It's a small-town population, but it has a sly sophistication. The residents may seem backward and out of things, but that is an inaccurate observation. There is an undercurrent. Like the river, they have been there and done that many times. They can choose to be the way they are. River people are different. They have seen the best and the worst of life and are not surprised by anything in between.

These are tough people, forged by hard times, a fluid landscape, and the constant presence of the river. There has never been the luxury of time to put on airs. You had to take what the river brought you and earn a living, feast or famine, drought or flood. Use what floats by and send the rest on its way.

I came here several years ago after I left my husband. I had a little dream about owning a place of my own where I could be peaceful and think and sit on a porch. And be left alone. I wanted to paint. And create a place where other women like me—throwaway women, I call us, women wounded by life or just plain tired—could come and rest or just catch a breath. It was just a dream.

But if you don't have dreams, you don't have anything. And I wasn't willing to give mine up and become poor in spirit.

So I came to this little river town and ended up staying. The town barely noticed my arrival, but it's not that I was ignored. I'm just not peculiar enough to warrant a mention in the newspaper.

Anyway, the river treats me as if I belong here. And that is enough.

Chapter One

I sit in the shade of my own tree *now*, but it wasn't too long ago, I didn't have a twig, much less a tree to sit under. I was running from a marriage that was no good. It took me fifteen years to take that first step, but once I did, I just kept going. Now, several years have come and gone. Already! Time flies when you're having fun. Or running for your life.

I married my college boyfriend, Ted, when I was twenty-one.

After a few years of marriage, I knew that I had made a terrible mistake.

But once I was in, I didn't know how to get out. It was like being in prison. And I had a life sentence with no chance of parole.

I got three squares a day and had a bed, but that was it. There was hard labor and solitary confinement if I was uncooperative. Or if, as in Ted's words, I acted like a "sassy, smart-mouth bitch."

Even when it got as hot as hell in the summer, I wore long sleeves. My arms were always bruised. One August, I wore turtleneck sweaters to work for two weeks until the marks of Ted's handprints faded where he had tried to choke me.

I know what you're thinking: *She sounds so articulate! She could get a job anywhere. Why didn't she just leave? Why did she stay and put up with that?*

How many times have I asked myself those questions? How many times did *I* beat myself up after Ted beat me up? I'll turn the tables on you. You don't understand what I was dealing with. And for years, I didn't understand, either. By the time I did, it was almost too late.

The slaps, pushes, kicks, and punches didn't start right away of course. The insults, put-downs, scoldings, and verbal abuse began slowly. He started with "constructive criticism." I knew that I was in for it when he said, "Don't take this the wrong way, but . . ." or, "This is for your own good." By the time he finished with me, I felt like I was six inches tall and three years old, standing in the corner for bad behavior.

Ted was charming in college. Smart and handsome, athletic and talented, he played a saxophone that Sonny Rollins would have been jealous of. Everyone loved Ted. Especially women. The cutest girls on campus threw themselves at him. I, on the other hand, was awkward and strange. I liked Bach, the Indian-influenced music of Alice Coltrane, Herbert Marcuse, and *Jane Eyre*. Ted could dance. I had two right feet and that is worse than two left ones. Ted talked and dressed "cool." I didn't.

So when Ted Hearn asked the tall, gangly, studious-looking redbone girl from Ohio with straw-colored hair, braces, and glasses with lenses thicker than bullet-proof glass for a date, everyone was shocked. Especially me. I had never had a boyfriend like Ted before. I was thrilled and proud to be seen with him. I was finally "cool." Ted took care of everything. He was wonderful. He made sure that my friends didn't take advantage of my weakness for loaning out books and albums and helping with term papers. He helped me deal with my mother, who had a tendency to be a little overbearing and critical. Ted helped me with my class schedules; he even started to suggest the subjects for the paintings that I did, because I thought that I was a painter. He was so protective of me. At least, that's what I thought at the time.

By the time we got married, the trap was nearly set. I was already isolated from my friends, who had been cut out of my life by Ted, who wanted only to be with me. He had alienated me from my mother, and my poor easygoing father accepted without question what he interpreted as a natural transition of authority: from father to husband.

Two weeks after our honeymoon, Ted and I moved to Atlanta, where he had taken a job. I was now three states and fourteen hours away from home. I had a new house, a car of my own (that was in Ted's name), and a part-time job. I was pregnant and I didn't know anybody in the big, long state of Georgia, not one soul. By the time our daughter, Imani, was born, the cheese was in the trap.

It started with an argument, I think. I don't remember now what the argument was about. It ended with Ted backhanding me and then apologizing. It happened so fast. And then we made love. And it didn't happen again for six months. I remember saying to myself, *Maybe I imagined that. Maybe it didn't really happen.*

But, of course, it happened again. A push and a shove into the stove. Dinner was late that night. It was early the next night and I was slapped because it was cold. This was before microwaves.

I thought about calling for help. But who was I going to

call? Imani? My friends? I didn't have any friends. The only people I knew were the people Ted knew. And he was very careful to make sure that I didn't get too friendly with anyone. I couldn't call my parents, either. In my family, whining is not allowed. Thanks to Ted, Mother and I were barely speaking. And Dad's gentle nature hid a strong resolve when it came to working out your own issues in a marriage. "If you make your bed too hard," he always said, "be ready to turn over more often." I turned over and over and over.

So I did nothing. The years of my life flew by.

Unlike prison, there was never time off for good behavior, because Ted beat me whether I was "good" or not. What was "good"? He made me feel small.

As the years passed, I became numb. I did not feel at all. The only thing that made me smile was Imani, our daughter. And yet there were days when, even with her, I couldn't remember how. My voice grew softer and quieter and then went silent. I nearly disappeared altogether. Except when I screamed. I had volume control. There was loud. And there was louder. When Ted told me to shut up, I bit through my bottom lip and sent the screams deep inside.

I saw a silly movie once about voodoo and zombies. I watched the campy-looking zombie stagger through the scenes with its black-circled eyes and a blank expression. I could have performed that role myself without makeup, script, or rehearsal. Ted had beaten the humanity out of me.

I did ask for help a few times when I could get up the courage and get past the humiliation.

I just didn't take the advice that I got.

I called a domestic violence hot line. The woman told me to pack up my daughter and leave Ted. Right then. Take only my purse and my keys. They had a shelter on

Peachtree. Leave Ted and do what? I was only working part-time then. Imani was six. What would I do for money? Where would I live? *How* would I live?

Another time, after we moved north, a hospital social worker visited me, uninvited. I had been kept overnight for observation after Ted kicked me in the abdomen and broke a couple of my ribs. She touched one of the dark red roses that Ted had sent me from an expensive florist. I know that she saw the card that read: "I don't know what got into me. I love you so much. I would die if you left me. Ted"

The woman sat down in the chair next to my bed and looked me straight in the eye. She didn't say good morning; she didn't say, "How are you feeling?" She just looked at me without smiling.

"If you don't leave him, *you* will die."

And then, there was the memorable occasion that I talked with Miss Thelma, one of the elders at my church. She clucked her tongue at me.

"Honey, there ain't no problem with that man. Now he's got a good job at the auto plant and he brings home good money. You-all have that nice house over there on the east side and you got your own car. You ain't got nothin' to complain about. What's the matter with you?"

Well, that was no advice at all.

I was afraid to leave Ted. And I was afraid to stay.

I left him four times. And I came back four times. I called the police so often that they knew me by my first name: "Opal, are you going to let us lock him up?"

And I did a few times.

Ted called me from jail: "Are you gonna come and get me out? I'll kick your ass if you don't." Ted wasn't charming anymore.

I pretty much lost everything.

The few friends I'd made stopped calling because I always canceled lunch and girls' night out at the last minute. And I wouldn't return their telephone calls. I didn't want to hear what they were telling me.

I missed the sermons and the music at church that gave me so much comfort. I stopped going to church because I dropped out of the choir. And I dropped out of the choir because I missed too many rehearsals. I missed too many rehearsals because I was ashamed. I didn't want God to see my black eyes, bruises, and swollen lips. I didn't want him to know.

Except for work and the grocery store, I became a recluse. I hardly saw anyone. I learned, well, sort of, what set Ted off. I could walk on eggshells in high heels. I was good. I could sense an electricity in the air; I could tell from the set of his jaw or the look in his eye. Sometimes I could tell whether I was going to be slapped or kicked. Or both. I should have used that ESP on better things.

It's true that you can lead a horse to water, but you can't make it drink. I call it the ruby slippers syndrome: you can wear those shoes all over the place, but until you click your heels together and chant the magic words, nothing will happen.

I eventually made up with my mother and my parents offered me sanctuary. They knew what was going on. But I wouldn't take it.

My brother, JT, threatened to just show up one day with a U-Haul to take me, Imani, and all of our furniture and other belongings away. I refused to go.

Even my cats left. There was a time, some years ago, when Ted would come home after he'd been drinking and pick up one of them and throw him against the wall to see if cats would bounce.

They don't.

You don't have to tell cats anything twice.

By the time Imani was ten, she knew that her mommy and daddy weren't like other mommies and daddies or like the ones that she saw on TV. The households of her friends may have been noisy and hectic, but the muffled sounds of shrieks, screams, and banging furniture were absent. The mothers of her girlfriends didn't have bruises or black eyes. My daughter is a smart kid. She never brought her friends home with her.

And I was stupid and blind enough to believe that because Imani was a child, she didn't notice what was happening in her home.

"Mommy, did Daddy hurt you?"

Imani asked this question again and again over the years until it became more of a statement than an inquiry.

"No," I lied. "Daddy was just a little upset." My eyes were puffy because Daddy was "a little upset." The kitchen chair was a pile of sticks because Daddy was "a little upset."

Who was I kidding?

Certainly not my daughter. I became a "shadow" mommy, there but not there, lurking around the edges of my daughter's life.

Imani left for college when she was eighteen, and she hasn't really been home since. She spent the holidays with my parents. Ted got worse after she left. Once she was gone, there was no more need for me to bite my lip to keep from screaming. There was no one to hear.

And still, I stayed.

I must have been waiting for a sign from God. It finally came.

Ted and I went to Kmart. I think we were looking for a lawn mower or some yard tools or something, I don't really remember now what it was. We didn't find the lawn mower, but we picked up a few other things, moved at a snail's pace through the checkout line, then headed home.

Ted was quiet in the car.

I knew then.

The automatic garage door hadn't finished its descent before he started in on me.

"Think you're pretty slick, don't you?"

My stomach began to churn.

"Ted, what are you talking about?"

His voice got louder and he clenched and unclenched his fists.

"I saw you looking at that man in the white shirt. I saw him looking at you! Who is he?"

The first punch caught me on the back of my head. The second one grazed my right eye. I saw stars and dropped to the floor.

"What man?"

"Bitch! I am tired of this shit! Do you think that you can sneak around on me!"

He kicked me in the ribs and in the stomach. My head was ringing and I remember thinking that now I knew how a football felt. A stupid thought, really, when you're being beaten. But my mind was desperately trying to separate itself from the pain and the fear. I tried to open my eyes and look at Ted as I defended myself. But my left eye was bleary from the tears. And my right eye was swollen shut.

"I don't know who—"

"You're *my* goddamn wife and don't you forget it!" he bellowed as he dragged me up from the floor by the collar of my shirt. "I'll take care of this shit right now!"

He threw me against the wall and stormed off into the family room. I thought for a moment that he was going to get a gun and shoot me, but Ted doesn't have a gun. His fists and feet have always been lethal-enough weapons. I just pressed against the wall where he had thrown me, stuck there like a piece of gum. My legs were so wobbly that I could barely stand up. And my vision was so blurred that I couldn't see to run.

But I saw him approaching, his form dark and ominous. In his hand was a lighted cigarette.

"I'll take care of this right now," he repeated. "Your lover boy will know that you're my wife. And you, you stupid bitch, you'll know, too."

He burned me in three places with that cigarette.

Ted left me in a heap on the floor of the foyer whimpering and moaning, my right eye cut and bleeding, my ribs sore, my kidneys bruised, and my arm and neck burned from the small glowing tip of a cigarette.

He went out to meet some friends for drinks at a sports bar.

I didn't leave him that night.

I didn't even leave him the next night.

To this day, I don't remember a white-shirted man in Kmart who gave a hippy, tired-looking middle-aged woman the eye.

I slept in the same bed with Ted for two more nights.

On the third night, the straw broke the camel's back.

I was brushing my teeth.

It was late and Ted wasn't home yet. I was tired and had to work the next day, but I knew that I would probably be up all night because he would come home drunk and we would fight about God knows what. I turned off the faucet and caught a glimpse of the woman in the mirror.

I didn't know who she was.

I hadn't studied myself in the mirror for years. I usually did just enough to get my hair combed and put my glasses on straight.

My hair was white at the temples and there were pouches under my eyes. My right eye was a mess, completely black-and-blue and still huge. My nose was crooked (it had been broken twice) and there were deep gorges in my cheeks like the Grand Canyon. My complexion was gray. There was a welt on my neck that was several weeks old, but it wasn't healing right. I'd have an ugly scar there no matter what I did.

And there were small circular sores on my arm and neck where Ted had burned me with the cigarette. I had been putting salve on them, but they still looked raw and nasty.

I looked like an old crack head.

I stared at that woman for a long time. And she stared back with sad, tired eyes.

My mind was confused. The Opal that it remembered was a caramel-colored woman with hair the same color and brown eyes. It remembered a woman with dimples in her cheeks when she smiled and a pointed nose and a little more meat on her bones. Where was the woman who liked fusion jazz, Latin American literature, and Egyptian mythology? The one who dreamed of studying art in Paris and living in a loft? What happened to the Opal who wanted to wear a beret on top of her Afro and find out what was so great about *Whistler's Mother*?

"What is this shit?" Ted would ask, looking over my shoulder when I was painting. When he was sober and mean (as opposed to being drunk and mean) he said nothing at all. I'm not sure which was worse.

When Ted began to take out his frustrations on my canvasses, I only painted when he wasn't home, hiding the pieces in the basement behind the furnace. I pulled them out once a week, then once a month, and then I stopped pulling them out at all. As I looked into the eyes of the defeated-looking woman in the mirror, I realized that I hadn't looked at those canvasses in over ten years.

Hey! Didn't you used to be Opal Sullivan? Didn't you used to be her?

I didn't know the woman in the mirror and I wasn't sure that I wanted to. She was the scariest thing I'd seen in years. And she was *me*.

Then I noticed the ugly red burn on my upper arm.

Over the past fifteen or so years, I had been punched, slapped, backhanded, beaten with a belt, and kicked. I had been belittled and ridiculed. I had been "restrained" (a polite word to use when you have been locked in a closet) and almost choked. I had been smacked and pinched.

But I had never been branded.

And that's just what Ted had done. He had branded me just like they used to brand slaves.

What was next? Would he stick pins in my feet? Tie me down and put wet bamboo sticks under my fingernails? Would he kill me?

The woman inside me had an answer to that question. The social worker's words came back: "If you don't leave him, *you* will die."

Ted had his own litany: "If you try to leave me, bitch, I'll fucking kill you."

Well, maybe he would and maybe he wouldn't. I might end up dead.

But I'd be *free*.

The woman in the mirror was so angry that her face almost split open.

I would be a lot of things in this life, but I would be damned in hell if I'd be branded like a steer.

I left with the clothes on my back and my purse.

I wasn't sure what to do next.

My parents lived in Florida, and Pam, the only friend I

had left that Ted hadn't run off, was out of town. I was too embarrassed to call anyone else or go to a neighbor's. With shaking fingers I leafed through the phone book until I found the number that I was looking for.

"Women's Crisis Center, LaDonna speaking."

"I, uh . . . I need a place to stay. Just for a few days."

LaDonna's voice was calm. "What's your name, dear?"

"O-Opal Hearn."

"Are you in a public place, Opal?" she asked.

I told her that I was.

"Is he around?"

"No, no, he's gone. I'm in my car. At a gas station."

"Good. You have transportation. All right, here's what I want you to do. . . ."

The directions were crystal clear. I parked in the small lot behind the innocuous-looking apartment building. A woman holding a flashlight stood in the middle of the lot. She waved me over like she was directing an airplane on landing.

"I'm LaDonna," she said, smiling. "Come on; let's get you settled."

She was petite and wore her waist-length bleached blond hair teased up in a style that I hadn't even seen on a country and western singer in twenty years. At least two layers of makeup covered her fifty-plus-year-old face. She was dressed in blue jeans, cowboy boots, and a fringed Western-style shirt. Her earrings were almost as big as she was. She looked like Dale Evans on acid. But LaDonna wasn't singing "Happy Trails." There was a no-nonsense tone in her voice. This was a woman who was used to giving orders and having them obeyed. A small frown darkened her features. She touched my chin gently and turned my face to the side.

"Has anyone looked at your eye?"

I could barely talk. I shook my head.

She smiled sympathetically and passed me a handful of tissues.

"We'll take care of it," she said confidently. She took me by the arm and led me toward a taupe-colored door that was discreetly set in the recessed entryway. "You don't want to go blind in that eye."

"Opal R. . . . what's the R stand for?" LaDonna asked as she filled out a form.

"Renee," I told her, still blowing my nose.

"Nice name," she commented. "Just sign here."

I scribbled something that looked like my signature.

"I'm going to recommend that you not go to work tomorrow. You need a thorough medical exam. I'll ask Christine, that's the nurse-practitioner, to look at your eye tonight. But you should see a doctor just to make sure it's nothing serious," LaDonna said. "I'll call your supervisor in the morning and—"

"No!" I shouted, suddenly getting my voice back. "No! Please . . . I'll . . . I'll just call in . . . sick or take a vacation day or something." A lump was forming in my throat. I started crying again. "I—I don't want them to know. . . ."

LaDonna's expression was warm, but her words were as sharp as razor blades: "Opal, they know already."

The humiliation and embarrassment swept over me like a tidal wave.

Of course they knew. I have had black eyes and bruises that paint and plaster couldn't cover up. I wanted to crawl under LaDonna's desk and hide.

She smiled and patted me on the arm. "It's a form of denial, Opal; we've all been through it. It's the work-ethic shit. We are raised from the cradle to get over it. Suck it up! Ignore it," she said matter-of-factly. "The son of a bitch that I was married to was six feet, five inches tall and weighed over three hundred pounds. I'm barely five feet tall and weigh one hundred pounds. He threw me against a wall once and cracked my pelvis. I went to work the next day with a cane telling everyone that I was having trouble with my arthritis! Who was I kidding? Only myself."

My ribs hurt when I laughed. So I cried instead.

Christine's fingers were cool and firm. Her blue eyes were nearly unblinking as she listened to my heart and probed my abdomen and back.

"Does this hurt? This?"

I shook my head.

"Let me have a look at that eye again." She turned her head slightly to the left as she studied me. "Good. I don't think anything is broken. Bruised ribs, that's all. I want a specialist to check out your eye, though." She wrote something on a notepad, tore off the top sheet, and handed it to me. "Here's the name of an ophthalmologist. She'll see you without an appointment; just tell her receptionist that you're a client of the Center."

"OK," I said. "Thank you."

"No problem," the nurse replied. "Just be sure that you go see the doctor. You can't take black eyes for granted. I should know. The last one I got nearly blinded me. I'll never be able to see more than shadows out of my right eye."

I must have gasped, because the nurse smiled at me and folded her arms across her chest.

"I know. I don't look like 'the type.'" Christine sighed dramatically, then flashed me an impish grin. "I get that a lot. But there are all types, Opal, and that's what you have to understand. This can happen to anyone. Unfortunately, our society has insulated itself with an antiquated image of a battering husband. They don't all wear T-shirts and dirty blue jeans and guzzle beer all day. They are mayors, ministers, corporate types, and teachers. They are police-men, believe it or not. They are your coworkers and your funeral director. They are everywhere." She bandaged my forehead.

"My boyfriend was a medical student. He came from a 'nice home,' whatever that is. And went to 'nice schools' and lived in an 'upscale neighborhood.'" She paused for a moment and looked at me.

I noticed then that one of her eyes didn't move in sync with the other one.

"He was so 'nice' that he tortured cats and squirrels when he was a kid. I found out later that he had punched his prom date and broke her jaw when he was seventeen. When he grew up, he graduated from small animals and prom dates to girlfriends." She smirked. "And I wanted to be a doctor's wife. Can you imagine?" Then she gave me an engaging grin. "After I spent two weeks in the hospital after he tried to kill me because I was leaving him, I de-cided that I would rather be a doctor myself. I'm going to medical school in the fall."

LaDonna settled me into a small room with three beds.

"We're under capacity tonight, so you'll be on your own. The room across the hall and the room next to yours are occupied, but I don't think you'll be disturbed. Oh, and just ignore any clanging you hear from the basement. We had a broken pipe scare and the maintenance man is fin-ishing up down there."

She set an extra pillow on the bed and patted me on the shoulder.

"Sleep well, Opal. You're safe now."

...

I sat in the corner of the TV room by myself.

The woman in the room next to mine walked in on bare feet and got a Coke out of the vending machine. She nodded at me and padded out. I heard the maintenance man coming up the basement steps with the gait of King Kong. The basement door creaked when it closed and he clomped down the hall and stepped into the TV room, setting his toolbox on the floor. He, too, went to the vending machine to get a can of soda.

"Oh! Excuse me; I didn't know that anyone was in here," he said apologetically when he noticed me.

I turned my face away from his and scooted the chair quickly into a shadow. I wasn't ready to face anyone else with a fat lip and one eye that was swollen and multi-colored.

"It's OK," I told him. "I was just sitting here."

He paused for a moment. "Do you want me to turn on more lights for you?"

I shook my head. "No, thank you."

"Then I'll let you get back to it," he said, giving me a nod and a quick smile. He had a nice face. And then he was gone. I heard his footsteps as he moved down the hall.

I smiled. He was trying to walk quietly on tiptoe in his heavy work boots with his huge feet. He wasn't having much luck with it. He still sounded like King Kong.

It was now after eleven o'clock in the evening. With shaking fingers I smoked a cigarette, something I had not done since college. I still had the jitters. According to LaDonna, the "point of separation," the phrase coined to describe the transitional period when women leave their abusers, is the most dangerous time of your life. I had tensed up my muscles so much that they hurt. My shoulders felt as if they were resting at the bottom of my ears.

I exhaled and blew the smoke into a cloud in front of my face.

Through the window, I watched the lights in the apartment building across the street go out one by one. I tried to imagine the lives behind the drawn shades and closed curtains.

The late-night TV shows were about to come on. Work clothes for the next day were laid out; showers had been taken. People with normal lives checked the locks on the front door before they went to bed. They had walked the dog. They fluffed the pillows and set the alarm clock. People with normal lives clicked off the lamp on the nightstand. People with normal lives.

Normal lives.

What was a normal life?

I was a woman with a college degree, my name on a mortgage, one car note, a Sears bill, and a "good job." Wasn't that "normal"? And here I sat with three cigarette burns, bruised ribs, scratched knuckles, and a swollen eye.

"Sleep well, Opal. You're safe now." LaDonna's words echoed in my head.

For years I slept curled up in a ball on the edge of the bed with one eye open. How in the world had I ever thought that I had a normal life?

I would try to have one now.

That night I stretched out in the little bed and buried my face into the pillow. And slept. Well.

Chapter Two

I thought that when I walked through the doors of the women's shelter I would be able to leave Ted behind, leave that life behind, and salvage something for myself now that Imani was pretty much grown and on her own. I was half-right.

"Leaving him is only part of it," LaDonna told me. "Staying alive long enough to have a life after him is the other part."

"What?" I exclaimed, feeling the cold concrete feeling settle in my stomach again. "I thought that all I had to do was leave!"

LaDonna shook her head. "No. You have to survive."

Ted's message on my voice mail at work hinted at what I would be up against: "If you don't come back, I'll kill you."

There was an ironic twist to that. Even if I stayed he might kill me. But bad choices are better than no choices at all. And freedom beats bondage any day.

I stayed away.

I filed for divorce. Ted countersued. He accused me of

"inhuman treatment" and "mental cruelty." I had a good laugh over that. He claimed that I was "mentally deficient" and needed treatment. He asked for the house, the cars, his 401(k), *my* 401(k), all of the furniture and household property. He probably would have asked for the dog if we'd had one. Surprisingly, for a while at least, the restraining order kept him at bay. The harassing telephone calls stopped and I didn't feel as if I was being followed anymore.

But it was the calm before a storm. Ted was doing his best to leave me with nothing. His lawyers sent over a decree that pretty much gave him everything we had. All I would get out of the deal was the divorce. After weeks of haggling, I was just through.

"I want to be separated from that son of a bitch once and for all. I don't care what the paper says." I tried to snatch the document out of my lawyer's hand. "I'll sign it, lick it, put my fingerprints and footprints on it. I just want my divorce."

My lawyer, George Cox, quickly moved the blue-bound documents out of my reach.

I had been staying with my friend, Pam, and her family, but I couldn't do that forever. I needed to get a place of my own. And I wanted to put Ted behind me. If I could.

George shook his head and pulled off his glasses, probably in an attempt to look more scholarly or judicial or something. It didn't work. In my mind, he still looked like "Georgy Porgy" from the nursery rhyme.

"Opal, you know we are talking about more than pennies. If you give up your rights to his pension and the mutual fund accounts, it's going to take you years to make up that kind of retirement savings."

"Make it stop, George. Let's just get it over with." I could feel my eyes filling with tears.

"OK. Look. You've just gotten out of a bad situation. And I know . . . I know that you want out. But we're only in the beginning phase of this thing. You don't have to make any decisions right this minute. Give yourself some time. Now, so far anyway, he's abiding by the restraining order, but I have to be honest with you: he probably won't continue that forever, so you'll need to be alert. You have the use of your bank accounts, plus you can get your personal possessions out of the house. We'll get the sheriff to escort you." George's eyes were kind behind his thick lenses. "Opal, I want you to get what is fair. What you have earned by being married to that asshole for twenty-plus years."

I stopped sniffling long enough to take in his words.

He was right. I *had* earned a few things in that marriage with Ted. And I had earned them punch by punch.

"One thing, though," I said, my words muffled by the tissue that I was using to blow my nose. "Can I add one thing to the temporary order?"

George's eyebrows raised. "That depends. What do you want to add?"

"I want my name back. I don't want my identity tied up with his anymore. I want to be me again. And I think that taking back my name will help."

George smiled and started writing on his yellow pad again. "Plaintiff requests that she be allowed to regain the use of her maiden name: Sullivan."

The temporary order went in the next day and the judge signed it. Opal Renee Sullivan was born again that day. Not like a river-baptized Christian, but it certainly did feel that way.

Ted called me at work the next week and started cursing at me. So much for the strength of restraining orders.

"Bitch, who do you think you are?"

I was so mad that I forgot to be scared. "Ted," I said, "kiss my high-yalla ass." My coworkers just stared. The "old" Opal would never have said *that*. I knew that it was like throwing gasoline on a campfire, but man, did it feel *good*.

Things would never be the same again.

That evening after dinner, I sat at Pam's kitchen table, sipped coffee, read the classifieds, and thought about who the "new" Opal Sullivan was and what she was going to do next. It had been so long since I had been able to think without fear that even with the shouts and giggles coming from the bathroom where Pam was getting her little ones ready for bed, I felt as if I were sitting alone at the top of a mountain.

I called my family. Mother was so relieved that I had left Ted. She and Dad were after me to come to St. Augustine and live with them.

"Opal, now that you're free of that jerk, you can start living like a normal person." I could hear Mother's concern despite the sharpness of her words.

"He's not harassing you on the job, is he?" my dad's voice piped in on the other extension.

"No, Dad, I have a restraining order. . . ."

"Well." (When Mother says "well" it has two syllables.) "Opal, toilet paper has more lead in it than those damn things," my mother responded. "You need to get a gun. I can show you how to shoot. I used to shoot squirrels when I was a girl."

"Lena, for God's sake!" Dad's aristocratic sensibilities had been wounded. I smiled. He and Mother had been going at it for fifty years. Dad, the child of the black bourgeoisie of New Orleans, was refined and soft-spoken. He was a man of an era long gone, when men tipped hats and didn't spit in front of ladies.

Mother was the opposite. When you put her into her Sunday church suit and pearls with her still nearly black hair pulled up into a French twist, she appeared to be a lady out for afternoon tea. Until she opened her mouth. ArLena Powell was from a "holler" up in the craggy hills of eastern West Virginia that was so small, it didn't have a post office.

"Martin, a pistol is a great equalizer. If she puts some lead in his ass I bet he'll leave her alone." Mother's words were truer than she realized, but now was not the time to raise her blood pressure more.

I left them to it. Besides, I had already had that conversation with my brother, JT, long-distance from Oakland.

"Opie, are you sure that you should stay there? Is it safe?"

"JT, I've made up my mind," I told him. My much taller and larger but younger brother had been acting like my protector ever since he could walk. And, to answer his question, no, it wasn't safe. It would never be safe. I could move to California. But what good would that do if Ted followed me there? Where would I go next? Tahiti?

"What about Imani?" JT asked.

"She's still in India; she won't be back until September. I'll have my own place by then," I told him, hoping that my lack of confidence wasn't transmitting over the telephone lines.

"OK," my brother said in a voice that was sweetly reminiscent of the little boy who had been my shadow over forty years ago. "But you keep in touch, all right? I worry about you."

I finally got a connection to Imani's dorm in a small town outside of New Delhi. The static was so bad that I had to practically push the telephone receiver into my ear in order to make out Imani's words.

"I hear you fine. . . . Momma, can you hear me?"

"Yes, sweetie, I can hear you. Are you all right?"

The static cut off the first part of her reply.

". . . left Daddy! . . . about time! I was afraid that he would kill you, Momma. And I couldn't do anything about it."

"That wasn't going to happen," I lied to her. Of course, it could have happened. It had almost happened many times and we both knew it.

"Don't worry about me, Imani. Everything will be fine. I'm staying with Pam, Ron, and the boys, but I am looking for a house or apartment. I'll be moved in and situated by the time you come back in the fall."

"Momma, do you want me to come home now?"

"Absolutely not! You stay there and finish your classes."

The static must have drowned out my answer.

"What? Momma, I can't hear you!"

I screamed out again that she should stay where she was and that I would be all right.

This time she did hear me. And I heard her.

". . . love you, Momma. A bunch."

It was what we had always said to each other ever since she was little.

"I love you, Imani."

"How much, Mommy?"

"A bunch."

I had to wipe my eyes after I clicked off the phone. Throughout the years of terror and numbness, I had forgotten how much I had been loved. And how much I loved in return.

I turned back to the real estate classifieds. Next Friday afternoon I was supposed to pick up my things from the house. Ted had been ordered to stay away, and the court had arranged for a sheriff to escort me. It all sounded very safe and dramatic. And it made me nervous. What made me more nervous was the fact that I didn't have a place to live. I took the pink highlighter and went to work. A half hour later, when Pam joined me, the newspaper was covered with pink marks. But I was discouraged. Nothing appealed to me or to my bank account.

I didn't know whether I needed to look close by or far away. Change my name, get another job? It all sounded as if I were joining the Federal Witness Protection Program. It didn't sound like much of a life to me.

"Having any luck?" she asked.

"Nope. Either too far away, too expensive, or too small."

Pam poured some coffee into her cream. "What are you looking for? An apartment? What about a condo or a small house? That might give you a little more room and privacy. The walls of most apartments are pretty thin. You can hear everything that's going on with your neighbors. It gets old after a while."

"Yeah, I know, but I just don't think that I can afford to buy anything right now. Ted's screwed up his credit and mine, too. And a house . . . well, that's probably out of the question."

Pam frowned and then reached for the huge backpack that she called her purse. "You know," the sound of rummaging interrupted her train of thought, "I met a woman at Tré's school a few weeks ago. A realtor. She gave a seminar on women and finance. Investments, insurance, stuff like that. She really had it going on—ha! Here it is!"

The card was red, white, and blue and had a wad of pink bubble gum stuck on the back, but I could read the name.

"Bette Smith . . . Realtor Extraordinaire . . ." There was a tiny picture on the card of a woman with daffodil-colored hair and bright red lips. Hmmm. . . .

Pam giggled and handed me a butter knife so that I could scrape off the gum.

"Sorry about that. . . . The boys have been in my purse again." Noticing my expression as I gazed at the rather flamboyant-looking woman, she smiled. "I know what you're thinking, and she's even more extraordinary-looking in person. She started the lecture with some background on herself. Her family was dirt-poor and moved around a lot. West Virginia, Georgia, Kentucky, places like that. She said that she was the first person in her family to graduate from high school. That really impressed me. Maybe she could help you find something that you can afford."

I wanted a haven, a sanctuary.

What was the going price for paradise these days?

I called Bette Smith, the extraordinary realtor with the very ordinary name, the next day and arranged to meet with her.

Pam was right about one thing.

Bette was quite extraordinary.

She picked me up in a fire engine red Cadillac with white leather seats and zebra-striped faux-fur floor mats. The vanity license plate read: BETTE. She was wearing a red knit suit (very expensive; I recognized the designer from the buttons), two strands of quarter-sized pearls, a diamond bezeled watch, and a pair of three-inch-high mules that she walked in as if they were sneakers. She caught me staring and grinned, her perfectly made-up face beaming with pride.

"Manolo Blahnik," she said. "I have ten pairs of these things. They're more comfortable than my house slippers."

I had to wonder what kind of house slippers *she* wore.

Her hair was no longer the color of daffodils. She'd just had it colored, she told me, because she needed a change.

It was now the color of ripe cantaloupe. I hope that's what she wanted. Her cell phone was attached via an earpiece, and a red beeper was clipped to her purse strap. The Louis Vuitton bag that she carried was larger than my suitcase.

"How are you!" she exclaimed in a crisp, sharp voice that blended the best elements of West Virginia, eastern Kentucky, and a little taste of northern Tennessee into one. "I'm Bette Smith!" What she really said was, "Ahm Bettay Smith!"

Her beautifully manicured fingers clasped mine in a warm handshake and her green eyes twinkled. "Now, I took the liberty of running some numbers so that I can prequalify you for a house of your own. You don't need to be payin' out rent money when you can have a deed in your hand."

I slid across the smooth white leather and sank into the plush seat. Wonderful.

"Um, Bette." My nose began to itch. I am allergic to some perfumes and I've found that a little bit of L'air du Temps goes a long way. "I, uh, think perhaps a lease option deal might work better for me. I don't have much of a down payment. Prob'bly won't until my divorce goes through." I was being optimistic. I'd be lucky to get out of this soup with my life, much less extra cash.

The Cadillac moved like a panther on tiptoe through the streets. She raised her bejeweled hand with its scarlet-tipped fingertips to silence me.

"I know my business, hon," she said in a tone that would quiet a crowd at a football game on a Sunday afternoon. "You may not know this, but I'm called the 'James Brown' of the real estate business. I am the hardest-workin' realtor in four counties. If I can't get you into a house, no one can!"

It was a statement of fact, not a sales pitch.

Her sideways glance at me was steely and determined.
I had seen that look before—on my mother. And I knew
that Bette Smith had pulled herself up over thirty years
from nothing to red Cadillacs and designer suits. This was
not a woman to mess around with.

"OK," I said, acquiescing. "I am in your hands."

She patted me gently on the arm. "That's a girl. I will
not accept 'no' as an answer. My first husband says that I
am a force of nature."

I heard that.

She stuck a folder in my face. "Now, inside you'll find
your financial profile, the prequalification amount, a list
of recommended lenders that I've personally worked with,
and, most importantly, the profiles of fifteen properties,
including the five that we're going to look at tonight."

She had outlined and inventoried my entire financial
life in less than five hours! The only thing she left out was
my shoe size.

"I just called you today at one! How on earth did you
get all this done in so short a time?"

"Hon, I *told* you. I'm the hardest-working woman in the
real estate business!"

For three evenings straight, I looked at houses and con-
dos. I discussed lease options, buy-back options, land contracts, lease-purchase programs, and mortgage rates. My
head was spinning with all the details.

But nothing appealed to me in an emotional way. I was
trying to find that something special. Maybe it was going
to take longer than I thought. Even with the prequalifica-
tions, preapprovals, low interest rates, and budget utility
plans, I wasn't comfortable with the numbers that were
thrown at me. And I wasn't ready to go out on a limb where
money was concerned. The restraining order was holding

so far, but as LaDonna had warned me (and my mother had confirmed), it was only as binding as Ted thought it was. I felt as if I were watching granules flow through an hourglass. How long before Ted began a reign of terror and I had to escape again? Maybe across-country? I wrestled with the rent versus buy scenarios until my head hurt. Finally, as we started toward the fifteenth house (and this was only the third day of looking) I made up my mind.

"Bette, this is it. If I don't like this one, I'll just shelve the house hunting for a year or two and get an apartment over at Hill Run." I could rent on a month-to-month arrangement there. That way, if I had to leave again in the middle of the night, I wouldn't be left tied up financially.

"Hill Run!" Bette's yelp was more like "He-yull Runn!"
"Opal, you simply cannot equate rentin' with buyin'; they just don't match up. Now let's stop here and look at this house, and if you don't like it, we'll go over to the Starbucks and get a cup of coffee and I'll see what else I can pull outa my inventory. I hate to see an independent woman rentin'."

Seven-forty South Mitchell was a Victorian-era Italianate painted light gray with purple, charcoal, and burgundy trim accents. The little house had been completely renovated, and the current owner had done an exquisite job of decorating. The period furniture in the cozy parlor was picture perfect, the dining room was stately, and the upstairs "morning room" was something out of an Edwardian novel. There was just one little problem.

The house was haunted.

I wandered up to the third floor while Bette checked in at her office. After seeing the lavish furnishings on the first and second floors, I was a little surprised to find the third floor completely finished but nearly empty. There were a few boxes stashed in a corner—CHRISTMAS marked prominently on one of them—and an old bureau that looked ripe for refinishing. That was it.

Here on the top floor of the house, there wasn't any air-conditioning and the windows were closed, so it was stuffy and the air was stale. I walked over to the front window and looked out, not thinking of anything more particular than the fact that we were probably in for another hot summer if this early May heat kept up.

I thought I heard something behind me. Thinking that Bette had decided to risk climbing the steep narrow stairs in her high heels, I turned and caught a glimpse of something out of the corner of my eye. But there wasn't anything there, not even a bug. My stomach muscles tensed. I blinked. *Something* had floated past me. Where was it? *What* was it?

Then the room got cold. Freezing, bone-chilling, west wind–blowing cold.

I stood completely still. My fingers went numb and I shivered. My nose started to run.

And so did I.

All the way down two flights of stairs and out the front door.

I stood in the beautiful little English garden, rubbing my arms. Bette followed me, her stiletto heels clicking on the old slate sidewalk.

"You didn't like the house?" She dropped the cell phone into her huge purse and returned the key to the lockbox.

"I, uh . . . No. That house . . . I didn't get a good feeling about that house," I stammered.

Bette looked at me for a second, then sighed. "Let me guess," she said, her lips hardening into a straight line. "You think you saw somethin' on the third floor."

I cocked my head sideways. "Yes."

"Then the room got cold?"

"Yes. Do you know something about that?"

"Hold on a moment." Bette dug the phone out of her purse and tapped out a number with the tip of one long scarlet nail.

"Deb?" she barked into the tiny phone with the warmth of a marine drill sergeant. "I thought you told me that Father McEachern did the exorcism last week."

Exorcism?

"Ah see. Well, that doesn't hold any water with me, Deb. If you want me to sell this house, then you'll have to get the spirits out. Nobody wants a house that has non-payin' guests even if they don't eat anything."

I wanted to hear the other side of this conversation.

"Exorcism? Spirits?"

Bette looked at me as if I had just landed from the moon. "Now, Opal, in an area like this, with all these old homes, they've seen a lot. Folks have been born, died, killed, burned up, and anything else you can think of in the two hundred years that these structures have been standing. You're bound to have one or two with resident ghosts that don't want to leave. Believe me, darlin', before I sell any of these old homes, I always have Father McEachern do a 'spirit sweep.' "

"A spirit sweep?"

"Of course! I can't very well go round sellin' haunted houses to people!"

She was right about that.

"What happened here exactly?" I asked.

Bette popped on her Chanel sunglasses and grabbed me by the elbow. I never saw anyone move so fast in high heels.

"Believe me, hon, you don't want to know."

Chapter Three

Historic Home for lease or sale.
Needs TLC. B&B license.
1010 Burning Church Road, Prestonn.
Call Bette Smith, Realtor Extraordinaire.

There were five telephone numbers listed: Betty's office, home office, home, cell phone, and pager. Her E-mail address was bettesmith@bette.com. Bette is an original.

It was 7:30 in the morning and the office was still quiet. I'd come to work early that day to get caught up with some paperwork before the phone calls, E-mails, faxes, and meetings started. I also wanted to use the time to check the classifieds in case there was an interesting apartment or house ad that I could check on. Not that Bette would ever miss anything. The Burning Church Road listing caught me by surprise.

At the dawn of time, the area that is now Prestonn was a summer settlement for hunting parties of the Cherokee.

The river bottom land was rich and the surrounding areas were teeming with game, including bison if I remember my local history. The white man came in the early 1700s and settled there, too. The town charter says "1792," but it was probably settled much earlier than that. The founding father's last name was Preston, but sometime during the past three hundred years the extra *n* was added. No one knows why.

In the early 1800s, Prestonn had a great reputation as a lawless river town complete with gambling, houses of "ill repute," opium dens, and life-or-death card games. There were so many duels and gunfights that the sheriff formed a guild with the sole purpose of picking up bodies and cleaning up the streets. There were thirty saloons and two churches for the three thousand semipermanent residents.

In the middle 1800s, the town ran off the undesirable elements and transformed itself into a retreat destination for the wealthy who built palatial summer homes along the river road. In the 1960s, Prestonn fell into an economic slump because it didn't have a base of manufacturing or service industries. Many of the grand residences fell into disrepair and decay.

The late 1980s brought another transformation when a historic district designation was granted and the old river town got a facelift. The Victorian and pre-Victorian era houses were restored and rehabilitated. Antique shops, boutiques, restaurants, and trendy bistros moved onto the main drag and the tax coffers bulged. Prestonn was born again.

I hadn't considered Prestonn. It was close enough and yet far away. Folks didn't pass through it to get to the town I lived in now, and unless you were going there for a reason, it was not on the way to anywhere. The main bridge to the big city was three miles downriver. Would I be safe in Prestonn? Would I be happy there?

I smelled a bargain (I love bargains) and punched out Bette's home number, then her home office number, then her office number, *then* her cell number. She was at the gym working out with the personal trainer she'd told me about, a twenty-something named Charles. Yeah, right.

"Hi, hon!" her voice came through even over the sound of the music accompanying her "workout." She was breathing hard. I would have given anything to see if she was really on that treadmill.

"Bette, you've been holding out on me," I started. "You didn't tell me that you had anything on Burning Church Road."

The sound of Meredith Wilson's "Seventy-six Trombones" came blaring over the receiver.

"Hold on; I can't hear you. Just a minute." There was rustling in the background. Then the music stopped. "Now. What's this about Brendan Woods?"

"No, Burning Church. What about your listing on Burning Church Road?"

"Opal, you don't want that house! It's too big, it's too far away, it's too damn old, *and* it's a dump! Nothin's been done to that barn since Caroline Xavier was in pigtails, and she lived to be over ninety!"

"I'm not opposed to using a little elbow grease," I said eagerly. Especially if the price was right. I had always loved old houses. Besides, a big old house would have a room that I could fix up for my studio. I could start painting again. Not to mention room for other throwaway women who might need a place to stay for a couple of nights. I had decided that if I got out of my situation, I would help other women get out of theirs.

"Elbow grease! You won't have any elbows left when you get finished scubbin', tearin' down, wipin' up, and plasterin' that pit! Besides—"

"How much, Bette?" I interrupted her. I had better get that question answered before I argued with her any further. When she told me, I was surprised.

"It's not haunted, is it?"

Her laughter trickled through the phone line. "No, sugar. I went there myself right after Miss Caroline died to make sure that she made it over to the other side OK. She could be a contrary old woman. The house seemed fine to me, but I had Father McEachern do a spirit sweep anyway."

What a relief.

"Opal. It's pretty antebellum, especially the kitchen. I don't think that house has been touched since before Sherman went through Kentucky."

"Bette, Sherman didn't go through Kentucky."

"You know what I mean."

I made an appointment to see the house. How bad could it be?

It was awful.

The house was an Italianate painted a soft yellow color that reminded me of lemon custard. Part of the porch was falling down. Correction. Part of the porch had fallen down. On one side of the house, there wasn't enough wood left to build a fire. The electrical system was new and all of the lights worked. The plumbing was old. Really old. When I flushed the toilet it sounded like an elephant with gas.

As I looked at the slimy water, I thought I saw something *move*. I blinked. The water was still. Sort of. I flew out of the bathroom on Bette's heels.

There were, literally, bats in the belfry, and an owl was living in the attic of the coach house. When Bette clicked the light on in the basement, I saw something small, dark, and furry scurrying into the shadows. I froze at the top of the stairs. Bette was already halfway down the steps.

"Bette, what was that?" I asked.

"Just one of those fuzzy brown things," she answered calmly. "Nothin' to worry about."

Fuzzy brown things. Well, that was helpful. I'd look them up in the encyclopedia.

"OK . . ." I said as I took the stairs very, very slowly. "How many legs do they have?"

"Five or six," was the reply.

"Oh, that's all right then," I commented sarcastically. "Spiders have eight."

Bette rolled her eyes at me.

"Coming!" I yelled back.

The basement was dark and scary and housed a furnace the size of Montana. The walls were stone, and several sections appeared to have been bricked over sometime in the Jurassic Age. Human torture probably took place here in the Dark Ages.

Bette was wrong about the kitchen. It wasn't antebellum. It was prehistoric. The walls were water-stained and the refrigerator was a relic from the 1940s. As I glanced at the ancient sink and the huge stove, I imagined a family of Neanderthals gathered around waiting for the mammoth roast to get done.

The second-floor commode backed up with greenish burgundy-colored water and a smell that could fry your liver. Bette wasn't concerned.

"I have a plumber who'll fix you right up," she said brightly, making a note on her pad.

I was skeptical.

"Unless he's going to take out the entire sewer line, I don't think it will do much good."

Bette saw my expression and chuckled. "I told you that it was a dump."

But the house did have its good points.

The rooms were spacious and the tall windows let the sunlight shine through in all of the right places. The wallpaper, where there was any, was peeling, and the fireplaces were small and narrow. The hardwood floors were original, and Miss Xavier had kept them in perfect shape. The thin slats of wood gleamed in the warm sunlight, highlighting the rich hazel color of the grain. Where the kitchen made me anxious, the parlor won me over. It was small but had an alcove with three windows on each side that faced the street. I could picture a tall Christmas tree standing there during the holidays and a little couch nestled in for reading during the rest of the year.

The dining room was grand.

I had never had a "dining room" before. The house that I owned with Ted had one big room that combined a dining room, living room, and family room together.

The dining room in the yellow house was for "dining." In my daydream, I saw a well-set table with gleaming silver and delicate floral-patterned china and crystal wineglasses. Bette pointed out the peeling plaster and commented that the room would need to be redone since there had been some water damage from the bathroom above. But the faded brown stains on the ceiling didn't ruin the effect of the intricate crown molding around the chandelier. The tiny lights reflected like diamonds.

I noticed peeling wallpaper at the end of the room near the door to the kitchen.

"Prob'bly four layers of wallpaper under there," Bette said, scratching at the edges with her fingernail. "Folks

didn't bother with scrapin' paint or peelin' off the old paper back then. If the styles changed, they just painted or
papered right over it."

The upstairs rooms were cozy and charming. Even in
their careworn state, I could see the majesty of the house
in the strong woodwork, beautiful brass-trimmed light fix-
tures and now-peeling floral-patterned wallpaper. But if I
was frightened in the dungeonlike basement, overwhelmed
by the 19th-century kitchen, and concerned about the peeling plaster in the dining room, the third floor took care of
all of that.

Once I got up there, that is.

"In the days when these gracious homes were built, the
family used the front stairs, which were, gen'rally speakin',
wide and long, with a generous banister or handrail. So, o'
course, the lady of the house swept down those stairs
with her long crinolines rustling. I'm sure it made quite a
picture!" Betty explained.

"The real business of the house took place in the back,
however," she went on, gesturing toward the dark and
narrow stairs at the back of the house that led directly
into the kitchen. "That's why this staircase leads into the
kitchen. It is merely functional."

"And unsafe," I said under my breath as I struggled up
the stairs behind her. I had to wonder how many maids
and laundry women nearly died trying to move up and
down these stairs wearing long skirts and high-buttoned
shoes, carrying trays of food, tubs of water, armfuls of
laundry, and smelly slop jars.

"Here we are! You're gonna *love* this! It's darling."

We rounded the corner of the hall and Bette pulled
open a tiny door.

I looked up. Straight up. The steps were barely two

feet long and less than a foot wide. They stretched into the clouds. I felt a little dizzy.

Maybe I could take Bette's word for it that the third floor was "darling."

"I won't need a Stairmaster after a few weeks in *this* house," I complained as I climbed, almost on all fours, up the steep stairs to the third floor. My thighs were calling me everything but a child of God. I could feel my hamstrings and the backs of my calves crying. My chest was getting tight. I thought I was having a heart attack.

Ahead of me, Bette climbed the steps like a Sherpa strolling up Mount Everest. I hated her.

"Bette, I trust your judgment." I was still breathing hard from coming up the last staircase.

"Opal, I'm gonna have to get you to the gym. You should get an appointment with Charles. He'll get you in shape."

I thought about the last time I had called her and heard Charles's voice in the background. Perfect shape, my ass.

When I finally reached the top I thought I was going to have to lie down. And die. There was a buzzing sound in my ears.

"What's the altitude up here?" I whined as I breathed heavily. "Have we reached base camp yet?"

"Hush up and look!" Bette ordered.

I did look.

The front room was filled with sunlight.

Two windows, one facing east and one facing west, gave me enough light to see all that I could want to see. The room was at the very top of the house, so I was, literally, standing on the roof. The view was wonderful. I could see the river. There was so much space. At the very back was a closet-sized space that held only a commode and sink. The ceiling was stained from roof damage, but the floors were sound. And there were bookshelves.

"Miss Caroline was plannin' to use the room as a library, but she fell in the tub and broke her hip."

"I thought you said that she was over ninety years old!" I could not imagine an old lady climbing up and down these steps.

Bette smiled. "She was old, but she didn't act old. Scampered up and down these stairs like a mountain goat. Had all her own teeth and could see a ladybug on a leaf on the tree across the street without binoculars." Bette shook her head in a gesture of appropriate sympathy. "But you know, after they break a hip, things are just never the same."

I made a mental note to be careful.

I walked around the room and placed all of the furniture that I hadn't bought yet (and couldn't afford) in their proper places. The wrought-iron bed, the antique chest of drawers, the white crockery pitcher and bowl on a stand, an easel and worktable that I didn't have yet. There was a tiny closet on the side that was large enough for the few clothes that I had. In my mind I added up what I thought would be the cost of putting a shower in and fixing up the sad little bathroom.

I had it all planned out.

I stood in the neglected rose garden only halflistening as Bette rattled on about the history of the place, the Xavier family and the legendary Lorene Xavier, Miss Caroline's great-great-aunt, who was beautiful and accomplished and who had presided over a salon during the summers when wealthy folks came to Prestonn. I wasn't paying much attention when Bette talked about the Xavier secret that Miss Caroline bragged about or the suitor who died of diphtheria in the Philippines in the thirties. I was off in another world thinking about pruning the roses and fixing a cup of tea on the stove. I was thinking about three rooms that could give some woman a break for a few days while she got herself together. And I was thinking about a dog or two and perhaps a cat to keep in the coach house to keep the mice away. I was thinking about painting the studio a pristine white and mopping the floors until they were sterile, then throwing down old-fashioned rag rugs and covering my couch with a throw I found at the flea market last week. I loved the way the yellow house looked in the sunlight. It was warm and soft and welcoming, despite the basement dungeon, the questionable plumbing, and the Mount Everest climb to the third floor.

"How much again?"

The figure that she quoted wasn't bad. But I had let my daydreams run away with me. I started running down the "minus" column:

No air-conditioning. This was a river valley. Even the Devil would ask for air-conditioning in this valley in the summer.

Heating. The old house probably wasn't well insulated, although I didn't know that for sure. I made a mental note to have the elephant-sized furnace checked.

I had to do something with that Stone Age kitchen. Even if I had previous lives, there was no way I could remember how to cook on a woodstove! And the plumbing.

I can rough it with the best of them and I was prepared to make sacrifices, but I have to have indoor plumbing that works. Plus there was the small problem of the creature in the burgundy lagoon in the second-floor bath.

The dollar signs got larger and larger.

"What do you think?" Bette asked.

"I don't know, Bette," I told her dejectedly. "It'll take more cash than I'll ever have to get this barn together. I think I need a place that already has indoor plumbing."

Bette stuck out her tongue at me. Then she glanced at her notes. "Don't bail on me yet, hon," she said confidently. "I told you, the seller just wants to be rid of this place. He's willing to . . ." She flipped up one of the pages. "He's willing to replace the kitchen appliances and fix up that third-floor bath so that it's functional. Maybe we can negotiate some other repairs."

"What about the roof?"

Bette didn't bat one long mascara-coated eyelash. She flipped through her book and pulled out a business card. "Call this guy. I use him all the time. He's a house inspector. Plus he's single," she added with a wink.

Second to finding me a piece of real estate, Bette's primary mission in life is to find me a man.

I rolled my eyes at her. Anything male was simply not on my "to do" list.

"Hon," I said, using her favorite word of endearment, "the last damn thing I need in my life is another man!"

She laughed and handed me a folder. The front cover had her picture on it, red lipstick, cantaloupe-colored hair, and all. "Bette Smith! *The* Hardest-Working Woman in the Real Estate Business!

"That's everything you'll ever want to know about this house," she said as she turned quickly on her heel. I had to jump out of the way to keep from being body-slammed by her huge purse.

"Think it over, hon, then give me a call," she called over her shoulder as she marched off to the red Cadillac.

I stood there in the rose garden and watched her drive away.

I didn't know what I wanted to do.

My mind was crowded with information. And the cir-
cuits were beginning to overload. Money, always money.
Imani. Moving. Would the restraining order hold? Money
again. Ted. *Ted*. All of a sudden, I didn't know which way
to turn. I could barely find my car keys. There was so
much to think about.

Bette's car was just a red streak in the distance. I sat in
mine and stared off into space.

I had to decide if I was going to be myself again. And if
I was going to stick my neck out and lease this old yellow
house or play it safe.

As it turned out, other things decided for me.

Chapter Four

When I got back to Pam's, all hell had broken loose.

The water heater broke, leaving water all over the basement floor. One of the boys was running a temperature. Pam had a class at noon and the baby-sitter called to say that she couldn't come. Pam's husband, Ron, a policeman, was working a double shift and wouldn't be off until midnight. On top of this, there was a very large, ferocious-looking beast sprawled across the sidewalk leading to the front door. I came in through the side door.

Pam was hysterical: "I'll have to miss class! The plumber hasn't called me back! Ron's shift isn't up until midnight!" she sniffled. "Tyler's temperature is up to a hundred and two and I don't have any dog food! It can't *get* any worse!"

I glanced over at Tyler, who was just about to throw up. *Actually,* I thought, *it can.*

I sprang into action.

Once a mother, always a mother. You never forget how to leap tall buildings in a single bound, send a fax, cook chili, and manage a sick child while splitting the atom.

I handed a box of tissues to Pam, cleaned up the kitchen

floor and Tyler, and put him to bed with a cup of ice chips and a video. I sent Pam's older son, Tré, next door to play for the afternoon. I fixed Pam a sandwich and gave her a Tylenol. Then I called Bette (who knows every plumber, electrician, caterer, painter, tile man, window washer, *and* masseuse in ten counties) and got the name of a reliable plumber who could come right away.

I told Pam that I would watch the boys.

What else did I have to do aside from trying to decide what I was going to do for the rest of my life?

In no time, the house was calm again. Tyler fell asleep. Relieved, Pam went off to class. I put in a load of laundry.

But there was something I'd forgotten.

Why was I thinking about dog food?

I checked on Tyler, then looked out the front door.

Yep. "It" was still there.

The beast was sprawled across the sidewalk. It looked like a dirty shag rug with legs. One ear was clipped, one ear wasn't. The fur around its neck was matted and there were sores in a few places. It had a paw that looked as if it had been broken and hadn't healed right. It lifted its gigantic head to look at me with the saddest dark brown eyes I'd ever seen.

It wagged its tail as I got closer and looked up expectantly.

But I was downwind.

"I'd love to pet you, whatever-your-name-is," I told it, "but you stink."

The animal whined as if it understood what I had said.

I mapped out a plan of action.

Food and water first. Next the vet and then a bath. Maybe two baths. A distinct odor hit my nose again. Cancel that. Food and water first, then baths, *then* vet.

The beast was Pam's former neighbor's dog from across

the street. They moved out and just left the poor thing tied to a tree in the front yard with no food, no water, and no forwarding address. It had been there for almost a day before folks realized it had been abandoned.

The vet who examined him shook his head. He really did look baffled.

"My professional opinion is that he, that much I was able to figure out, he is a five-year old . . . something. Combination golden retriever . . . without the gold . . . Bouvier de Flandres . . . with only a little Bouvier. German shepherd I think . . . and Labrador maybe."

"Any grizzly bear?" I asked jokingly.

"Could be," he said, his expression solemn. "Perhaps some Newfoundland."

"Newfoundland?" I asked. I hadn't heard of that breed before.

"Yes," he said, trying to sound more convincing. "Newfoundland. Perhaps . . ."

I called the walking shag rug "Bear".

Later, I hovered over the calculator trying to make the numbers on the house work. With a dog as large as Bear, I would have a hard time finding an apartment that would take us. Besides, I rationalized, Bear would make a wonderful guard dog. Once he got over his fear of chipmunks.

In one week, I had to pick up all of my stuff.

And move it. Where?

A sensible two-bedroom place five minutes from work?

A stylish town house with beige walls and matching carpets with a carport, heated pool, and workout facility?

Or a faded Victorian beauty with a coach house, overgrown rose garden, no insulation, prehistoric kitchen, *and* rumored family secret?

I have discovered something about human nature. If

you don't know where you're going or what *you* want to do, everybody (and I mean *everybody*), their momma, their daddy, and all of the neighbors, will be happy to tell you what to do with your time, your money, and your life. My family and friends were no exception.

Dad tried to keep it light and philosophical. "Baby girl, you don't want to bite off more than you can chew," my father said, his voice filled with worry.

Mother was more pragmatic: "Are you crazy? The gas bill alone will eat you alive!" she snapped. "Are you planning to pay the bonuses of the utility hotshots all by yourself?"

Bonnie at work (I know her last name, it's Stegman, but when I think of her, she's just "Bonnie at work") also had an opinion. Bonnie has an opinion on everything. She makes it her business to know as much as she can about her coworkers' business. That includes me.

"Uh, uh. Prestonn has . . . a kind of a reputation. You know what I mean?" Her voice dropped to a loud whisper. "Some of the people in Prestonn are a little . . . you know . . . peculiar."

Pam's husband, Ron, took another approach: scare me into submission.

"You would be safer in an apartment complex with lots of people around."

Ron is a policeman and I knew that he meant well, but please, this was making me tired.

"Ron, a woman was shot to death by her boyfriend in a third-floor apartment at Autumn Chase just last month. It was all over the TV; don't you remember?"

He did. How could anyone forget?

The woman's neighbors listened to her screams and pleas for almost half an hour before they called the police. Safety in numbers? I didn't think so.

"If Ted wants to find me, he'll find me," I told Ron. Saying it aloud was sobering. It was a reminder to me not to get too comfortable. It really didn't matter where I lived. It really didn't matter how far away I moved. Unless I could make myself invisible, Ted could probably find me. That reality would be part of my way of life from now on.

Pam just smiled at me and said, "Do what you want to do, Opal."

Now I had to decide what that was.

It was a Sunday afternoon. Pam, Ron, and the boys were at a soccer tournament and would be gone until evening. I took Bear to the dog groomer, who looked at him doubtfully. "I'll do my best," the woman said with a grimace. "But I have to be honest with you: when I'm finished I think he'll still look like a bear."

With time on my hands and a tank full of gas, I found myself driving around in circles as I thought about what I was going to do.

My mind kept spinning. And I kept driving. Not going anywhere.

Then I did something really stupid.

Without thinking, I drove to the house that I had shared with Ted for over twelve years. Like a homing pigeon, I had returned to my base.

It wasn't safe for me to be there except that Ted was working second shift. He was the assistant plant manager at an automotive supplier.

Our house was in a neat little neighborhood that looked like something out of a cereal commercial. Wide boulevards, tree-lined sidewalks dotted with children riding bikes

or folks walking dogs. The lawns were neatly manicured—
the neighborhood association sent you a friendly reminder
if you forgot—and every third house was identical, so
there wasn't much individuality here. Brown trash cans
dotted the edge of each lawn. Monday was trash day.
Fourteen-thirty-five Fallen Brush Lane was no exception.
Except for one thing.

Five trash cans and a tower of boxes stood at the edge
of the curb. They were completely filled. With my things.

I don't remember parking the car. I may have left it
running.

I was like a crazy woman.

I pulled my winter coat out of one can, a pair of pumps
out of another, and a stack of books from one of the
boxes. Practically everything I owned was in those trash
cans and boxes. Some of my clothes had been cut to
shreds. The heels or toes of my shoes had been hacked
off. He'd thrown out my canceled checks, cosmetics, family
pictures, even sanitary pads. Nearly every damn thing
that was mine he had thrown out. Many of the "personal
belongings" that the court had allowed for me to pick up
next week were in those trash cans.

Then I noticed a long, flat box crate leaning up against
one of the cans. My breath caught in my throat.

Oh, Lord.

The canvasses I'd hidden behind the furnace years ago.
The ones that I told myself I would recover someday
when it was "safe." Only it was never safe.

I knew what I would find before I pulled the first painting out.

It was in shreds.

I pulled out another one and then the rest of them.

All of them were in shreds. A few were sliced up so

badly that they looked like painted icicles ready for a Christmas tree.

I'd painted some of them almost thirty years ago in high school. Many were from my college art classes, and a few were the slowly evolving works I had begun after my marriage. These last ones were the most precious to me because they were painted in the stolen moments of my life, when Ted was out of the house or when Imani was napping or in school. They were the "me" that I hadn't been able to express anywhere else. A brush stroke here, a brush stroke there, sometimes two brush strokes was all I could get done in a sitting. It's a wonder that I had finished them at all. I could only paint a few times a month, and many months, then years would go by when I wasn't able to paint at all.

Now they were gone forever.

I cried. I wanted to shut myself up in a room and stay there for a month. I thought about dressing myself in black as if I was in mourning and never smiling again. A part of me was gone. A part that I had ignored and forgotten about was gone forever because of my fear.

I could buy a new coat, new shoes. They sold cosmetics at Walgreens and I could even replace my books. But my paintings? I had put myself into the colors and shapes on those canvasses.

I saw Ted's car coming down the street.

It was the first time that I had seen Ted since I left him. I knew that he wouldn't be in a good mood. He was angry with me for making him throw out all of my stuff. Angry at me for making him spend money on an attorney and having to take time off from work for court dates. He left me voice-mail messages at work threatening me because of what I was doing to him. This situation was entirely my fault.

The dark gray car was coming closer.

I was supposed to run for my life. I was supposed to be frightened.

But the body snatchers arrived on time and returned the real me, the one that had been missing for nearly twenty years. I felt something warm seep through the soles of my shoes into my feet and surge up my body, exploding into my brain like a jolt of electricity. My hair was standing on end. My eyes felt as if they were on fire.

The bitch was back.

And she was mad as hell and looking for a pair of boxing gloves.

Have you heard people talk about "seeing red"?

Ted was just turning into the driveway when I approached. His car was still running. He had barely gotten the words, "Stupid bitch," out when I marched up to him, reached through the open window, and grabbed him by the collar with both hands. Ted is a good-sized man, but when you see red, size means nothing. I figured that I could pull at least half of him out of the window and if the other half broke off, oh well. He was able to pry my hands loose a few times, but it took more effort than he ever planned to expend on the likes of me. He was shouting at me, but the buzzing in my ears (you "hear" red, too) blocked out the sound. I just saw his lips moving. I heard my *own* voice, though. I was calling him a bastard and a mean, nasty son of a bitch. I kept smacking him on the head over and over. And, for the first time, I saw fear in *his* eyes.

For one tiny moment, Ted was afraid.

Of me.

It was enough.

In retrospect, I can imagine what I looked like: a brown Medusa with teeth bared, hair flying every which way, and eyes shooting bolts of lightning. No wonder he was scared. He had never seen me this angry in his life! I had never *been* this angry in my life.

He fumbled with the door handle, but it wouldn't open.

"If I get out of this car, Opal, I'm gonna kick your ass!"

"You'll have a fight on your hands, you son of a bitch!" I yelled back at him, tightening my grasp on his collar as he tried to pry my fingers off. "You threw out my stuff! My books! You cut up my clothes! And my paintings!

"Who gave you the right? *Who?*" I bellowed.

He swatted at me, still trying to open the car door. But I had a death grip. All I could see in my mind was his open mouth against the background of my shredded paintings. The more I thought about those canvasses, the more pissed off I got.

"Just wait till I get outa this car," he finally managed to growl.

"Take your best shot, asshole," I growled back. "This won't be a knockout." My voice came out deep and mean, like the bark of a big dog just before he bites you on the ass.

Ted just stared at me, his mouth open in amazement.

This was a new thing for Ted. He had always been the angry one. He had always had the upper hand, making me say, "I'm sorry," while I cried and cowered in pain and fear.

Not this time.

Now he heard a voice that he didn't recognize.

Mine.

And it scared the shit out of him. (Excuse my French.)

Ted finally pried my fingers from his collar and pushed me away. I whirled around ready to defend myself, but instead of getting out of the car, he put it in reverse and zipped out of the driveway. I couldn't have been more surprised. In the middle of the street, he screamed out of the car window at me.

"Bitch! You forget who you are!"

I just stood there, staring, as he flew down the street at fifty miles an hour.

I have to give Ted credit. He is an abusive, mean, drunk-ass son of a bitch, but his parting shot to me was and still is one of the most inspirational things I have ever heard. Sometimes you really do have to give the Devil his due. Ted reminded me of what I had left behind and what I needed to do to get it back. I *had* forgotten who I was. I had buried her, hidden and neglected her. I thought that I was keeping her safe, but I almost let her die.

But those days are over, I swore to myself, savoring the memory of Ted's panic-stricken expression. I knew that it wasn't over. That he would find a way to even the score. But I had my voice back. No matter what happened, no matter if he stalked me, threatened me, killed me, no matter what.

I would not forget again.

In Prestonn, I walked on the path that follows the river. A few joggers passed me panting and several young families pushing the huge European strollers moved like semi-trailers along the trail. I stopped and watched a family of ducks quarreling in the water near the bank. Geese had taken over part of the sidewalk, leaving a trail of goose shit everywhere. Nice touch. Two winos sat in the grass enjoying the sunshine, their bottles securely wrapped in brown paper bags. I meandered along the trail and then crossed over the main road into the town's square.

The "new" downtown is a hub of boutiques, hair "design

studios," and antique shops. The restaurants are always written up in the food sections of the local papers. But they don't serve real food. As far as I can tell, they serve thin strips of meat decorated with weeds, twigs, and edible flowers. I decided right then and there that I wouldn't eat in any of these places. I don't care how good they are for you; I am not eating weeds.

There's an Oriental rug "boutique," a mirror and glass "boutique," and a row of "interior design" studios. Beamers, Jags, and Benzes populate the street-side parking spaces.

But while the "new" downtown receives more press, it is only part of the picture. It is wrapped around the "old" downtown, and that is the real heart of Prestonn. Next to the Oriental rug boutique is Earl's Gun & Bait. The Main Street Hair Design Studio and Spa patrons share a parking lot with the Prestonn Bar & Grill (no extra *e* there), where breakfast is served twenty-four hours a day and hamburgers are fried in their own grease, by God. Designs by Sylvia Gold is right across the street from the Red Fox, a rough, worn-out-looking place that, according to its sign, specializes in GIRLS, GIRLS, GIRLS.

The superthin, very blond things who come out of the restaurants (no wonder they're thin; they're only eating weeds!) share the sidewalks with good old boys who wear oil-stained ball caps and drive trucks that the Chevy dealership doesn't carry parts for anymore. And they know how to make use of tobacco in this state. If they don't smoke it or sniff it, they chew it. Spittoons dot the tree-lined street. Very thoughtful.

Miss Pearl's Place de Beauty is about the only salon I know of that rolls, perms, teases, and sprays hair that can stand up to the summer humidity and the tornadoes that come through this part of the state two or three times a year. They don't set hair like *that* in the Main Street Hair Design Studio & Spa.

I turned off Main Street and it was an entirely different world. This is where people lived. Houses and yards and kids and bikes and gazebos and few driveways. The houses are all museum pieces whether they are restored or falling down. In front of some houses, a boxy Volvo or BMW sits gleaming in the sunlight. In front of others, an old Oldsmobile rests on cement blocks.

The Confederate flag fluttering gently in the breeze caught my eye. Something about that thing always makes my blood boil. I don't care about that part of southern heritage. Maybe I wasn't born to. I had stopped for a moment to meditate on the Stars and Bars when a gravelly voice assaulted my thoughts.

"Hey there! How're you? Lovely day, ain't it?"

I lowered my gaze and found myself looking at a two-hundred-year-old man.

Now I understood why he was flying that flag. He probably *was* a Confederate.

He had a grizzled gray beard, and tufts of white hair fuzzed out from beneath his fishing cap. His clothes were at least as old as he was, and his shoes were older. His house was a dilapidated Queen Anne that might not survive the next strong wind. Two mats of fur lay on a concrete slab next to a pickup truck that belonged in the Ford Motor Company antique car museum. The mats moved, so I think that they were dogs. Something that smelled horrible burned in a huge barrel. Oblivious to it all, the little man sat in a lawn chair in the middle of the small yard, with a six-pack at his side, a beer can in his hand, and a cigar stuck in the side of his jaw. He was grinning at me.

"Excuse me?"

"Lovely day, ain't it?" he repeated. Reaching down to his side, he pulled a can out of the pack. "You the colored girl's thinking about buyin' Caroline's place?"

I had to think about this question. I hadn't been colored or a girl since 1965. But to this talking relic I probably was both.

"Thinkin' about it," I echoed his words. *How did he know?*

"Good house," he commented. He spit out a wad of gnawed cigar and mumbled something. I thought that I heard him say, "Caroline was a good woman."

"Want a beer?"

"Um . . . no, thank you," I said.

"Suit yourself," he said, shrugging. "But if you change your mind, I'll be right here." He stuck the stubby piece of cigar back into his mouth. "I'm here all the time."

The grin never left his face.

"Thank you," I said.

He nodded and held the beer can aloft before guzzling it down.

I kept walking.

There was laundry hanging on the clotheslines. There was a chicken coop in one backyard, a state-of-the-art wood play set in another, and a pair of model types power-walked past me wearing designer athletic wear with matching sneakers. They carried bottled water. Another woman with a cigarette hanging out of her mouth walked by carrying a soda. She was probably only thirty years old, but her face already spoke of a hard life that had gone on too long. The sun was shining and the sky was blue, but I could tell by the way she walked and the dead look in her eyes that she didn't notice or care.

She wore the face of a woman who doesn't think that life is much worth living. It is the face of a woman who doesn't see beauty or love anymore. The face of a woman who doesn't see herself anymore.

I have worn that face myself.

I turned down Burning Church Road.

The church that lent its name to the road had long since burned down but left its pioneer cemetery. I wandered through the gates and glanced at the tombstones marking the passage of time of Prestonn from the early 1800s through the early 1900s. It was quiet.

The yellow house stood like a bastion at the end of the street. Even from here, I could see Bette's FOR SALE sign, the new one with her pink/orangeade colored hair. But this tag of American enterprise had not ruined the majesty of the house. It stood with the confidence of a woman "of a certain age" who has come into her own, a little worn and somewhat beaten up and disappointed but still poised, still lovely. And still alive. The sunlight left a warm glow around the house that said, *Come on in and have a cold drink.*

The house had stood through the Civil War and tornadoes. It had survived lightning, locusts, and yellow fever epidemics. It was standing beneath trees that watched the last of the Shawnee and the Miami move west never to return.

The paint was peeling and the porch was falling down. The plumbing was a nightmare and the roof was questionable. The garden needed attention. And the house had a past. It had been neglected and taken for granted.

But it had survived.

Like me.

There was a slight breeze and for a moment I felt a chill. Then I heard it.

Caroline Xavier had left a set of wind chimes hanging

from the rafters of the only part of the porch that wasn't falling down. The tune they played was soft, light, and pleasant. It fit like poetry on the day. I walked toward the sound.

The yellow house deserved a second chance.

And so did I.

Chapter Five

There is a saying that when the gods want to punish
you, they answer your prayers. I think that's true. I am just
trying to figure out what I did to make them so mad at *me*.

I called Jack Neal, the inspector whose name was on
the card that Bette gave me. I arrived a little before six to
unlock the house. Most of Miss Xavier's furniture and personal things had been removed, so there wasn't any place
to sit except on the porch or on the front steps. I stepped
on to the south porch, then wandered out into the rose
garden. I counted nearly fifty bushes in all. I thought I'd
better get my mother up here quick before I killed them. I
can grow mold and that's it. I have a "purple" thumb when
it comes to plants. One of the bushes was budding early;
the tiny buds were soft and smooth to the touch. I pulled
my hand back before I got too carried away. I didn't want
to kill the little blooms before they got a good chance at
survival.

"Ms. Sullivan? Ms. Sullivan?"

The house inspector.

"Yes! I'm back here."

I headed toward him and then stopped. The inspector smiled and marched in my direction, clipboard in his hand. My stomach turned to concrete.

He was the maintenance man from the Women's Crisis Center.

I wanted the ground to open up and swallow me whole. My embarrassment went into high gear. Had he gotten a good look at me in the TV room at the shelter? And if he had, what did he think? I was humiliated. LaDonna's words about everyone knowing about my situation still stung.

"Opal, they know already."

I was embarrassed before he said one word.

"Ms. Sullivan, I'm Jack Neal. Bette Smith called me right after I left you that message." He chuckled. "She gave me a whole list of items to check on and a page full of instructions." He looked up from his clipboard. His eyes were friendly. "She's all over my case about this inspection report. Wants me to turn it around in twelve hours. Is she your guardian angel or something?"

It didn't help that he was so good-looking.

If Jack Neal remembered seeing me before, he was too polite to mention it. I was grateful.

He slipped on a pair of reading glasses as he went down "Bette's list," which was two times as long as mine. Tall and a little bulky, he had a shaved head, a broad grin with dimples when he smiled, and dark eyes. He looked like a chocolate Mr. Clean. His shoulders were broad and his movements reminded me of football players that I had seen. He chuckled when I mentioned it.

"That football stuff is great when you're young. But when you get old? The knees go, the ankles go, and your hips ache. Old football players don't die; they just fall to pieces!"

We headed towards the house.

"I just want to make sure that I'm not being a total fool over this house," I told him as I opened the door. "If it ought to be burned to the ground, you've got to let me know before I sign on the dotted line."

"Got it," he said with a nod. "Let's see what we have here. . . ."

An hour and a half later, he was finished. I glanced at Jack's clipboard. The inspection report was the size of a telephone book.

"All right," he said, "The house needs work, no doubt about it." He slid on the glasses again and started on the first page. "You're going to need some roof repairs. Not an entirely new roof, but you don't have any flashings around your chimneys and there are some loose bricks up there. That will need to be fixed. There are some venting problems. . . ."

He had only gotten through the first three pages of the report when I decided that I needed a break and a swig of Pepto-Bismol.

"Look, Mr. Neal," I interrupted him.

"Just call me Jack," he said.

Startled, I lost my train of thought. I looked up at him and noticed that he was smiling again.

"I'm getting indigestion here," I snapped. "Can you break it down for me?"

He flipped the pages back and took off his glasses. For a moment, I blinked. For an old fart, he *was* a pretty nice-looking man. Too bad I wasn't in the market for one right now or anytime in the next four hundred years.

"OK," he said slowly. "The best way I can say it is . . . about the only things that you don't have in this house are termites and a ghost."

That was comforting. And he was right about the ghost. The "spirit sweep" performed by Father McEachern had come up clean.

"I see," I said in a low voice. My heart sank.

Like an old broad with varicose veins, cellulite, hot flashes, and graying hair hidden under control-top panty hose and slacks, a fan, and Clairol, the house had done an excellent job of covering up her real secrets.

"Mr. Neal—"

"Look, Ms. Sullivan, I know that you think this old house is a pile of junk and that somebody should light a match and put it out of its misery." He looked up at the box gutters and the south porch that was the only solid piece of porch there was.

"But the things that I've outlined on my report are pretty common in houses of this age. This house is over one hundred and fifty years old. You can't expect it not to have a few things wrong with it."

"A few things!" I waved a hand at the two-inch-thick document attached to his clipboard. "From what you're telling me, I might as well tear the damn thing down and start over." I said those words with a sigh. The yellow house had gotten into my blood. I had begun to feel that fixing it up was like fixing up myself. That both of us would become whole together.

Neal laughed.

"No, no, this is a day's work!" he said. "Your report is only ten pages long. It's not really that bad. This place was built by craftsmen who knew their stuff. It's hardwood construction, virtually termite-proof, by the way. It's been here a long time. It'll be here a few hundred more years. The roof is slate. Once you have it repaired, it'll last you forever. You have a real treasure, Ms. Sullivan. Just needs a face-lift, that's all."

He smiled at me this time. And I smiled back.

OK, Opal, I said to myself, *it is time to get off the fence. You can't play it safe forever. If you're going to see a rainbow, you might have to dance on the roof a little.* And I was about to do just that. In high heels.

Between Neal and Bette, I got a list of contractors to bid on the roof, the plumbing, and some of the plaster-work that was needed to get the yellow house into shape. The rest of it I would do myself.

Georgy Porgy got the social services agency to waive some of the restrictions for respite care for victims of domestic violence. As long as the electricity was on and the Loch Ness monster was out of the toilet, they would make referrals. I was spinning around in circles, trying to juggle my job, coordinate the move, call plumbers, roofers, plasterers, electricians, and so on.

By the time moving day was over I was too tired to sleep.

"Ma'am? Where does this go?"

I couldn't see the owner of this voice because he was hidden behind a tower of boxes labeled BOOKS. He was huffing and puffing and sounded as if he were about to have a heart attack. I tried to look innocent. I only have a few hundred books. How heavy could they be?

"Uh . . . third floor," I answered apologetically.

I thought I heard him say, "Shit!"

"Basement," I said quickly to the man behind him before he had a chance to open his mouth. I heard his heavy footsteps clomp through the dining room. When did I get so much stuff?

Pam and Ron unloaded my car. Ron started organizing the garage under the coach house. Even little Tyler and Tré "helped," bless their hearts.

"I'm moving, Aunt Opal!" Tré exclaimed as he proudly carried a small box of Tupperware into the kitchen.

"Yes, you are, sweetie." I gave him a pat on the head and watched him toddle into the kitchen where his mother was waiting.

"Opal! This kitchen is prehistoric!" Pam yelled.

"I know!" I yelled back.

"Hope you like camping out," she added under her breath.

"I heard that!" I yelled back.

I went back to my "business plan." At Jack Neal's suggestion, I decided to do the most urgent things first. Plumbing, roof, kitchen, then plasterwork.

One of the plumbers was coming at noon. It was only 10:30. Next item.

I drew a line through the name of one plasterer in my notebook. Never call a man named Jean Pierre to do any work with his hands. At least, not in the U.S.

He'd shown up earlier this morning dressed in shirt and tie. He had a clipboard in one hand, a latte in the other, and an attitude. He surveyed the house—and me—with his nose turned up. My dining room, he declared, was "hopeless."

"Ms. Sullivan? The roofer wants to see you," the moving company supervisor's voice came from behind the huge chest that was going into what would be Imani's bedroom, because it wouldn't fit up the third-floor stairwell. For someone who would only be home for about thirty days a year, that child was going to have a lot of furniture.

One of the first things you learn in these old houses is that half of the furniture that you want to put on the third floor won't fit up the third-floor stairwell. Those third-floor stairways were made for an elite segment of the population: elves and gnomes.

The roofer was scribbling quickly in his notebook as I

approached. I knew that I was in trouble when he looked up with a tragic expression on his face. I wondered if the director had yelled, "Action!" yet.

"I don't know how to tell you this, Ms. Sullivan," he said with the solemnity of a doctor pronouncing a sentence of imminent death. "You have a lot of things going on up there. It's a wonder that you don't have more leaks." He shook his head with the appropriate amount of pathos. Richard Burton would have been jealous. I wanted to put my hand on my forehead and sigh loudly, but I managed to restrain myself.

"Give me the damage, Jimmy," I said. If I didn't stop him now, this performance could go on forever.

With barely undisguised glee, Jimmy ticked off the different pieces of the job and the total. I had to take a deep breath. My financial plan was looking more like a financial science fiction plan. Now I needed to sit down.

But I had company.

I had set up some lawn furniture on the only part of the porch that wasn't falling down. Two cats, one a tiger, the other a calico, were sprawled across my new cushions enjoying the sun. Bear lay on the floor in his usual position in front of the door with his huge head on his paws.

"Some watchdog you are," I grumbled at him, and looked at my newest guests.

The cats didn't move. The tiger looked at me without interest, yawned, and rolled over. The huge calico opened one eye, blinked a few times, then went on with her nap.

"Beat it," I said.

The cats didn't move.

Bear looked up at me, whined, and lumbered off the porch.

"Not *you*," I said, watching him go.

"Them!"

The cats glared up at me as if I were sitting on *their* porch.

"Must be ghetto cats," I mumbled to myself, lifting the cushions so that the cats would have to get up. "Not afraid of anything. *Beat* it."

The calico shrugged and disappeared. The tiger gave me a withering gaze, then followed.

They both slinked away toward the coach house.

Wonderful. They probably had a litter of kittens hidden in there. I decided to name them Ice Tray and Calico With an Attitude (CW for short). I couldn't keep them in the house because I was allergic to cats now, but if they kept the place free of mice, then they could stay in the coach house.

Two of the movers struggled with a huge armoire that had been in my grandmother's house in New Orleans. They gave me a hopeful look.

"Ms. Sullivan?"

I lied and told them to try the front bedroom on the second floor. I just wasn't ready to see two grown men cry because I had asked them to take that four-thousand-pound piece of mahogany up those narrow steps to the third floor. It wouldn't fit anyway.

The second plasterer came.

He wasn't wearing a shirt or a tie, but he wanted $5,000 just to redo the east wall in the dining room. He was the first person that I told to have his head examined. But he wasn't the last.

Plumber Number Two came right on time and I walked with him back to the kitchen.

"The current owner has put in the new refrigerator and stove, but—"

The man's face was turning red and he was grinning from ear to ear. Bellows of laughter spilled out of his mouth.

"There hasn't been any plumbing work done in this kitchen since the turn of the century!"

I had heard all of this before.

"Which century? Nineteenth? Or twentieth?"

"Twentieth," he said without missing a beat. "I will have to rip out everything that's here and start from scratch." He was so thrilled that he could barely control himself.

I turned to let Plumber Number Two out the back door just in time to see two of the movers at the front door performing a juggling act with my mattress and box spring. They looked like dancing bears in the circus. They looked up at me hopefully. "Third floor," I said.

A duet of groans followed by a "shit!" followed. I tried to look busy with the cap on my ink pen.

A little person tugged on the hem of my skirt.

"Auntie Opal? Where's this?" Tyler was having a wonderful time. His eyes were shining with excitement.

"Take that to Mommy, Tyler." I pointed him in the direction of the kitchen, where Pam's monologue was continuing on the ancient age of my sink.

"I can't *believe* these cabinets!"

"Give it a rest, Pam!" I shouted.

Just as I turned away, I heard someone call my name. I almost bumped into a man who had appeared at my elbow.

"Oh! Excuse me!"

"Ms. Sullivan?"

A stocky man dressed in a T-shirt, paint-splattered jeans, and work boots leaned into the doorway. He slid off his baseball cap, revealing a bald head.

"I'm Rodney Hayes," he said with a friendly grin. He extended his hand and gave me a bone-crushing handshake. "I called about the plasterwork."

"Oh, yes, Rodney!" I exclaimed, looking at my watch.

Twelve noon, right on time. I loved it when folks were on time. "Come on in."

Rodney wiped his feet about twenty times on the door-mat, then stepped gingerly into the front hall. Obviously, the man had good home training.

"Solid house," he commented, stroking the wall as if he were caressing his girlfriend. He closed his eyes as his hand stopped on the center of the wall, and then he moved it gently in a circular motion. Obviously Rodney has a thing for walls.

It was 12:30; the movers were almost finished, I had a plumber and electrician picked out, the exterminator had done his work, my new refrigerator and stove had been delivered, *and* I had contracted with Rodney for the plasterwork. Suddenly I was tired. A nap sounded like a good idea.

But something caught my eye outside. Coming from around the side of the moving van were a woman and a boy. The woman had a piece of paper in her hand and she stopped once to look at it, said something to the boy, then continued up the driveway. Just before she reached the front sidewalk, she threw down the cigarette that had been hanging out of her mouth. I headed toward the front door.

"Can I help you?"

"Are . . . are you Opal Sullivan?" she asked in an uncertain tone.

"Yes, I am," I answered. "Something I can do for you?"

Her eyes flickered for a second, then narrowed.

"Is . . . is this your house?"

"Yes, it is," I told her. For just a second, I was angry. *Do you want to see the deed? My driver's license, maybe?* I counted to ten.

"Oh. I'm Gloria Estepp," she told me in a voice sanded down by Marlboros and beer. "My social worker told me to come here." It was more of a question than a statement. She reached into her tote bag and pulled out a sheaf of papers that she pushed into my hand. Then she remembered the little boy standing beside her. "This here's my son, Troy."

"Won't you come in?" I said.

She stepped into the foyer holding her son by the hand. With wary dark blue eyes, she sized up the front parlor to the right and the dining room to the left. Then she sized me up.

I didn't have to look at the papers in my hand to know what I was dealing with.

All I needed to know about Gloria Estepp was written on her face.

She was small and thin, with pale freckled skin that was the texture of parchment paper. Her frizzy hair had been dyed so many times I couldn't tell what color it was supposed to be. She had the shadow of a recent black eye and there was a large bruise on her forehead that was still purple and gold.

Troy was a scrawny little boy.

But it was the scrawniness of an active child, not a starving one. His cheeks were rosy and his strawberry-colored hair was neatly cut and shiny. His eyes, dark blue like his mother's, were bright and intelligent. His clothes were worn and old, but his blue jeans had been ironed and had a knife-sharp crease in them.

Gloria had used the energy that she had left after fighting with her husband to take care of her son. I could tell from looking at her that there was never enough money, energy, or time left to spend on herself.

I closed the door behind her and glanced at the papers. Early thirties, GED course work, laid off from the paper plant, husband set fire to their home (and himself) when he passed out while smoking a cigarette. He was in the hospital and would be for a while. And Mrs. Estepp was taking this opportunity to get out of Dodge. Permanently.

"It says there on that paper," she pointed to the documents that I was holding, "that I can get some res . . . respite housing with you. Until I can find a place for me and Troy." She glanced down at her son. He looked up and smiled at his mother, but his dark eyes were serious.

"Yes," I said, handing the papers back to her. "Two rooms. Well, I will have two rooms. But not for three weeks."

Gloria's eyes narrowed.

"I can't wait no three weeks," she said. "Troy and me are sleeping on the couch at my brother's house, but we can't stay there much longer. My sister-in-law is threatening to throw all our stuff out in the yard."

OK, I said to myself, taking a deep breath while I tried to think.

"I'm sorry, Mrs. Estepp, but . . ." I gestured toward the towers of boxes in the dining room and the mess that was growing in the front parlor. "I'm just moving in today myself. I've got to paint some of the rooms, and only one of the bathrooms is even functional. I'm not even close to being ready."

Gloria glanced into the dining room and then looked at the staircase that wound its way toward the second floor in a graceful curve.

"The social worker said that you might not have anything for a while. . . ." Her voice trailed off. "It don't look so bad to me, though."

"Look," I said, trying to buy some time. "Do you have someplace that you could stay just for another, say, two weeks? That would at least give me time to get the room painted and repair the bathroom." I was trying to think ahead. She wasn't in any physical danger, since her husband was safely anesthetized in the burn unit of the hospital.

She looked at me as if I were the man in the moon. Her eyes were hard.

"Yeah, the social worker said I could try the women's homeless shelter over in the city." Her voice was harsh, angry, and dripping with sarcasm.

That wouldn't work. A woman running for her life, from either a burned-out house or a messed-up home situation, will take a mat on the floor if the mat is clean, the floor is warm, and she will be left alone. But that's only if you are alone. The homeless shelter, with its population of wandering alcoholics and troubled souls, was not the place for a little boy like Troy.

Gloria barely gave me time to change my mind.

"I ain't begging you for nothing," she snapped, grabbing Troy by the arm. "Come on, Troy."

"Mrs. Estepp," I said quickly.

She kept walking.

"Mrs. Estepp!"

She whirled around.

"What?" Her expression was like granite.

"I have a half-painted room with twin beds, towers of unpacked boxes stacked in the corners, one hardly working bathroom on the second floor with an antique sink and a Loch Ness monster swimming in the toilet. If you can overlook those," I paused, "minor inconveniences, then bring your stuff day after tomorrow if you want."

"Thank you," she said, her voice still harsh. But I saw the gratitude in her eyes and it made me feel small.

"Thank you," came a strong little voice from the boy standing at her side. He gave me a smile.

"You're welcome," I told him, wondering how I could get that room ready in less than twenty-four hours.

By evening, the place had settled down. The movers left at six, and the last of the contractors (a roofer who

was overpriced) left at seven. Neither of the prospective
tenants showed up to look at the coach house, and that
was disappointing. But there was so much to do that I decided to worry about that tomorrow.

Bear and I spent the evening on the south porch watching the day turn into dusk, him with his pig's ear, me with
a cold drink. In the South, you have either a cup of coffee
or a "cold drink." There is nothing in between. The phone
rang a couple of times. Bear is very sensitive to noise.
Every time the phone rang, he dived under the wicker
settee.

Let me rephrase that.

Every time the phone rang, that damn dog tried to dive
under the wicker settee. Since he is too large to fit beneath it, I had to keep rearranging the settee after he had
knocked it over. I decided then and there I'd better get a
Pekingese, Yorkie, or Chihuahua. I needed a watchdog.
Bear wasn't going to be of any use at all.

But later, when I got ready to go in, Bear suddenly stood
up, his one unclipped ear perked up, his tail rigid.

"Bear? What is it? What's out there?"

The yard was dark and the street was empty as far as I
could tell. Light twinkled from the porches of my neighbors. Another dog barked in the distance.

A low, menacing growl came from Bear's throat as he
slunk to the edge of the porch and stood at attention on
the top step. I grabbed his collar and looked out into the
darkness. I didn't see anything. Bear growled again, then
barked.

Then, just across the street, the lights of a car that I
had not noticed before came on. Bear tensed. The car
idled for a moment, then pulled out from the curb and
sped down the street. It was too dark for me to really see
if I recognized it. But a chill crawled down my spine.

Was it Ted? Was he out there in the darkness watching? And waiting?

"It's all right, boy." I scratched Bear's head. I strained my eyes trying to see in the darkness. "It's OK, just someone visiting the neighbors." I could tell that Bear wasn't buying it. I wasn't even convincing myself.

Bear didn't move until the taillights disappeared.

Cars had been coming and going all night, but this was the first time I had ever seen him act like that.

I shivered in the warm summer air and stepped inside.

I had to call Bear several times before he followed me.

Chapter Six

One of the most sobering truths that I have had to wrestle with since my "liberation" is the fact that there is really no escape from a situation like mine. You are never completely "out." When I was in my marriage with Ted, I figured that I was beaten because I was, physically, *there*. I couldn't leave Ted (this is what I told myself) because he threatened to kill me, he threatened to hurt Imani, he threatened my cats, and on and on. So I stayed out of fear. But it was the most insidious kind of fear. I was afraid to stay with Ted. And I was afraid to leave him. So I did nothing.

In my daydreams, I always imagined taking a road to freedom, much like the clandestine route that fugitive slaves took to the North before the Civil War. In those rosy scenarios, I lived in a utopian community where I was safe and free from the violence that had dominated the most intimate layers of my existence. Ted was no longer a factor in my life.

I did not realize that physical escape from my marriage and our home was only the smallest part of my new life.

The rest of it focused on staying alive. The first time I heard this, I was ready to give up, go back to Ted, and forget all about going it alone. What was the use?

LaDonna was sympathetic but unyielding.

"Look, when I left my husband, he took it out on my son. But Junior was eighteen, so he left, too. Then Winslow trashed the yard at my new place, slit my tires while I was at work, and called me so much on the phone that I almost lost my job. He caught me at the grocery store once and I thought he was going to kill me then over the cantaloupes. He stalked me, he harassed my mother, who was in a nursing home by the way, and he even threatened the nice little high school teacher that I had started dating."

LaDonna fiddled with her saucer-sized earrings.

"I'm not the brightest bulb on the tree, but it finally dawned on me that the bastard was never gonna let me go. Either I'd have to die or he would have to die. It was never really going to be over." She pounded the table to emphasize each word.

I felt sick to my stomach.

This was not what I wanted to hear from LaDonna. She was supposed to encourage me and support me, tell me that everything was going to be all right now that I had walked out on Ted. I felt as if she had cut my legs off.

"What about the restraining order?" I ventured in a weak voice. LaDonna gave me a withering look. "Counseling?" I offered.

LaDonna let out a hoot of laughter at the mention of the C word.

"Yeah, yeah, the latest thing is sending the men to 'anger management' and group counseling sessions." Her laughter was bitter. She shook her head and the silver satellite dish–shaped earbobs swayed. "How effective is the anger

management course for an angry man who has been ordered by a court to attend and who doesn't want to be
there? And don't get me started on counseling sessions!"
She was grinning from ear to ear. I was too upset to find
any humor in what she was saying. "They are usually all
male. Don't you know that the bastards sit around and
swap trade secrets about better ways to abuse and harass
their wives and girlfriends? Without leaving marks or getting caught? Isn't that brilliant? The sessions set up to correct this horrendous behavior are making the guys better
at it!"

I closed my eyes, said a prayer, and waited for the floor
to swallow me whole.

"It's never going to be over," I murmured, wondering
now about the wisdom of entangling myself in a house
that was only forty minutes away from Ted. And what
about the other women who needed help? Their troubles
would follow them to my doorstep. So much for serenity
and a new life.

LaDonna sensed what I was thinking and patted me on
the arm.

"I've been where you are," she said. Her eyes were soft.
"You want to give up. But you can't give up, Opal; you
can't. Not only are you saving yourself; you're saving others, too."

"But what kind of life is that?" I asked, frustrated. "I feel
like I should be in Witness Protection. Change my name,
dye my hair red, join the Foreign Legion. What kind of
life am I going to have, being afraid all the time?"

I was already paranoid. I circled parking lots at least
three times before deciding on a strategic spot. Bear and I
patrolled the yard every night before turning in. Then I
locked the doors and windows and set the alarm. I checked

the locks again. And the windows again. And the alarm. Over and over. Answering the telephone had become a game of Russian roulette. Was it Ted? Was it my parents? Was it Imani? I couldn't not answer. And caller ID was no help at all. It was always a guessing game as to who would be on the other end: "Who the hell do you think you are?" or "Hello, Opal? This is Sue; how are you doing today?"

LaDonna shrugged her shoulders.

"Well, that's up to you."

Now it was my turn to shake my head.

"No. It's up to Ted." I felt like giving up.

The corners of LaDonna's mouth began to curve upward into a wry smile.

"Only if you *let* it be," she said. "It's *your* life. You can let Ted control it as he's always done. Or you can control it yourself."

The very thought of Ted having power over my life, after I'd left him, after I'd divorced him, was enough to make my blood boil. Who did he think *he* was? OK, I had to be realistic, and LaDonna pulled me back to the real world once I'd gotten over my ranting.

"He'll always be angry at you; he may still threaten you and stalk you. Your challenge is to live safely, violence-free, and in your own way."

The war stories I'd heard made me painfully aware that moving to China was no guarantee. And shooting him dead, an option that I had considered, probably wouldn't work, either. For some reason, the legal system takes a dim view of that, despite a substantiated claim of domestic violence.

My only choice was to be careful, mindful, and alert. And get a watchdog.

"Bitch, who do you think you are?" had been Ted's parting words to me.

Both he and I were about to find out.

The yellow house filled up faster than I imagined with
both two-legged and four-legged visitors. I had hoped to
have the house cleaned up, stripped, painted, and completely repaired by the time my first "guests" arrived. But
it just did not work out that way.

Life with Gloria and Troy Estepp began with a cloud of
smoke and the smell of stale beer and old cigarette butts.

Her brother dropped them off. He drove up with a
screech of tires and a toxic cloud of dark bluish-gray smoke
in a rusted-out truck that had rolled off the Ford assembly
line forty years ago. The antique truck groaned when he
jerked the gears into neutral and threw on the parking
brake. The scraping sound of metal on metal made my
teeth hurt. Then he jumped down from the cab and ran to
the back of the truck. A cigarette dangled from his lips.
With a grunt, he hauled out four garbage bags and a couple of boxes full of stuff, threw them onto the front walk,
and hopped back into the cab. I thought that I heard him
say something like, "Is that it?" Judging by his expression,
however, what he probably said was, "Get the hell out."

Gloria and Troy had just enough time to close the door
on the truck before he backed down the driveway, flying
like a bat out of hell. The gearbox jammed for a split second and I thought for sure there'd be a pile of metal left
in the middle of the street. But he managed to move the
gearshift around again and pulled off. The brakes squealed
with such a high-pitched whine that Bear groaned and ran
around to the back of the house. I wondered if the man
had to stop the truck with his feet like Fred Flintstone.

Gloria watched her brother with an expression like granite. Neither she nor Troy said a word. Not even "good-bye."

"Let's get your things into the house," I said, grabbing one of the huge overstuffed bags.

I explained the rules as we dragged Gloria's things into the front hall and up the stairs. I had, finally, talked with the social worker this morning. Gloria could stay for up to six weeks while she looked for a full-time job and an apartment. LaDonna had signed her up for weekly counseling appointments at the Center.

"You and Troy will share this room. The bathroom is next door." I said this triumphantly. The plumber finished up last night. The Loch Ness monster was officially dead.

"Quiet time from ten o'clock until seven, no alcohol, no smoking in the house. It's OK on the porch. Troy, there's a TV in the room down the hall." I set the garbage bag containing his clothes and toys next to the bed. "You can pay toward your room and board in kind." I glanced up at the ugly grayish-beige wall. "There's a lot of work that needs to be done around here."

"In kind," echoed Gloria. "What does that mean?"

"Instead of paying money, you'll pay by helping out with the cooking, cleaning, or gardening, painting—"

Her face hardened and she stuck out her jaw.

"Nobody said nothin' about doing any work. I ain't cleaning out no toilets."

I counted to ten before I said anything.

"You'll clean out the toilet that *you* use," I told her. "That's only fair. I'm not asking you to do anything that I'm not doing myself. If you want to stay here, you've got to help."

We glared at each other. Troy looked first at his mother and then at me.

Gloria fiddled with her purse strap as she considered her choices. Finally, she said, "OK." She dragged the word out like a bald tire over gravel. "I guess I could help paint a little. And I like to work outside with flowers and plants and things." She looked over at her son. "Troy can do chores. Take out the trash and wash dishes, stuff like that."

Troy scowled.

Gloria was still looking around the room when I left. I couldn't read her expression.

As I reached the landing to the first floor, I heard Bear lumbering around in the kitchen. Then I heard a series of sharp barks followed by a low *woof*. The *woof* belonged to Bear. The barks didn't.

I marched through the dining room into the kitchen.

"Bear! What's going on in here?"

Bear, standing by the screen door, looked guilty as hell with his "what did I do?" expression.

The expression of the other four-legged creature in the room was another story.

Standing over Bear's gigantic food and water dishes was a small, muscular box-shaped dog with a smushed-in face and a turned-up nose. If this pug weighed twenty pounds, I would have been surprised. He gave me a look that said I had the importance of a flea on his butt, then turned his attention back to the dog food that he was enthusiastically eating out of Bear's bowl.

"Where did you come from? Bear?" I looked at my two-hundred-pound mutt as if I expected him to speak to me. I have got to stop doing that.

Bear whined as if to say, "What do you want from me?" and flopped into a heap on the floor.

"You're no help." I turned to the intruder. "Excuse me?" Now I know that you aren't supposed to approach animals when they are eating. But this dog was not intimidated or distracted. He gave me the look an English butler gives just before he says, "Madam is not at home," and slams the door in your face.

"Who let you in anyway?" But the screen door was unlatched and Bear had gotten into the habit of leaning into it so that it would open. I glared at Bear, who sighed and looked contrite.

The pug continued to eat as if I were talking to myself. And, when he had finished, he delicately drank a few sips of water as if cleansing his palate. Good grief, a dog with better manners than mine! I would not be treated like hired help in my own house.

Three days later, the pug was still hanging around my house. I posted flyers, but in the meantime I named him Wellington and let him stay. He and Bear patrolled the yard, chased squirrels, and kept the coach house cats from taking over my porch furniture. Wells was earning his keep.

Oh, I had him neutered after I caught him marking each corner in the dining room. I don't think Wells has forgiven me for that yet.

After the first few weeks, between dealing with Gloria and Troy, housebreaking Wells, coordinating home repairs and my own dismal efforts at painting (wall painting, that is), I wondered if my sanctuary idea was going to work. Dealing with "OPP" (other people's problems) and "OPC" (other people's children) was taking me to the limit of my coping skills.

The first confrontation with Gloria took place one afternoon when I came home early from a dentist's appointment. That was when I discovered that Gloria's daily routine was a little different than I thought. I came in the back door and almost did a neutron dance.

The kitchen looked as if a tornado had hit. There were dirty dishes in the sink. Dishcloths lay in a heap on the

stove. The linoleum floor was covered with black footprints. In the parlor, the sofa pillows were now stacked on
the floor as if someone (someone small) had tried to make
a fort out of them. There was something wet and sticky
on the coffee table. The second-floor hall had a mound of
dirty clothes on the floor and the bathroom was a fright.
For a moment, I thought that the toilet bowl creature had
returned.

I tapped on the bedroom door, then peeked in. Gloria
was sleeping soundly, a half-full ashtray of cigarette butts
on the floor beside the bed. So much for the no-smoking-
in-the-house rule.

"What the hell is going on around here?"

Gloria nearly jumped out of her skin.

"Wh-what? What is it? What's wrong?"

"There are dirty dishes in the sink, clothes on the floor
in the hall; the parlor is a mess; *this* room is a mess. And
what happened in the bathroom?"

"I-I was getting ready to clean that up," she began.

"Same way you were 'getting ready' to go to your appointment with Nancy?" I charged, referring to the counselor at the shelter. Gloria hadn't shown up for her last
appointment.

"I can't sit through that 'I'm all right and it's OK' shit,"
she snapped back. She fumbled with the cigarette pack.

"No smoking in the house, remember?" I said. "And
what about your interview yesterday? Did you sleep
through that, too?"

Her blue eyes widened and then darkened with anger.

"I don't 'preciate you talking to me like I was a kid or
somethin'," she growled. "I'm a grown woman. I take care
of my own business."

"Well, you're doing a piss poor job of it," I growled

back. Not very diplomatic of me, but you should have seen that *bathroom!* "You agreed to stay here and follow the rules. You also agreed to see Nancy once a week. As far as I can see, all you've done is sleep, smoke, watch TV, and use the bathroom. You aren't helping me with the painting and you're not doing much anywhere else around the house, either."

"I've been pruning the rosebushes," she shot back.

"One branch at a time?"

She tightened her jaw. "That's how you prune rosebushes."

"I see." As far as I could tell, the garden was still an overgrown tangle of weeds and thorns.

"I'm a little depressed," Gloria said. She wasn't very convincing.

"Bullshit," I snapped. "You're the one who said she didn't like that 'I'm all right; you're all right' stuff. A little lazy if you ask me." Wrong thing to say.

At that, Gloria's eyes blazed and her cigarette-sanded voice raised with anger.

"What the hell would you know about it? No, I am not goin' to counseling. I don't want to sit there with Nancy lookin' down her nose at me like I'm dirt on her shoe. Feelin' sorry for me. Her degree don't tell her nothin' about my life. And now, I got nowhere to go and I've got to depend on you and your fancy house and nice things and all your goddamn rules. I just want to sleep it away. I want it all to go away." She glared at me and took a deep puff on the cigarette that she had just lit. The smoke poured out of her nose. "I want *you* to go away."

Her eyes were wet, but her voice was still strong. "You don't know shit about how I feel. Did you have your house burned out from underneath you? All your stuff and your kid's toys turned to ashes? Have you had your arms broke and your face beat up? And no place to go, no one to help you with a kid to feed?" A sob escaped from her lips and the weight of it hit me in the chest. "Scared half to death all the time? All the time?"

Besides when I was with Pam and LaDonna, I kept it all inside. I hadn't shared my pain with anyone. I mean, what was the point? My life was laid out like a freeway littered with broken glass and bloody washcloths, dark, ugly purple bruises, scratches, four broken ribs, three concussions, and two sprained ankles. If I'd put it to music, it would sound like a perverted version of *"The Twelve Days of Christmas"*:

> *On the fourth day of Christmas, my true love gave to me*
> *Four side punches, three bruised ribs, two black eyes,*
> *And a partridge in a pear tree*

I had kept it all to myself. But that was wrong. I was wrong.

"Yes." The word came out in a whisper, but Gloria heard it. She almost dropped her cigarette.

"I used to sleep in a tight little ball because my back could take the punches better than my stomach could and . . . and because I'd already had broken ribs and if he hit me on the back of my head, it didn't . . ." I stopped. This was a lot harder than I thought. "It didn't leave marks that you could see and I could go to work the next day and not have a punched-in face."

Gloria was staring at me as if she'd seen a ghost.

"I-I didn't know. Nancy didn't tell me that. I'm sorry; I—" Her words poured out in a rush.

I blinked the tears back. "It's OK. I should have told

you. You're not alone, Gloria. But the hardest part of this . . . this thing is that getting out of it is something that only you can do. I know this because it took me almost fifteen years to take that first step. And I suffered because of it. And my child suffered." I looked at her. "I won't lie to you and say that everything will be rosy going forward; it won't." Our eyes locked. "The dirty little secret is that it will never really be over. But you still have to take the first step. And leave."

It was a conversation that left both of us exhausted and sad. But it helped me to see things more clearly as I stumbled through my dream to make the yellow house a sanctuary for myself and for others. And Gloria's attitude changed, too. She went to her next appointment with Nancy. Soon I noticed that the rosebushes in the front yard had been pruned.

But there was still Troy.

When I decided to open the yellow house to women refugees from violent marriages and relationships, I guess I forgot that many of them have children. Apparently, LaDonna felt that I could manage at least one child.

I think she was wrong about that.

Every day I found myself offering up the same prayer: *"Dear Lord, please give me enough patience and restraint to keep from murdering this smart-mouth boy and burying him under the tomato plants. Amen."*

It was a constant battle. A continuing litany of "quit" and "stop that." His mother was never around when he was acting like a little ass. As far as she was concerned, he was a "good boy." I referred to him as "the Beast."

He had taken to exploring the house, looking for secret passageways, hidden doors, and buried treasure. In the beginning, it was annoying because he would jump out from behind chairs or out of closets. After a while, though, I began to hope he would actually find a secret tunnel and get lost in it.

Greasy spots appeared on my lace curtains in the parlor.

"Troy, don't wipe your hands on the curtains. That's what paper towels are for."

"I don't have to do what you say."

The delicate handle of a demitasse cup had been broken. That cup had belonged to a great-grandmother whom I remembered in the pleasant fog of childhood memories, a woman of white hair, vanilla cookies, and a Bible held in strong but arthritic hands. I fingered the little broken piece and wondered if Superglue would work. I could glue his nasty little fingers together and then he wouldn't be able to bother my china treasures anymore.

"*Troy!* Come here please!" I said this through clenched teeth. There were chunks of mud and grass on the rug in the front hall and scuff marks and tracks all over the kitchen floor.

The screen door slammed and the little monster appeared wearing a surly expression.

"What?"

That does it. If there is one thing that I cannot stand, it is disrespectful children. I must be old-fashioned. The positive parenting/time-out/count-to-five stuff came in when Imani was little, but I couldn't get into it. I watched the children that she went to school with terrorize their parents and challenge the teachers. Their punishment was a "time-out" that they blew off like birthday candles on a cake. At the mall, I held my daughter's hand tightly as other children ran through the stores and their smiling parents (afraid to dampen "independent spirits") threatened to count to three. They were never clear about what would happen when they got to three. It didn't matter, though, because the little brats didn't listen and their pleading parents ended up counting to three hundred.

"Not 'what,' " I told Troy, my jaw tightening. "You say 'yes, ma'am.' "

"I can say whatever I want," he snapped. "My mom says I don't have to do what you tell me to."

That was it.

I grabbed him by the ear and marched off to find the source of my troubles.

She was in the rose garden wrestling with a tenacious dandelion. The dandelion was winning.

Gloria has a green thumb and the yard was beginning to flourish under her care. She can make any plant thrive, and landscape with the best of them. But she has a purple thumb when it comes to disciplining her child. I dragged that boy down the cobblestone path toward the back of the yard where his mother was working.

Gloria was designing an English garden like one she'd seen in a magazine once. She had filled the beds around the porches with bright flowers. I now had "herbaceous borders" along the walk and near the coach house. I had lavender, holly, and even lilies.

I was going to miss her. Because if she didn't get this ten-year-old brat into shape they were both going out onto the sidewalk.

"Mom! She's hurting me!" Troy's voice piped in.

I released his ear.

Gloria looked up and shielded her eyes from the brightness of the late-afternoon sun. "What's going on? Troy, what's the matter?"

The little monster explained, "She grabbed me by the ear and it hurt!" He rubbed his ear and his sandy-colored eyebrows crunched together in a scowl as he glared at me.

This remark got his mother's attention.

"What are you talking about?" Gloria stood up. She smashed out the cigarette she had been holding between her lips. Looking at me, she said, "What did you do to him?"

"Troy, go into the house; your mom and I have to talk."

"Wait a minute! Who do you think you are, telling my kid what to do? That's my job!"

OK, if you want to play it that way.

"Good, I'm glad that you told me that. Since you are the only person to tell him what to do, will you please tell your boy to stay out of the front room, keep his hands off the curtains, not break my china, and wipe his feet when he comes in from outside so that he won't track grass, mud, and dirt all over the house? Oh, and if he talks back again, I'll spank him. I will not be disrespected in my own house."

Gloria stared at me. Troy looked up at his mother with a hopeful expression.

Gloria looked down at Troy.

"Go into the house, Troy."

"But, Mom—"

She silenced him with a look. He disappeared.

"You have a lot of nerve putting your hands on my kid—"

"Then you need to get him under control. I won't have monsters in my house."

"My boy is not a monster—"

"Brat, then." I was on a roll.

She threw the spade down.

"I don't have to put up with this shit."

"No, you don't. And neither do I. There is such a thing as consideration and respect. There will be other women in and out of here. There's the tenant in the coach house.

I can't have Troy running wild, breaking things and talking back."

She didn't say anything for a moment. We just glared at each other with the small ivy-covered stone wall acting as a demilitarized zone. Then she blinked.

"I'll talk to him."

"Fine," I said.

"But don't *you* touch him," she added, emphasizing her point with one dirt-covered finger.

"OK," I replied. *Probably best I didn't touch him anyway. If I got hold of him again, he was toast.*

Chapter Seven

Dana Drew joined my cast of "characters" not long after Wellington came to stay. As the writers of old would say, "thence" began a period of intrigue and speculation.

She called so early one Sunday morning that I almost didn't answer the phone and I had to resist the temptation to throw it against the wall. I didn't because it might have been Bette (who likes to call early when she's on her treadmill with Charles . . .) or Imani (I could never keep the time difference between Prestonn and India straight). So I cleared my throat and picked up the phone.

"Hello?"

"I am calling about the apartment advertised in the paper."

The voice in my ear was deep and husky, with an exotic accent.

"Yes?" I managed to croak out as I reached for a pen.

"Is it still available?"

She sounded like Greta Garbo, who, from all the reports that I had read, was still dead.

"Yes, it is."

"Good. Then I would like to make an appointment to see it," the voice said. "May I come this evening?"

"Of course." I fumbled with the notepad on my night-stand. "How about five-thirty?"

"No, that is too early," the woman stated firmly. "It must be after dark."

"OK . . . then, eight o'clock? I think the sun should be going down by then," I added facetiously. What was she? A vampire? I would come to regret that thought.

"Eight o'clock will be fine. I will be there. And it is on Burning Church Road in Prestonn, that is right?"

I confirmed the address and thanked her for calling.

Dana Drew was her name. Interesting. Maybe the reports of Miss Garbo's death had been exaggerated.

She showed up at eight o'clock sharp driven by a chauffeur in a large Mercedes with tinted windows. The car was so black and shiny that it looked like patent leather. When Dana Drew stepped out of the car, I wondered if it was too late to tell her that the apartment had been rented.

She made the Goths I had seen around the art school look like they were Catholic school students. Aside from red lipstick and fingernail polish, she was dressed entirely in black. Only her skin was white.

Her black hair hung to her waist. She was wearing a black T-shirt, slacks, and high heeled mules. Her silver chain belt had a miniature pair of handcuffs hanging from it. Interesting. There were interlocking Cs on her black quilted shoulder bag and sunglasses. Expensive.

She looked like a gumbo of Morticia Adams and Ozzy Osbourne with a sprinkling of Elvira thrown in.

"I'm Dana Drew," she said. It was nearly dark, but she did not take off her sunglasses. Scary.

"It's, uh, nice to meet you," I said, shaking her hand. I

led the way to the coach house, Miss Drew's heels clicking on the stone walk. Her chauffeur, a nondescript man
of average looks, height, and weight, followed quietly behind us. He was also dressed in black and wearing sunglasses. Dana did not introduce him.

They didn't stay long. There were only certain things
that Dana was really interested in. She glanced around
the huge room, checked out the bathroom, and made sure
that "the shades didn't let any light in." She tested the "integrity" of the floors. (I made a mental note to ask Jack
Neal about floor integrity the next time I saw him.) She
was interested in soundproofing. When I told her that
there was only a garage on the first floor, she seemed relieved. I could only wonder what kind of music she would
be playing.

The rest of the time was spent signing the lease. She
paid in cash. I watched her count out the security deposit
and two months' rent in tens and twenties. The money
came from a black briefcase that her chauffeur brought
from the car. I couldn't believe what I was seeing.

"I'll move my things in Tuesday night," she said in her
deep voice.

"That will be fine," I said, trying not to gawk as she
counted out the last twenty-dollar bill. My curiosity was
eating me up. "Uh, what do you do, Dana?" I asked. On
the application, she had written "Self-employed."

Dana adjusted her sunglasses with one touch of a long
bloodred-painted fingernail.

"I am a sculptor," she said.

And I'm Queen Elizabeth, I said to myself.

The black car disappeared silently into the night like a
panther wearing socks. Despite the cash that was soon to
make its way to my bank account, I had to wonder what I
had gotten myself into.

Gloria, who had come out onto the porch to smoke a cigarette, watched the car retreat into the early-summer darkness.

We had declared a truce, Gloria and I. We would probably never be the best of friends, but we weren't going to fight like pit bulls, either. Just a few border skirmishes here and there. She often had a clear-eyed view of things, and I smiled at her one-liners. Her initial comment about Dana was a classic.

Gloria took a drag on her cigarette and shook her head.

"If she ain't a pro, she's on the waiting list," she said.

I busied myself with my untied sneakers.

"She says that she's a sculptor," I said matter-of-factly, remembering the length of Dana's beautifully manicured nails.

"Yeah, right," said Gloria.

I looked up and we chuckled together.

Two evenings later, around seven o'clock, Gloria, Troy, and I watched from the porch when the moving van carrying Dana's things pulled up the driveway. First we stared. Then we exchanged glances. Finally, we dashed into the house, falling all over one another (and Bear, who had, as usual, parked himself across the threshold of the front door) like the Marx Brothers in *A Night at the Opera* to get cigarettes, iced tea, and a bowl of popcorn. Dana Drew's arrival was a performance we did not want to miss.

First, there was the moving van itself.

A semitrailer rig pulled up and it was, like Dana's clothing, completely black, no moving company logo on the trailer, no signs or lettering on the cab. Gloria and I looked at each other, both of us thinking the same thing: *Hmmmmm.*

Troy's reaction was what it usually was when things interested him.

"Cool," he said, his eyes wide with curiosity.

Nor were the movers' uniforms helpful in satisfying our curiosity. They were also unmarked except for generic name tags: JOE, BILL, JOHN, GREG.

And Dana's "stuff"?

Nearly everything was in large brown boxes. Unlabeled boxes. Some of them were huge. Others were much smaller. Two black leather chairs, which were too oddly shaped to fit into a box, were carried in separately. Our eyes widened when we saw them. They looked like something used for persuasion purposes during the Inquisition.

Not that we were being nosy or anything, but it was such a lovely evening for porch sitting. And in Prestonn, as in most small towns, porch sitting has been elevated to an art form. There is skill involved, and a degree of subtlety is needed.

It takes real skill to be able to sit in a lawn chair or on a stoop, sip a cold drink, and appear to be preoccupied with a newspaper, book, or conversation while taking in every detail of whatever is going on next door or across the street.

Outright staring is rude. To lean or even sway toward the conversation that one wants to hear is unacceptable. To yell outright across the street or driveway? A punishable offense.

Gloria and Troy were seasoned porch sitters and I was impressed. Troy, as young as he was, knew the rules like an expert. He busied himself with a game while his mother smoked a cigarette and appeared to be perusing a magazine. I was fiddling with Wells's dog harness, the citronella candles, and a make-believe mosquito bite on my leg and positioning the bookmark in my latest book club selection. I have to keep busy when porch sitting or I am always found out. We all appeared to be very occupied with our own pursuits.

Nothing could have been further from the truth.

Our eyes were glued to each and every box and crate that came out of the black moving van.

One of the crates was over six feet long, two feet deep, and oblong in shape. It looked suspiciously like a coffin.

My nose twitched. Gloria glanced across the porch at me with a gleam in her eyes.

"Did you see that?"

"Cool," Troy commented under his breath. He didn't even look up. "I'll bet she's a vampire." He was thrilled.

I couldn't stand it anymore. I strolled over to one of the movers who was writing something on a clipboard. I strained my eyes trying to see if there was a company name on the top of that piece of paper.

"Hello?"

The man put his pen down and smiled. He tucked the clipboard safely under his arm. Darn.

"Yes, ma'am?"

"I, uh, is Miss Drew with you?"

The man shook his head.

"No, ma'am. She'll be over later this evening. We're just dropping off her things."

His answer was not encouraging.

Sure, I had run a credit check. But what good is that? Does it tell you if your new tenant is a high-priced prostitute or if a she sleeps in a coffin during the day?

The owl hooted. Wellington barked in reply as if to say, "Cut that out!"

Now I not only had bats in the belfry but a vampire in the coach house. So much for creating a peaceful haven of normalcy.

Everybody had a theory about Dana Drew.

Gloria, as usual, didn't mince words. We caught a glimpse of my mysterious tenant carrying a long tubelike container into the apartment. We exchanged glances.

"That look like a kiln or some clay to you?" Gloria asked sarcastically.

"Nope." What else could I say?

"She's a pro," Gloria said matter-of-factly, turning her attention back to the begonias. "Sculptor, my ass."

Troy was just as sure that Dana was a vampire. I had to admit that his case was a good one: black clothing, pale skin, only nocturnal appearances. Lately Troy had taken to exploring the house carrying a little notebook, pencil, and magnifying glass. He was looking for a secret room and buried treasure. Sometimes, he was gone for hours and then he'd just appear from around a corner or jump out of a closet. He was trying to find out if Dana had a sleeping space in the house. Lordy!

Whatever he was up to, he was usually behaving himself. For that, I was grateful.

Bette's meticulously drawn eyebrows knit together as she listened to the story about my tenant and her affinity for an all-ebony wardrobe and interior decorating scheme. It was the decorating that bothered Bette the most. As she was a woman of many colors, the black-on-black color scheme offended her personal sense of style.

"I've studied interior design at the art school. Black this and black that doesn't sound like anything I ever heard about. And I've tried to keep up with the New York and LA trends and also that new Arizona Southwest fusion style. This sounds like neo-modern Gothic dungeon to me. Where'd you say this gal was from?"

Bette's solution to my problems was like Jack's: to run a background check, of sorts. With a huge network of family that included two sons, four brothers, three sisters, and hundreds of nieces, nephews, and cousins, Bette knew everyone worth knowing.

"If she's from anyplace around here, I'll know it," she

said with satisfaction, jotting down information in her bulging planner. "I'll call my ex-husband in Frankfort; he's in the legislature there."

I frowned.

"I thought your ex-husbands were in Atlanta, Knoxville, and Cleveland."

"Three of 'em are." She scribbled something into her notebook, then reached for her cell phone. "The fourth one is in Frankfort."

Fourth?

"How many times *have* you been married?"

She gave me a belly laugh.

"Hon, let's just say that the county domestic relations judge and I are on a first-name basis. I make Elizabeth Taylor look like a girl at her first prom."

Bette was too much.

"But these days, Bette, why on earth get married? Why not just take a lover? Or move in together?"

Bette almost dropped her two-ton Louis Vuitton on her Jimmy Choo's.

"Why, that's the most improper thing I've ever heard!" Her indignation was as fake as her Bambi-length eyelashes.

That comment came out as "Y that's the most *im*-propah thang A've evah hurd!"

"B'sides," she added with a wink as she delicately tapped out a telephone number. "When you get married, you get a lovely diamond engagement ring that you *don't* have to give back! Hello? . . . Templeton! How are you, sweetheart? . . . Fine, fine. . . ." As she talked, she waved her rose-tipped fingers at me, tapped the four carats' worth of diamond studs in her ears, and gently lifted the car headlight–sized diamond pendant that dangled from a chain that hung around her neck.

"Temp, I would *luv* to chat with you 'bout old times, but

I've got a showin' in about fifteen minutes, darlin', and I'm runnin' late. . . . What? . . . I'm still partial to that red teddy, too. Now listen, hon, I need a favah. . . ."

Deliver me from red teddies.

It was only 5:30 in the afternoon when Jack Neal proposed his Dana Drew theory, so the subject in question was nowhere in sight. She only showed up after the sun went down and then only on Tuesdays, Wednesdays, and Thursdays. Sometimes I caught a glimpse of her on Saturday evenings. Late. Like one o'clock in the morning late.

Jack sipped the soda that I had brought him and glanced up at the now black-curtained windows on the second floor of the coach house. He was keeping me company while I scraped a particularly hideous baby-poop yellow wallpaper fragment from the dining room wall. He had been "in the neighborhood" and thought that he would stop by and deliver the historic register info he had copied for me. Jack Neal lives a half hour away, so his being "in the neighborhood" was fiction. A fax or E-mail would have been more efficient. But I was glad to see him and (OK, I'll say it) flattered that he had taken the time to stop. Even though I wasn't thrilled with his Dana Drew theory.

"Is she growing mushrooms or what?"

"She, uh, works best with most of the natural light blocked out."

"Oh," he said. He looked confused. "Is she a photographer?"

"Nooooo . . . she says . . . she's a sculptor." I coughed. "She'd like to put a kiln in."

"Bullshit. What kind of sculpture is *she* doing?" He pointed to the odd-looking shades that Dana had installed over the weekend. "I think she's got a meth lab in there. You said that she paid in cash money."

Meth lab?

"Yeah . . . but lots of people pay cash these days." I would have to do better. I wasn't even convincing myself.

Jack gave me another look that said, *Bullshit.*

"I have a buddy who works for the sheriff's department. He owes me a favor or two. Do you want me to call him?"

"No, no, I'm sure it will be all right. Her credit check came back fine. In fact, it was perfect."

"I'd still be careful if I were you. There's something that's not quite right about that woman. All that exclusively *nocturnal* activity."

"Maybe she's just a night person," I said optimistically.

Jack gave me a look that said, *Get real.*

Then, out of the blue, he asked me to dinner. I was so surprised that I stared at him with my mouth open.

"Uh, you mean . . . ," I paused as I struggled to find the right words in English, as opposed to the gibberish that was pouring out of my mouth. "Dinner? With you?" I stammered. "I don't eat dinner," I finally said with some authority.

Well, that was a really stupid thing to say, my conscience scolded me. *He can look at you and tell that you haven't missed many meals lately, especially dinner. What's the matter with you?*

Jack smiled and offered a polite response.

"Oh, I didn't know that. Do you eat lunch?"

Yes and breakfast and afternoon snacks, too, my conscience commented acidly. *Not to mention Dove bars and buttered popcorn.*

"Yes, I do," I managed to spit out. I was suddenly too nervous to look at him. I busied myself with a glob of wallpaper paste that had become troublesome. "Actually, I do eat dinner." I didn't know what else to say. I felt as if I were twelve years old.

"Oh. Great. Sorry." Now it was Jack's turn to be at a loss for words. He probably thought I was a nut. "I'd like to take you out sometime. Nothing fancy. But we could have a good time."

He paused and looked at me, an uncertain smile on his face. "That is, if you're sure that you do eat dinner."

I nodded, wiping the paint chips off my nose with the back of my hand as delicately as I knew how.

"I would like that," I admitted to myself as much as to him. We actually set a date two weeks in the future. And I stopped scraping long enough to watch him climb into his huge SUV and drive away.

A date? Me? Why would he want to go out with me? Especially the way I looked today! A pair of khaki shorts that were ten years old and a T-shirt that Imani had threatened to throw away because it was so raggedy. Sneakers older than the Keds label, and the crown jewel, a lovely navy bandanna wrapped around my head. I looked like who-did-it-what-for-and-don't-do-it-again.

Since I'd left Ted I had thought about a lot of new experiences, but they had been fairly mundane: living without a black eye, sleeping peacefully through the night, not being cursed at or verbally demeaned. I hadn't figured on dating.

I wasn't ready. I wasn't even divorced yet. Why was he asking *me* out?

My conscience had no patience with me at all.

Why me?

Why not you?

I stood there for a moment stupidly reflecting on why a nice-looking man who seemed to have it going on would ask me out when a flash of blue caught my eye. I saw Gloria making her way through the garden, yelling and obviously looking for something.

I needed a break from the dried paste and peeling wallpaper, so I headed outside.

"Have you seen Troy lately?" Gloria was squinting in the strong sunlight. "I'm taking him to a cookout tonight. I've been looking for him for fifteen minutes."

"He's not in the house," I told her then, watching her expression change from mild frown to near panic. "But I haven't been upstairs in a while. I'll go look."

"I don't know where he could have gone!" She sounded really worried. "He was over by the shed one minute; the next minute, he wasn't."

But no sooner had we stepped into the front hall than Troy appeared. Out of nowhere. His checks were flushed and his shirt was filthy, a combination of mud, twigs, cobwebs, and grass stains. He smelled.

"Hi, Mom!" he said a little too brightly.

Gloria was so glad to see him that she forgot to be mad.

"Where did you go? I was calling all over the place for you!"

Troy's eyes were alive with excitement.

"I was in my secret tunnel," he told her, barely able to keep still. He looked at me. "I'm digging for pirate's treasure."

I ruffled his hair.

"Whew! You look and smell as if you were digging for worms!" My hand was now black with what looked like soot and spiderwebs. Yuck.

Gloria sighed and pushed him toward the staircase.

"Go upstairs now; go into the bathroom; run the water. Take off all of those clothes. Get into the tub." She raised Troy's face to hers. "Soap up everywhere, and I mean everywhere. Rinse off; get out of the tub. Dry off and get dressed."

"But, Mom, I found—"

"Now, Troy," Gloria's voice was firm.

"I found—"

"Troy!"

"OK." He trudged up the stairs as if he were carrying the weight of the world on his small shoulders. Gloria watched him.

"I wonder where he was," she murmured.

"In the secret tunnel," I said, smiling.

Gloria rolled her eyes.

"I have got to get him some kids to play with. His imagination is just plain running away with him. He starts day camp next week, thank goodness! Oh! I almost forgot." She thrust four pale eggnog-colored roses into my hand. "They're called 'Florabunda.' I have a ton of 'em; they're popping up everywhere. Thought they might look good in there." She gestured toward the front parlor, which I was decorating in a traditional Victorian style.

The roses were beautiful. And Gloria was right; they were perfect for the parlor.

"They are lovely," I said, turning them over in my hands.

She nodded, trying without success to suppress her pride.

When Gloria walks into a garden, she is transformed into a wizard, wise, subtle, and powerful. She uses the little grace notes of her art to tame the delicate blooms of the pink tea rose and sings an aria in a language only grass understands. It is the mystery of her craft and there isn't any point in her trying to share it with me. I couldn't understand it if I tried.

It was magical to see the same fingers that usually held a cigarette or were wrapped around a can of light beer gently stroking the petals of a newly blossomed rose or tapping the side of a thorn until it fell off. Gloria's hands are wide and square and her fingers are muscular. Her skin is rough and flaking because she plunges her hands into hot water without gloves and once worked on an assembly line. She doesn't get manicures and she's forgotten that hand lotion was invented. Her fingernails are short and often dirty with the soil and grit that she works in. And the tips of her fingers are stained yellow from the nicotine of the cigarettes that she smokes one right after the other.

None of that matters. What matters is what she has done in the garden. It had become a place of wonder. Miss Caroline would have been proud.

Upstairs, we heard the water running. Troy was following instructions for once. Then I remembered something.

"Did you go to work yesterday? There was a message from the store on the answering machine." Gloria had been working part-time at the Quik-Mart in west Prestonn.

Gloria's shoulders stiffened.

"I was late. I had an interview at eight o'clock. I told the manager, but I guess she forgot." She lowered her head as if she were trying to duck under something.

"Oh," I said, trying not to sound too nosy. "How'd it go?"

"They said they'd call me."

Well, that usually means "no," I thought to myself.

"Didn't you have one this morning, too?"

Her shoulders practically welded themselves together. I could tell from the set of her jaw that she did not want to have this conversation.

"Yeah. I went. But I seen when I got there that I wasn't getting that job."

I sniffed one of the soft lemon–chiffon colored roses. It had a delicate fragrance. Nice.

"What made you think that?" I headed toward the pantry to get a vase.

Gloria followed.

"The girl at the front desk looked down her nose at me as if she was smelling shit."

I tried to seem really interested in the roses. Job interviewing was another subject on which Gloria and I had declared a truce. We didn't agree at all about how you interview for a job. Gloria believed in a bare-bones, what you see is what you get approach. She went to interviews armed with a one-paragraph résumé, dressed in slacks and a shirt and her hair pulled back. She was clean and she was neat, but she didn't look professional. I had offered to help her with her résumé, coach her through the interview process, and give her a complete makeover.

Gloria wasn't having any of that. Gloria Estepp didn't put on airs for anybody. She was what she was and that was that.

But, so far, her approach wasn't working. She still had the part-time job at the carryout, but no other prospects.

"Who cares what the receptionist thinks? Who did you interview with? A manager?"

Gloria sighed.

"Yeah. Some guy who looked like he was Troy's age. He was lookin' down his nose at me, too. I don't need that. That job wasn't for me anyhow."

I bit my tongue. I had promised myself, sort of, that I wouldn't go down this road with Gloria again unless it was her idea.

"Have you seen anything better?"

She pulled a piece of folded newspaper out of her

pocket. It was a section of the classifieds and it had been pressed, folded, and refolded. One two-inch-square box outlined in bold black lines was highlighted in bright pink:

Landscape Design Company needs project manager to design and implement residential and commercial landscapes. Experience required. Call Andy Lawrence at . . .

The address and telephone number were also highlighted. I glanced at the top of the page.

"This newspaper is four weeks old! They haven't called you back yet?"

She looked away.

"I haven't called 'em yet."

"You haven't called them yet?" I was amazed. "Why not?"

"I-I don't know. I guess . . . I guess I was just waiting."

I frowned.

"Waiting for . . ."

"Just waiting. To see if they hired someone else. I guess . . . to see if I could get the courage to apply for it." She took the clipping out of my fingers and refolded it. "They'd never hire me anyway."

"Why wouldn't they?"

Gloria looked at me as if I were from Mars.

"Why hire *me?*"

"Why *not* hire you? If the rose garden is an example of your work, they'd be stupid not to."

She looked out the kitchen door at the neatly trimmed hedges, the beginnings of a topiary that she was experimenting with, and the now-flourishing roses.

"Opal, what is a project manager, anyway?"

I shrugged my shoulders. "Corporate-speak for the person whose job it is to map out the placement of the trees, bushes, shrubbery, flowers, and other green things and put them into the ground or tell other people where to put them."

Gloria just looked at me. She seemed to be processing what I was saying. That was a good sign.

"Oh. I guess I could do that."

I shook my head in frustration. "Yes, I guess you can. You've single-handedly transformed this place. And it had been neglected for several years. Anyone who can do that can tell other people where to plant trees or bushes."

"Shrubbery."

"Shrubbery," I said. Anything green is completely out of my area of knowledge. If it weren't for Gloria, the grass on my front lawn would probably die.

"So, are you going to call them? Maybe they haven't filled the position yet." I wanted to say more, but I needed to restrain myself to avoid an argument. I arranged the roses in an old crystal vase.

"Yeah," Gloria said with finality, nodding her head. "I'll call 'em."

I took a deep breath before I asked the next question.

"Anything I can do?"

She saw through me immediately.

"Yeah, write me up a four-page résumé, paint my face, and make me look like somebody I'm not?"

Well, yes, I said to myself. *How did you know?*

To her, I said:

"It's all in the packaging."

"I'll do it my way, thank you."

"Fine," I said, turning my attention back to flower arranging.

Upstairs, the sound of water distracted us. Gloria looked at her watch and rolled her eyes.

"I'd better go up. That boy wasn't in the tub long enough to get a flea's ass clean."

I smiled.

Well said.

Chapter Eight

Tending to the rose garden began Gloria's transformation. Stripping off the layers of wallpaper in the house began mine.

At the beginning of the summer when I first moved in, I had planned to have a contractor do the plasterwork in the house, but the bids that I got were ridiculous. Even Rodney's initial "reasonable" bid grew like a dandelion. Five thousand here, two thousand there. But the rooms looked awful and I had to do something. Jack was the one who helped me get out of the corner.

He'd come by to deliver another bid from a contractor friend of his. My dismay must have been obvious.

"What's wrong?"

"Does this bid seem a little high? Or is it just me?"

"It's just you," he said from the opposite side of the room, where he was picking at the wallpaper that had peeled away. "A thousand more would still be within the range."

"Oh." The idea of bringing the house back to its glory days was slipping further away.

"Say, Opal," Jack squatted down and pulled off a small piece of the burgundy brocade, "the paper comes off pretty easy. You could save a lot of money by doing it yourself. Stripping off the wallpaper, I mean. Then, when you've finished, Rodney can do the rest. Here, let me show you."

I broke fingernails and stubbed my thumb. But I did get the hang of it. And started to enjoy myself. How sick is that? Jack had created a monster.

As I scraped, sweated, rubbed, peeled, and cursed Caroline Xavier's insatiable decorating zeal, I thought about all of the money I was saving. But I was really saving myself.

I was obsessed. I came home from work, checked on dinner, then headed to the dining room and forgot to eat. Another night, I stayed up until two o'clock scraping away old paper and dried-on paste. I did the west wall in a week, the east wall in three days. As I started in on the north wall, I realized that I was nearly finished. But the south wall would have to wait, because it needed plaster work that even my fanaticism couldn't help. And Rodney wasn't coming until the next week.

What would I do until then?

A movement caught my eye outside. Gloria was getting an early start on what would be another hot, humid river valley day. I watched her for a moment. Flowers, plants, anything with chlorophyll was her passion.

What was mine?

I had set up a studio on the third floor just after I moved in, but I had not lifted a paintbrush. I'd put in supplies, organized brushes, alphabetized art books. I had the prettiest, most immaculate studio that you ever saw.

And not one painting in the place.

The easel caught my eye. I had placed a canvas on it

weeks ago and it was still blank. If painting was my passion, why wasn't I doing it?

I painted for almost three hours that morning. I just let the colors pour out of my fingertips through the brushes and onto the canvas. I painted a bouillabaisse of twenty years of tears, bruises, car payments, school plays, torn panty hose, and headaches. I painted a stew of business meetings, accounts payable memos, and copier repairs. I remembered every art lesson that I ever had. Then I ignored them all and put what I wanted on the canvas. I fiddled around with shape and color. I put landscapes with portraits and blobs with no shape at all into still lifes. I had fun.

The "old" Opal would have been more meticulous. Well, I'd had to be; I was painting in secret then. Not anymore. If still lifes and Impressionism didn't go together, so what? If I made a mess on the floor or painted at four in the morning without any clothes on, who cared? No, the "old" Opal wouldn't have done that.

But she was gone. There was a crazy woman in her place and she was painting her soul.

My "soul" paintings began to appear everywhere. Once I filled up my bedroom walls, I headed downstairs. No empty wall space was safe: bathrooms, the parlor, the TV room.

The critics were not kind.

"Looks like the dog puked," Troy said.

Gloria frowned and cocked her head to the side.

"What is it?"

It was hard to control my disappointment. The horse and rider that I saw clearly looked like chocolate oatmeal in a puddle of black ink to her.

"Obviously, you know nothing about art," I sniffed, teasing Gloria.

She set her mouth into a straight line and cocked her head the other way.

"Maybe you're right," she admitted. "Because I don't care what you say; it still looks like chocolate oatmeal."

I only had one problem: finding just the right location for my studio. In the beginning, I thought the third floor would be perfect. It had great natural light, plenty of space for easels, works in process, and supplies. But it didn't work out. The ceilings were too low. And I didn't realize that the west-facing window sent the relentless afternoon sun into the room, making it stuffy and disintegrating my pastels.

So, I took my show on the road and moved, temporarily, to the sleeping porch that would become Imani's room when she returned from India. That didn't work out, either. The light was fine and the ceilings were tall enough, but the room was too crowded. All of the furniture that wouldn't fit in the stairwell to the third floor ended up in Imani's room.

Next, I set up quarters in the back parlor. I figured that I was moving into a landscape phase anyway and from the first floor it would be easier to take my stuff outside if I wanted.

Dana floated through one evening after the sun went down, wearing a black cape (yes, that's right, a black cape in July) and sunglasses. On the way out, she admired one of my paintings. From my "blue" period. How she could see the painting is still a mystery to me. She'd come to borrow duct tape. I didn't have the nerve to ask why she needed it.

"Maybe she's sealing up a box or something," commented Cynthia, a woman who was staying in the house for a couple of days. She stared with wide eyes at the vision in black.

"I like it," Dana purred after she had studied the painting. "It has," she paused as if looking for the right word, "texture."

I have to admit here that of all the things this piece had, I didn't think that texture was one of them. It was a screwup piece that I had accidentally dropped two blots of paint on. They had hardened into pimples—one grayish-brown, the other blue. But Dana bought it for fifty dollars. My first sale.

"You've put in a lot of vork in this room," she commented in her throaty Swedish (or was it German?) accent. She smiled and nodded appreciatively when I described my exploits with wallpaper scraping and midnight excursions to the mega–hardware store.

"I think you should rag roll the walls," Dana said firmly. "I could help you."

To my surprise, she went on to explain, in detail, the ins and outs of the rag-rolling art. She sounded like Martha Stewart. In latex. I thanked her for the suggestion.

Jack was kind enough to echo Troy's sentiments concerning my artistic endeavors, then tried to temper the blow with an invitation to take an evening drive and pick up some ice cream. I turned him down, too much to do right then. He pretended to be hurt and made a face that looked so pitiful that I laughed out loud. It just didn't fit his Macho Man GI Joe demeanor.

"Oh, it's like that, huh?" he growled. I pushed by him with a stack of folded laundry and he followed me through the dining room to the foyer.

"Uh-huh, it's like that."

"See, that's what I'm talkin' about there. Still mad at me because of what I said about your painting. You ask a black man to be open-minded and sensitive and what does he get? Criticized! Rejected!"

"Negro, please, you said it looked like an elephant threw up a spinach salad."

He tried to look serious.

"I was trying to be creative in the manner in which I convey appreciation for your use of color."

The exaggerated quasi-English accent was too much. I couldn't help but laugh. "Jack, take a laxative, will you?"

"OK, I will after you agree to go for a ride with me; what's up with this wall?"

He changed the subject so quickly that I got conversational whiplash. He'd stopped at the pocket doors leading to the foyer.

"Oh, that," I set down the laundry basket. "I'm not sure what it is. I've done the best that I can with it. Rodney starts next week; I'll let him figure it out."

Together we studied the wall. I had stripped and scraped down my dining room walls and I was pretty proud of myself. But the north wall presented a wrinkle that I hadn't counted on. After I peeled away the burgundy brocade, baby-poop gold, and robin's egg blue wallpaper, not to mention a busy rose floral number, the wall presented a brownish-greenish-gold-shaded goo that really *did* look like one of the dogs had puked.

"I wondered what it was," I said. "Mold from water damage upstairs? Another layer of wallpaper?"

Jack ran his fingers across the wall.

"I don't think so," he said slowly, fumbling in his pocket for his glasses. "It looks like paint. Not wall paint, latex. Or oil." He looked at me and smiled mischievously. "Like the paint you use in your *Dog's Innards* series."

I glared at him.

"Thought I'd try that one out on you," he said smugly. "I started to say '*Dog Guts*' but changed my mind."

"Out." I bumped him with the laundry basket. "It's better than *Dog Puke* but not by much!"

I was enjoying Jack. He brought humor and companionship, something I had not shared with Ted. Something that I needed when Beni Douglas burst into my life.

LaDonna called me at work from the Women's Crisis Center late one afternoon. I was up to my ears juggling two faxes, ten voice-mail messages, and more E-mail than I ever knew existed, plus a call from an irate attorney with whom I was having a really unpleasant conversation about his inflated bill. How can one attorney possibly bill 168 hours in one week unless he is working while he sits on the toilet?

"Hey, LaDonna, what can I do for you?"

"I'm referring Beni Douglas to you," she said.

I pulled out my little notebook and started writing. The fax machine beeped. Paper jam, darn.

"OK. I have room. When is she coming?"

A pause.

"I don't know."

"You don't know?"

"Well, I'm not sure."

I put my pen down. LaDonna was never unsure about anything.

"She's like the wind. Comes and goes. I won't see her for weeks; then, out of the blue, she just shows up or calls needing a place to stay for the night."

"OK," I said slowly. Beni Douglas sounded like a hemorrhoid to me.

LaDonna explained.

"She's young, a college student, artsy-fartsy type. Bright as all get out, but she's hooked up with this boyfriend." LaDonna paused. "You know."

Oh, yeah. I know.

"She's not from around here. Her folks live in Illinois, I think. I just want to leave a porch light on for her. Let her know that she has somewhere safe to go. Do you know what I mean?"

Yes, I did.

I first met Beni Douglas when she showed up on my front porch at two in the morning with a Coke in her hand, a cut on her left eye, and a busted lip. She grinned at me like a puppy. Her locks danced along her shoulders as she moved her head back and forth.

"Hi! I'm Beni Douglas. LaDonna sent me. Are you Opal?" She bopped into the front hall with the enthusiasm of a freshman pledge during rush. The only problem was I had expected her to arrive at 7:00 P.M., right after dinner.

I was sympathetic and irritated at the same time. And, of course, the "mother" in me came out. Beni was about Imani's age.

I turned her face toward me so that I could get a good look at her eye. With nearly twenty years of experience, I was an expert on black and soon-to-be-black eyes. Beni's soft brown eyes were bright but bloodshot.

"Do you know what time it is?" I scolded her. "You were supposed to be here hours ago! Has anyone looked at that eye?"

Beni was unfazed.

"Yeah, I know. Sorry about that. I stopped off at a party on campus. Do you still have a bed for me? I can't go back to the apartment yet. P-Bo is still pissed off."

I looked at her as if she had just landed from Mars.

"Yes, there's a bed for you," I said. "But I'll need to do something with that eye first. And you need to see LaDonna first thing in the morning. You can't go back to that apartment, Beni."

She shrugged her shoulders and looked at the hall now bathed in lamplight. The rest of the house was dark.

"Your house is beautiful," she said, running her fingertips

along the top of a small chest that was sitting under the French window. "That's a great window. It looks like stained glass."

"Beni, are you listening to me?" I sounded like a mother again.

She giggled. In the dim light I couldn't see her eyes clearly, but I could smell the burnt weed on her clothes. This time, she smiled sheepishly, as if she didn't have a care in the world. No, she wasn't listening to me.

"Yeah, yeah. It's just a little cut; it'll be fine. You got any ice?"

Cool as a cucumber, that Beni.

I briefly told her about the "house rules."

"No smoking," I said firmly as we walked to the kitchen. "Of *any* kind." I looked her in the eye when I said this. She grinned again, her eyes shiny. Nope, she wasn't listening.

I got her an ice pack and sent her to bed.

She was gone in the morning.

And I worried about her.

LaDonna tried to reassure me.

"Don't worry yourself to death about it. She'll be back," she told me grimly. "That's the sad part about these situations. She hasn't left her boyfriend for good. And that means she'll be back."

Beni was like the kamikaze. In Japanese, the word means "divine wind." She came out of nowhere and you never knew when she was coming, so it was impossible to prepare for her arrival. If there was a "sighting," then you were on alert. LaDonna would call from the crisis center. "Beni Douglas's boyfriend kicked her out. We're full. Can she stay at the yellow house tonight?"

And I wouldn't see Beni for a week.

Other times, she would just show up.

One of her visits lasted seven hours, just long enough for her to get some sleep and leave the bathroom a wreck.

On her next visit, she was subdued. Beni sat down at the kitchen table with a soda can in her hand. Her hair was a soggy mess and her face was rumpled. She looked like she hadn't slept. No almost-black eye or fat lip this time, the boyfriend was becoming more strategic in his abuse. Beni wore a long-sleeved cotton T-shirt that made me hot just looking at it. It was eighty degrees already this morning. I knew that if I rolled up Beni's sleeves, her arms would be finger-painted with bruises.

The animation in her eyes was gone. She looked as if something had sucked the personality out of her. Gloria and I glanced at each other. We knew a lot about that feeling.

Troy sat at the table eating his breakfast. Beni fascinated him. She had played chess with him on her last whirlwind visit and he thought she was "cool." This morning, he kept staring at her. She looked like a completely different person.

"Troy, don't gobble your food," his mother chided him. "It don't have . . . doesn't have legs; it won't run outa the bowl."

"All right," Troy mumbled, milk dribbling down his chin.

Gloria started to say something else, then thought better of it. We all sat in silence until Troy finished inhaling his cereal and juice and flew out the door with his backpack to catch the bus for day camp.

"You can't go back to him," Gloria said matter-of-factly. She wasn't waiting for an invitation to get into Beni's situation. "He'll just knock you around again."

Beni took a long gulp of her soda.

"He was just upset," she said in a low voice without

looking at either of us. "His portfolio was turned down by the art academy committee. He was really disappointed."

"Then he needs to take his disappointment out on the photographs and not on you," I said, setting a small plate of toast in front of her. "Here. You need to eat something, Beni."

She pushed the plate away.

"No. Thanks. My stomach is . . . a little shaky. I'll just drink the Coke."

Gloria's fingertips tapped the table. Whenever she did that, tapping like a pianist playing Bach, I knew that she either was agitated or wanted a cigarette or both. She looked at Beni as she raised her coffee cup. "You can't go back to him," she repeated.

Beni's eyes narrowed and, for the first time, I heard the voice of a frightened, confused girl instead of the hip, wise, gum-cracking college student.

"I-I know. But . . . but I don't have anywhere else to go," she said sadly. Hearing that tone in the voice of a girl so young ripped into my stomach.

"That's not true. You can stay here until you get another place. Stay as long as you want. That will give you time to recover."

She stared off into space.

"Frankie said I could move into their place."

Gloria's brows knit together.

"Who's Frankie?"

"One of my girlfriends. She and two other girls have a big old house like this one off River Road just a few blocks from school."

"Sounds like a good deal to me," Gloria commented, glancing at her watch as she put her dishes into the sink. "Maybe you should look into it. Because if you go back to P-Bo, he's going to hit you again."

"How do you know that?" Beni snapped.

Gloria's eyes widened.

"I mean, just how the hell would *you* know? Are you psychic? Some of kind of wisewoman?" Beni's tone was sharp and sarcastic. "P-Bo said he was sorry. He's . . . he's just temperamental. Moody. He feels really bad about what happened."

"They always do," I said to myself loud enough for Beni to hear.

"He *said* he was sorry! What do you want from him anyway? He's even taking me to dinner tonight to apologize!"

"If you're smart, you'll turn down that invitation," I said coldly. There was no other way to say it. How many apology dinners had I been on? How many "I'm sorry, sweetheart" roses had I gotten over the years? And boxes of chocolates? And scarves and jewelry? All not worth a damn.

"Don't go, Beni," Gloria said quietly.

Beni stood up, but her legs were wobbly and she sat down quickly. Her face was gray.

"Look. I don't mean to be ungrateful or anything. And I really appreciate your taking me in, but . . . you're older and you've got kids and . . . well, you've been putting up with this stuff for years with alcohol a-and other things. P-Bo doesn't have a drinking problem. He doesn't! And he's a brilliant artist! He just . . . He's just excitable, that's all. He didn't mean it."

This impassioned defense of one who was so undeserving exhausted her. She closed her eyes and leaned back into her chair.

"Anyway, I'm too tired to do anything right now. All I want to do is go to sleep."

I patted her on the shoulder and lifted her chin.

"Then go upstairs and get some rest. When you wake

up, call LaDonna. You need to talk with someone. You can stay here until you get it all sorted out. OK?"

Tears glinted from the corners of her eyes. She nodded, her lips pressed together.

"OK." Her voice came out in a whisper.

Gloria looked away.

Beni did not come back that night. I didn't see or hear from her again for almost a week. But, just like the kamikaze, that girl brought trouble to my door. We tried, in vain, Gloria and I, to help this girl and give her the benefit of our sorry experiences. But the young know best. It is only us old folks who are fools.

Chapter Nine

"P-Bo" showed up on my front porch at one o'clock in the morning screaming at the top of his lungs. Scared my intestines clean. He sounded like a pair of mating cats harmonized by nails pulled across a chalkboard. I sat up in bed so fast that I nearly gave myself whiplash. Wells yipped a few times and raced down the stairs. Bear woke with a start, woofed loudly, then ran after him. I heard Gloria and Marsha, a sixty-year-old refugee who was staying for a few days, rustling around downstairs. Gloria yelled from the bottom of the stairs.

"Opal! Opal! You hear that?"

"Yes, I'm coming right down. If it's not Ice Tray in heat, I'm calling the police."

It wasn't Ice Tray in heat, although the screeching woke Tray and CW and a few other cats that were rooming with them for the night. It did not wake Troy, who, as usual, slept the undisturbed sleep of the not-so-innocent.

We ran down the two flights of stairs and I turned on the porch lights.

"Do you want me to call the police?" Marsha asked, clutching her robe around her.

"Not yet," I said, peering out the front window. "I just want to make sure it's not the cats fighting again." Ice Tray and CW had notorious reputations on this corner of Burning Church Road. They challenged and attacked anything with legs that moved across the yard at night, human or animal.

The screeching came again. Its shrillness made my teeth hurt.

Marsha shook her head.

"That doesn't sound like cats fighting," she said.

No, it didn't.

A man stood in my yard. If this had been biblical times, I would have thought he was John the Baptist. As it was, I figured he was a poor slob who had drunk too much at a dive on the main drag and lost his way home. We get those in Prestonn from time to time. He was shirtless and his pants were falling down around his hips. I thanked God for the invention of boxer shorts or Gloria, Marsha, and I would have seen more than we needed to at that late hour of the night. He was bearded and his hair was long and twisted into thin dreadlocks. Wells took off before I could grab him and circled the intruder, yapping at him. I tried to hold Bear, but he weighs almost as much as I do, so he broke free and joined Wells. The man was surrounded by angry, barking dogs. But he didn't seem to notice.

I had just told Marsha to go ahead and call for Prestonn's finest when I actually heard the words he was saying.

"Benetia! Benetia!"

Beni.

"She's not here!" I yelled from the front porch. I started to go farther, but Gloria, very wisely, pulled me back.

"Opal, you don't know that boy. He might be crazy. Or he could have a knife or a gun. You might want to call the dogs back, too."

But this fool wasn't going to hurt the dogs.

"Beni! Beni!"

"She's not here, P-Bo," I told him. "And if you don't beat it, I'm calling the police."

His screeching, which was a combination of crying, sobbing, and yelling, stopped as my words finally sank in. He blubbered on incoherently while he ran his fingers through his matted hair. Then he dropped to his knees and continued to cry.

"Beni, I love you! Beni, where are you?" His voice was dripping with emotion and, well, drama. If he'd been singing, it would have been an opera.

"Get a grip," came Gloria's voice from behind me. Despite the seriousness of the moment, I smiled.

"Bear! Wells!" Bear gave one last *woof* and joined me at the bottom of the porch. Wells, as usual, did his own thing. The word *retreat* is not in his vocabulary. He backed off a few feet but remained in place, barking at intervals just to let the stranger know that he wasn't home free just yet.

"P-Bo, get the hell out of here or I'm calling the police!"

He sobbed for a few moments, still oblivious to the dogs. Then he seemed to wake up and struggled to his feet. Waving off Wells, who continued to yap at him, he stumbled away into the darkness yelling back at me, "Tell Beni I love her! I love her!"

Yeah, right.

Beni called the next day. I could tell from her voice that she knew what had happened. And I was madder than a hornet.

"Hey, Opal, what's going on?"

I couldn't keep the anger out of my voice. House Rule Number One is that under no circumstances do you tell the abusive partner where you are. In fact, depending on your situation, you don't tell anyone. There is an old saying: Two people can keep a secret if one of them is dead.

"Beni, you told P-Bo where you were."

"No, I didn't!"

Her denial was not at all believable.

"Yes, you did," I told her angrily. "He showed up here last night at one o'clock, screaming like a sick cat. I would have called the police, but he finally moved on."

There was silence on the line.

"I-I'm sorry. I didn't think—"

"No, you didn't!" I interrupted. "You had your head up your butt. When you tell people about this place, you put me and the other women who come here in danger!"

"P-Bo wouldn't hurt a fly!" Beni cried.

"He beat *you* up, didn't he?"

This time, my voice was cold. Reality can often be like ice water. It stuns you and then it wakes you up. I knew how Beni felt. Exactly as I had felt when LaDonna told me that everyone already knew that Ted was beating me up.

Beni's gasp came over the phone.

Then she hung up. After that, every time the telephone rang, especially if it was late at night, I hoped it might be Beni. But I didn't hear from her for a while. Instead, after weeks of blessed silence, I started hearing from Ted again.

First, it started at work. I'm an easy target there.

I was on another line, so Bonnie at work answered the first call. I could tell from the excitement in her voice that it tickled her to have to tell me that my soon-to-be ex-husband was on the line.

"Opal! I'm transferring a call to you," she said, barely able to control her glee. In a whisper loud enough for the rest of the office to hear, she added, "I think it's your ex-husband."

I sighed. I counted to ten. Georgy had said not to take calls from Ted. But legal advice and reality are two different things. Technically, you shouldn't talk to your soon-to-be-former spouse because you're in an active case and the negotiations can blow up on you. Not to mention the breach of a restraining order. The reality is that it happens all the time. You can hang up, you can put on your voice mail, or you can ask a coworker to take a message. But that gets old after a while. When it comes down to it, you have to take that call yourself. Because the asshole will keep calling until you do.

I took stock of what I was feeling and realized that, once again, there was no fear in my stomach. Just like the time that I practically pulled Ted out the window of the car, I was aggravated, pissed off, irritated, fed up, and mad as hell. But I wasn't afraid. Yep, the new Opal was still around.

"What do you want, Ted?"

"You're a conniving bitch, do you know that?"

"Unless you have something to say that involves Imani, I'm hanging up," I told him.

I heard him take a deep breath. Ted did not like the new Opal. She really *was* a sassy bitch.

"I've seen those papers my lawyer drew up. And I'm not going to sign them. That's my money and you won't get—"

I clicked over to my next call.

"Opal Sullivan, may I help you?"

The client call took several minutes, and by the time I finished it, my second line was blinking. Bonnie's head popped over the top of my cubicle. "It's your husband," she whispered. But this time, her expression was solemn and eyes were filled with worry as opposed to curiosity. I made a mental note to myself to apologize to Bonnie. Ted had obviously been ugly with her.

"What is it, Ted?"

"Don't hang up on me again, bitch. I know where you live now. You can't hide from me. I'll find you wherever you are. Think you can take my money—"

It was ten o'clock in the morning. I could hear the liquor dripping from his words like molasses over a biscuit. For just a second, I felt the cold heavy weight of fear settling into my stomach. I'd learned from the grapevine that his new girlfriend had left him. And, of course, that was my fault. I was taking all of his money. I was taking his manhood. He had to settle the score with me. I tried to shake off the fear and remember that, as I had told Beni, I could not go back. I would not go back.

I looked at the telephone receiver.

"Do you hear what I'm saying? You'd better come to your senses—"

"Go straight to hell, Ted," I replied, and hung up the phone.

To my surprise, Ted did not call again.

But his words left me nervous.

"I know where you live now." Retaliation was inevitable. To my chagrin, a tiny seed of fear had settled into my stomach, leaving it cold and jumpy, like when you accidentally swallow a sliver of ice. The new Opal was still around. But she was wary and suspicious. And every evening on the porch when I watched the lightning bugs, I searched the street for a car with its lights off and a man who was watching and waiting.

Gloria often sat on the porch, too, if she was home from work. Troy had made friends with a couple of kids down the street and was often away visiting. She took advantage of the free time to loaf and stare off into space. One evening, after Ted's telephone call, we sat there together in silence, listening to the birds chatter as they flew home for the night. From the settee in the corner I smelled the cigarette smoke and heard her gravelly voice come out of the darkness.

"It must be in the water," she commented after I told her about Ted's call. I had expected a wittier one-liner from Gloria about Ted. Instead she said, "Butch is out of the hospital. He wants me to come back with him." She was talking about her husband.

I almost dropped the glass of iced tea that I was holding.

"Gloria, he almost burned up you and Troy."

She took a long drag off her cigarette. "Don't I know that? But he's going to AA meetings. I can't credit that! Butch at an AA meeting! And . . . well, he's started going to church, too. Pool of Bethesda Congregation on Route 10 in Marysville. Says he's been born again." There was sarcasm in her voice.

I bit my tongue to keep from saying, "Bullshit."

Instead, I told her what we both had told Beni Douglas not too long ago.

"You can't go back to him."

The sandpaper voice came out of the darkness again; this time it sounded weary.

"I know. But it's Troy that I'm thinking of. Troy needs a dad around."

This time I didn't bite my tongue.

"But not if he's passed out all the time or smacking you around. Don't fall for this, Gloria."

"I *know*."

In the silence, we listened to the sounds of creatures scurrying around in the night. Ice Tray and CW were nowhere to be seen, but once in a while we heard an imperious *meow* issuing a warning to an interloping four-legged creature. The lightning bugs flickered back and forth. I caught one in the palm of my hand and let it go remembering a time, thousands of years ago, when I was small and my brother and I caught lightning bugs and put them into empty Miracle Whip jars. I wanted to say more, but I realized that there wasn't anything more to say. Gloria knew as well as I did how treacherous this high-wire act was. Balancing the needs of a child with safety, sanity, and security. It was a few minutes before her voice broke through the smoke-filled darkness again.

This time she didn't sound weary but harsh and angry.

"I had some nerve telling that girl what to do when I don't know what to do myself. Who am I to tell her not to go back with that artist boyfriend of hers? Here I am thinking about going back with Butch. Actually thinking about it. And he almost burned me up in a house fire. I must be crazy."

"No, you're not crazy," I said, feeling a tiredness creep over me that had nothing to do with the ten-hour day that I had put in at the office.

"It's just that," we both spoke at once. I stopped.

"Go ahead," Gloria offered.

She lit another cigarette. When the match struck, I could see that she was smiling.

"Despite everything, even though it was horrible, I just hate to think that I gave up. That I didn't try everything I could to make it work. I guess I keep thinking that a miracle will happen and Ted will turn into Prince Charming and everything will be all right."

Gloria's voice came out of the smoke-filled darkness to finish my thought.

"But it won't."

"No," I said. "It won't."

Bear growled and stood up, his tail stiff. Wells stood up, too, and went to the edge of the porch. He stood quietly, his square body stiff, his smushed-in ears perked. Gloria and I looked out into the darkness. The old-fashioned-looking street lamps flickered in the waning light. Nothing looked out of the ordinary. But Bear wouldn't budge and Wells let out a few yips of warning.

Gloria's hands were shaking as she lit another cigarette.

The last two weeks of July weren't a total depression drama, however. Gloria went after her dream job.

"I have an interview," she blurted out one day. "The project manager position with the landscaping company I told you about? They want me to come in for an interview."

"Is that right?" was all that I could think of to say at first. Then I added, "Gloria, that's wonderful."

She nodded and then, to my surprise, she asked for my help.

"I've thought about this for a long time," she said as we sat on the porch one evening waiting for our favorite activity to begin: Dana Drew watching. "This job pays good money. More'n Butch and I earned together when he was working," she added, referring to her still-recuperating husband. "If I get it, I can get a nice place for me and Troy and a car. I might have enough to put away for Troy to go to school."

She pondered that statement for a minute. No one in her family had ever been to college. And Troy was a bright little boy. Bad, but bright. He was the kind of kid who was always putting formulas and ideas together in his head. He had a mind that could engineer things like neutron bombs or heat-seeking missiles.

Gloria looked at me through a cloud of cigarette smoke.

"I want that job," she said firmly. "And maybe you're right about the packaging thing. I need to look like they look so that they'll listen when I tell them what I can do."

I couldn't have said it better.

"Marketing is only part of the game," I told her, reaching for the phone. "The package needs to look good, but there has to be substance behind it. And you've got the substance. You can make anything grow."

"Who are you calling?"

"Bette Smith. There's nothing she likes better than a good makeover."

Bette did the hair and makeup. I was responsible for wardrobe, interviewing strategy, and deportment. If I didn't do anything else, I was determined to purge the phrase "I seen" from Gloria's vocabulary.

At 8:20 on Thursday morning, Ms. Gloria Estepp stepped out onto the porch of the yellow house on Burning Church Road with a folder in her hand containing her résumé and a portfolio of the landscaping projects that she had planned and implemented, specifically the garden at my house.

She wore a navy suit (one of Bette's; I'm way too tall to loan clothes to anyone but the Green Giant's sister) with a pale pink sweater underneath and navy pumps. There were gold earrings clipped to her ears and a cameo pinned to her lapel that looked suspiciously like the one that my dad brought back from Italy after the war. I made a mental note to check my jewelry box and have a little chat with Troy once the festivities were over.

Bette has a knack for wielding a mascara wand and lip-stick tube. What she did for Gloria was nothing short of miraculous. "Hon, I can cover spots on a leopard!" Bette said gaily as she laid the makeup on Gloria's face with a spatula like she was spackling a ceiling. The ratty perm had been cut out of Gloria's hair, leaving her with a soft boyish hairdo that feathered around her face and soft-ened the hard edge of her jaw and pointed nose. When she looked into the mirror, she didn't recognize herself.

"Mom, you're beautiful," Troy said sincerely.

Gloria was too choked up to say anything. Bette stuck a tissue under her nose.

"Don't you *dare* cry!" she ordered. "We Kaintucky gals are made of tough stuff. Time to boo-hoo aftah you get the job, darlin'. Keep a stiff upper one till that happens. Then we'll celebrate with champagne regardless of the Baptist's rules!" she added, giving me a reproachful look.

"I guess I could make an exception," I said.

And I did. Gloria got the job.

I went in search of Troy that evening. Gloria told me that Troy "found" the cameo at a flea market they had vis-ited. The basement door was open. I caught him coming up the stairs. Yet another place he was not supposed to be. He froze at the sight of me.

"I know, I know, I'm not s'posed to be down there," he drawled, bounding by me as he prepared to escape.

"Not so fast, boy," I said sternly, catching him by the shoulder. "You sit down; we have something to talk about." I pointed him toward a kitchen chair.

Troy shrugged his shoulders.

"What did I do now?"

"Where'd your momma get that pin that she wore to her interview?"

Troy looked down at his feet, which were swinging back and forth bumping the legs of the chair.

"Stop that!" I told him.

He stopped, but he didn't say anything.

"Troy, I asked you a question."

"I found it," he answered with a defiant lift of his chin.

I had to chuckle at his nerve.

"You found it all right. You found it in my jewelry box upstairs on the third floor where you are not supposed to be."

He shrugged his shoulders again.

"You don't know that."

I took a deep breath. Children require a certain type of patience that I don't have much of anymore.

"I know that my father brought that cameo back with him from Italy when he came home from the war. He gave it to my mother, who gave it to me when Imani was born. I know that I keep it in a velvet-lined box that sits in the top drawer of my jewelry box. You know, the one that sits on top of my dresser upstairs?"

The little monster didn't even blink. "How'm I s'posed to know where your jewelry box is? I'm not s'posed to go to the third floor. Remember?"

I had to count to 300 to keep my language civil.

"I'm going to make you a deal. We'll say that you borrowed the pin for your mom's interview," I said, leaning over until I was looking the Beast straight in the eye. "But make sure that cameo sees the inside of that velvet box before I see daylight tomorrow morning. Otherwise, your momma is going to hear about it. And I can guarantee that you won't get to go to camp next week."

I have to admit that I told a lie there. Troy was set to go to a sleepover camp and he would be gone for seven days.

He had talked about nothing else for a week and was already packed. Considering the peace and quiet that would reign in the house while he was gone, there was no way that boy wasn't going if I had to drive him the four hours to Camp Rankin myself!

But Troy didn't know that.

"What am I gonna tell Mom?" he asked, falling into my trap.

"I don't care what you tell her," I said, turning to go. "Just as long as that pin is back in that box by morning."

He jumped off the chair to make his escape.

"Not so fast," I said, remembering something. "What were you doing in the basement?" I reached out to grab him. I missed. Darn!

"Nothing!" was his reply. I made a mental note to check the next time I did laundry down there. Just to make sure that the foundation of the house was still intact.

I also left the door to the third floor unlocked for the rest of the evening.

And the cameo mysteriously made its way into the little velvet-lined box by the time I closed my eyelids that night.

The bus stopped on Sunday morning to pick up Troy and take him to summer camp. I was beside myself. I could barely keep from grinning like a fool and dancing around in a circle. Instead, I said a little prayer: *"Thank you, Lord, for making sure this child is going to camp. Don't let him come back early. Amen."*

I yawned and picked up my coffee cup. It was 9:30 already and I was still wearing shorts and a paint-spotted T-shirt. I hadn't even combed my hair. If I hurried, I wouldn't have to dodge the dirty looks that Reverend Jenkins passed out when you were late for church.

"Did Troy return the pin?"

I was just pulling the screen door open when she spoke. I hated to turn around and look at her.

"Yes, he did."

"Good," Gloria said in her usual what-it-is voice. "I knew that he hadn't got it at the flea market when I saw it, but he kept saying over and over that he had." She sighed. "I hoped it was yours. Not that I want him stealin' from you, but . . ." Her voice trailed off. "It won't happen again, Opal, I promise. I won't have no thief in my family. Troy and I had a long talk about that. We had a long talk about lying, too."

"It's OK," I reassured her. "Raising a child by yourself is not easy. And things happen. The important thing is that you are working with Troy and have your hands on him, so to speak. He'll be all right." I opened the screen door, which responded with a loud creak. "Look, I've got to go or I'll be late for church."

But Gloria's mind was far away. I thought I heard her say, "He needs his father," but maybe I was mistaken. After all, Troy's father had almost burned him up in a fire.

With the new job, Gloria started looking for an apartment for her and Troy. She was happier than I had ever seen her.

Bette's family network of spies came up with nothing on Dana Drew. Jack's policeman friend came up empty, too. Why was I not surprised?

Ice Tray had kittens. I thought *she* was a *he*.

Imani would be home on August 26.

Oh, and I moved my studio. Again. The back parlor wasn't working. Too dark. I set up shop, temporarily, in the dining room.

Then, there was the hot, sticky evening when Dana came to the house in a black floor-length latex dress asking if we had any rope. That changed Gloria's opinion of Dana being a pro. Now she thought she was a serial killer. I didn't disagree.

The middle of July slinked toward August like a cat in the shadows without much incident, disaster, noise, or drama. It was too good to last.

Chapter Ten

The peace and quiet of the next few weeks were only camouflage for a sense of uneasiness that had settled over us. P-Bo's nocturnal screechfest, my encounter with Ted, and Gloria's conversation with Butch had an unsettling effect on all of us at the yellow house. They shattered the aura of serenity and safety that emanated from the old walls that I had painted cream, gold, and mauve. Even the roses that I picked from the garden seemed to droop once they were brought inside. And the bright colors in my paintings, which hung nearly everywhere in the house, did little to lift the gloom. It was beginning to feel like the House of Usher.

For a moment, just a moment, I thought that lighting the three gas fireplaces might lift the chill that had settled over everything. But the sticky haze of late summer had settled over Prestonn. In other words, it was hot as hell outside. I had the blues, all right, but I wasn't crazy.

Bear and Wells took to pacing the front hall, and they both stood guard on the porch steps now whenever we were outside. Their vigilance was unnerving.

Marsha, the genteel and elegantly dressed woman who had been a "guest" when P-Bo paid us a visit, left to stay a few weeks with her son in Wisconsin. She planned to move into a place of her own when she returned.

"Do you have a gun, Opal?" she asked as she was leaving.

I told her that I didn't, that guns made me nervous. She shook her beautifully coiffed head as she picked up her overnight bag.

"You might want to think about getting one," she said, her blue eyes stern as they bored into mine. "There are a lot of sick sons-of-bitches out there."

With that, she gracefully descended the front steps and walked in her shiny patent-leather Ferragamos toward the waiting cab.

Gloria and I watched as the cab pulled away.

"I don't believe *she* said that," Gloria commented, grinning.

"Neither do I," I countered.

But our smiles were only temporary. And for the first time since I came up with the idea of using the yellow house as a sanctuary, actually, for the first time in my whole life, I thought about getting a gun. I kept my thoughts to myself.

I wasn't allowed much time to brood, though. Troy had returned from summer camp, full of energy, mischief, and bright ideas. And it wasn't long before he distracted us with some of his schemes. Thank God. There is always room for a little silliness in life.

He had heard mystery stories at camp and decided to cook up one of his own. I had, unwittingly, obliged him. The yellow house was perfect for mysteries.

It started when Gloria found the wooden stakes in the toolshed.

I was being my usual ambitious self after dinner. I had

retired to the porch to think about thinking about balancing my checkbook and paying my due-by-the-fifteenth bills. I take a lot more time thinking about this process than actually doing it. But tonight I was distracted. Imani was coming home in two weeks. Wonderful. A little scary. What would she think of this place, her home, now filled with strangers? One of my guests' in-laws were pressuring her to return to her husband. Drama. Beni had called to say that she needed a place to stay tonight. More drama. Troy had taken to hiding around the house again, popping out of the oddest places at the oddest times. (He had frightened his mother "shitless," as she put it, when she was in the bathroom.) Mystery. And I was going to dinner with Jack Neal. Romance? I'll come back to that one. Mixed in with this hodgepodge came Gloria's voice over the fence post at the side of the house.

"Opal! Are these yours?"

Her gloved hands held a stack of wooden stakes. They were roughly cut and made out of small odd-sized pieces of wood that the carpenter left behind after he worked on the north porch. Gloria just stared at them, baffled.

"No. What are they?" I asked, taking one from her and studying it.

She shrugged her shoulders.

"I have no idea," she said. "I just found them stacked in the corner of the shed. I went out to get powder for those stupid beetles that have attacked the Japanese holly. And I found these."

"*Mom!* Leave those alone!"

The voice came from behind us, and in a flash Troy flew across the porch and landed next to his mother, a missile of red hair and huge feet in gray sneakers.

"Those are mine!"

Gloria handed them to her son. We both looked at each other.

"They're yours?" Gloria asked. "OK. But what are they?"

Troy gathered as many of them as he could into his small hands.

"They're stakes," he said proudly as he organized them by length.

His mother and I were still confused.

"Stakes," I said. "Stakes . . . for what? For the tomato plants?"

Troy looked at me as if I had two heads, four arms, and six legs.

"For the vampire o' course," he whispered loudly.

"What vamp—"

He pointed in the direction of the coach house.

"Oh, Lordy," I moaned.

Gloria couldn't help herself. She broke out into laughter. Soon I was laughing, too.

Troy did not see the humor at all.

"That's how you kill them," he told us as if we had been born yesterday. "You drive a stake through their hearts when they're sleeping in their caskets." He paused and looked over his shoulder at the coach house again. Dana's shades were drawn. But then, they were always drawn. The huge Mercedes wasn't parked in the turnaround space, but I had found, to my chagrin, that didn't mean anything, either. Sometimes I saw Dana and didn't see the car. Eerie.

"They sleep during the day, you know," Troy informed us.

Gloria nodded.

"Yes, I know," she said.

"Troy, what were you going to do?" I asked. "Sneak into her apartment and stab her through the heart?"

Troy's eyes widened.

"Well . . . yeah," he said simply.

Gloria began to take the stakes away from her son.

"Well, no," she countered.

"*Mom!*"

"Troy, you are not going to bother that woman. Now, she ain't . . . She isn't a vampire; there's no such thing. She's just a woman minding her own business, and you . . ." She leaned over and looked him directly in the eye. "You are going to leave her alone."

Troy looked away and frowned.

"Do you understand?" she asked him.

"Yes," he mumbled. "But—"

"No buts," Gloria said.

"Mom—"

"Excuse me." The voice that came from behind us was deep, husky, and had an exotic accent. We nearly jumped out of our skins.

Dana Drew stood on the cobblestone walk dressed in her usual black-on-black with a leather collar encircling her neck that was studded in what looked like diamonds. Interesting. Her eyes were covered, as they always were, in sunglasses. She was wearing high heels.

We had not heard one sound coming across those cobblestones. Not one tap. I walk across those things in sneakers and make noise.

Where the devil had she come from? Let me rephrase that question.

"Excuse me," she repeated. I tried to get a fix on that accent. At first, I'd thought Greta Garbo. Swedish. Then I thought, no, Marlene Dietrich. German. But the way Dana said "excuse me" reminded me of something else. When I remembered what it was, I almost laughed. It reminded me of Bela Lugosi in the old Dracula movies when he said, "Good evening." Is there such a place as Transylvania?

"How are you?" she asked graciously. Her accent had thickened.

We all stared at her.

Troy's eyes were as big as saucers. Vampires aren't supposed to be out before the sun sets.

"Ah, fine, thanks, Dana. I . . . uh . . . had no idea you were here," I stammered. "C-can I do something for you?"

Gloria and Troy were completely silent. For a moment I thought Gloria was trembling.

"I was wondering . . ." (This came out as "I vas vondering") "if you haf any WD-40. I need to oil some hinges."

"Oh. Oh, sure," I replied. "It's . . . it's in the toolshed; let me get it for you."

"Thank you," she said. She did not smile.

She followed me to the shed, took the oil, promised to return it tomorrow, and disappeared. I didn't hear her footsteps go back across the cobblestones, either. When I came back around the house, Gloria and Troy were still standing on the sidewalk. I couldn't think of anything to say.

"She, uh, needed oil," I said, repeating what they already knew.

"Yeah," Gloria said, picking up one of Troy's stakes and turning it over in her hand. "To oil the hinges on her coffin, I'll bet."

Troy was thrilled. "*See,* I told you. She's a vampire."

His words hung in the thick August air like ornaments on a Christmas tree.

"Troy, vampires aren't real," I told him in a tone that was completely unconvincing.

We looked up at the black-shaded windows in the coach house apartment.

"Aren't they?" Gloria asked.

It took me four hours to get ready for my dinner with Jack Neal. Yes, four hours.

You have to remember I'm an old broad. The last real date I went on was in 1974. That was a lifetime ago. My hair was all over my head in a straw-colored Afro and I wore flared jeans, a T-shirt, and a pair of platform shoes. It was the seventies. I didn't even carry a purse.

I didn't wear a bra with the T-shirt; we all went braless then. If I tried to do that now, I'd probably hurt myself or someone else. Flared jeans are "back", but I read some-where that if you have already worn an item that is back you are not allowed to wear it again. Probably be arrested by the fashion police.

As far as the platform shoes are concerned, that man-date won't be a problem. I fell off a pair of white platform shoes in 1973. Yes, fell off, stepping off of a curb to cross the street. I ended up spending that morning in the doc-tor's office having my leg bandaged up and getting a tetanus shot. I threw the shoes in the trash.

So thirty years later, here I am standing in front of my closet (bra on, thank you) trying to decide what to wear.

I had put Jack off for weeks because I just wasn't ready. He had become a friend; he was funny. He came with ref-erences (Bette had checked everything except his colon) and he was a nice guy. But I still made up lots of excuses for postponing our first real "date." I didn't want a re-bound situation. I wasn't divorced yet. I was too old. My hips were too wide. But it all came back to Ted. Why does it always come back to Ted?

He'd never leave me alone. Never. For the rest of my life (or his) I will look over my shoulder, pause before I answer a telephone, circle parking lots to make sure that his car isn't there, check and double-check my locks, doors, windows, and sleep with one eye open.

And any man that I married, dated, or was just friends with would be subjected to the same thing. How could I ask someone else to put up with this? What man would? Life is way too short to volunteer for drama, heartache, and danger. You'll get it anyway, but why stack the deck against yourself?

So what was I going to do about Jack?

I felt like a sixteen-year-old. Just that statement shows how behind the times I am. Girls today start dating at thirteen.

LaDonna laughed at me.

"Opal, it's like falling off a horse. You have to get back up in the saddle and ride again. If I hadn't done that, I never would have met my husband."

LaDonna's first marriage had left her battered, bruised, and alone caring for four children. Now she had been married for almost ten years to a teddy bear of a man who thought she square-danced on water.

Bette's approach was more mercenary.

"If it doesn't work out, go to the next name on your list." Bette shrugged her padded shoulders. "You *do* have a list, don't you?"

A list? *Me?*

"Bette, I'm forty-eight years old," I said. "The men my age want to date toddlers."

"That's your first mistake," she said sharply. "Assuming

that you have nothing to offer. You have confidence, experience, knowledge. In the right situation and wearing
the right lingerie, you can overcome any obstacles, whether
you're dating a man forty-eight or twenty-eight."

Twenty-eight?

Jack was fifty. I guess he'd obviously decided that he
didn't mind being seen out with an OBBWA (old black
broad with an attitude).

After three and a half hours had passed and I still hadn't
decided what to wear, I just grabbed something. It was a
colorful sundress, not too casual, not too dressy. I slid into
a pair of low-heeled mules and found a straw purse in the
bottom of a box at the back of my closet. With a sense of
resignation, I looked into the mirror.

I'll have to admit that I was surprised at what I saw
there.

I had pretty much given up mirror-looking months ago
when I saw the beaten-up, worn-down crack head—looking
creature with the cigarette burns on her shoulders and the
sunken-in eye sockets. Even after I moved out on Ted and
set up the yellow house, I continued my habit of doing
what I had to do to get ready for work and moving on.
Mirror-looking was a luxury that I could not afford. Plus,
it was depressing.

But for this dinner date, I had to make an exception. I
wanted to look nice and pulled together. That meant a
trip to the full-length mirror.

The woman standing there was a familiar stranger.

She was still tall and caramel-colored, but she didn't
look like the scary creature I'd seen four months ago.

Her hair was curled into long corkscrews that were
light brown, caramel, and auburn colored with highlights

of silver. Her dark eyes were shining and bright and the mascara on the eyelashes had, miraculously, not made its way to other areas of her face. Her skin was clear and smooth and healthy and her lips were parted into a smile. I looked her straight in the eye. And she looked back.

She looked like an older version of the twenty-two-year-old who'd worn the flared jeans and fallen off the platform shoes. She looked a lot like that girl who used to take art lessons and thought she was Mary Cassatt.

She looked a lot like me.

And when Jack arrived on my front porch and I opened the door, he smiled and said, "You look really nice."

And I felt good.

We had a reservation at Napa, a trendy bistro on the main drag of downtown Prestonn. It featured a "fusion" of Mediterranean/California cuisine and you had to make reservations weeks in advance. But Jack had done the owner a favor and we got a prime seating at seven o'clock. It was a beautiful August evening, so we walked.

We passed the Colonel, one of my neighbors who patrols the neighborhood as if it is his own private reserve. He was an older man and wore a ten-gallon hat rain or shine. Bette tells me that in the summer he wears the white hat and once Labor Day passes he wears the black one. He smiled and tipped the hat as we passed.

Another man approached on the sidewalk and extended his hand to Jack. He was a little man, about sixty years old, and he wore black-framed glasses with thick lenses. He was effusive and chatty. But he was a little strange.

"Hi, Cousin!" he said to Jack. "How you doin'?"

Jack smiled and shook his hand. "Fine, fine."

The man nodded at me and tipped his baseball cap. "How do."

"Hello," I said.

The little man turned his attention back to Jack. "You know, Susie ain't doin' too good, I was up there yesterday."

Jack's brow furrowed with concern. "No? I'm sorry to hear about that."

The man shook his head and sighed. "Yeah, it's sad, ain't it? But I'm satisfied that Aunt Florence and Bud and them will take care o' her."

Jack nodded in agreement. "Yes, you're probably right."

"You going up there anytime?"

Jack paused. "Not real soon. I have a few projects going on right now."

"Yes, well, I understand," the man responded. He shook his head. "Kinda sad."

"Yes, it is," Jack agreed. "Sad."

"Well, gotta go," the man said brightly. "Bye, Cousin!"

Jack waved. "Bye!"

The man walked briskly on.

I stared after him.

"Cousin? That white man was your cousin?"

Jack laughed.

"No, he's not my cousin!"

"He seemed to think that you're his cousin. And you didn't tell him any different."

Jack shrugged his shoulders. "He's a little confused. Been around here for years. Every time he sees me, he says, 'Hi, Cousin,' and talks as if he's known me forever. He's harmless. Just a good old boy with a few screws loose."

"It's strange, Jack," I commented.

Jack was not concerned. "What can I tell you? River people are different."

The owner of Napa gave us the best table, next to the window overlooking the river. He personally selected a wine for us and then sent it to the table with his compliments. I felt like Queen Elizabeth, only I was better dressed.

As usual, I alternated river watching with eating. The river was crowded with motor yachts, little fishing boats, and the occasional paddle wheeler. I was like a kid at the circus; I always am when it comes to rivers. And when the barge came through, filled with coal and sunk low in the water, it blew its horn in warning to the yachts that it dwarfed in comparison. The flotillas of dinner cruise boats parted and let the huge monolith float by, which it did in majestic style.

Jack thought I was ridiculous and teased me: "I don't get it. It's just a river."

I took a sip of my wine and grinned at him. "And you grew up here," I told him. "So, you're used to all this," I waved my hand at the window where a beautiful white paddle wheeler, the *Belle of Louisville*, made its way across our view.

He shrugged his shoulders. "Yeah, I guess that's it. My brother, sister, and I used to fish in the river, right off the banks near the River Road Bridge. We'd throw our lines out, catch catfish that wide around and that long," He showed me with his hands, and I couldn't imagine a catfish six inches around and over a foot long.

"Did you take 'em home and eat 'em?"

Jack made a face. "Oh, hell, no! I don't eat catfish. They're bottom dwellers; you don't know what they've been eating. Uh-uh," He shook his head vehemently and I couldn't help but giggle.

Yes, forty-eight-year-old women do giggle when the situation warrants it.

"What did you do with all the fish you caught, then?" I asked, completely clueless when it comes to a Tom Sawyer childhood.

"Threw 'em back," Jack said as if I should have known. "We were just fishing for fun anyway. We wrestled with them. It was something to do."

I smiled and looked out at the river again. If I live to be a hundred, I'll still be fascinated. I grew up in a flat, land-locked place, and the two creeks we called rivers don't hold a candle to this wide expanse of water that's seen it all. I am not a river person yet, but I'm working on it. But Jack disagrees.

"Nope. You may be a foreigner," he commented, refer-ring to the fact that I was not born in the state, "but I'd say that you're well on your way to being a bona fide river person, peculiarities and all."

I grinned at him. "I beg your pardon. I am not peculiar."

Jack raised his eyebrows. "Oh, really."

"Really. Oh! Look at that!" I was distracted by another barge slipping quickly through the water, scattering the pleasure craft in its path.

Jack shook his head. "Let me see. You're living in a huge yellow house. You paint pictures that look like—"

I held up my hand. "If you say 'elephant puke' we're gonna fight."

Jack cleared his throat. He tried to look innocent. "You can't keep holding that against me. I was trying to be more creative with my language."

I started laughing.

"Then, there's this movable-studio kick you're on."

I tried to look clueless. "I am trying to get the right light."

OK, so I've moved my painting studio from the third floor to the rear sleeping porch to the back parlor to the dining room. So what?

"Exactly. As I was saying before I was rudely interrupted," he continued, "you paint; you have a parade of unusual and, yes, somewhat fragile women coming and going. A noble enterprise, by the way. You have a huge bear of a dog, named Bear, that's afraid of his own shadow. And you have a piece of dog named Wellington who'll bite your ass off if you even look at him wrong. Two ghetto cats named Ice Tray and Calico With an Attitude who sweep the place like AWACS planes. The house ain't haunted, but it's definitely on the waiting list, and, the whipped cream on top of this sundae is that you have a vampire living in the coach house."

He stopped and looked at me, his dark eyes sparkling with merriment.

"We haven't confirmed that she's a vampire yet."

"I would say that her application has been accepted, wouldn't you?" Jack said sarcastically.

I shrugged my shoulders and busied myself with a piece of calamari that kept slipping off my fork. Finally, I just gave up, picked it up with my fingers, dipped it in the spicy Thai sauce, and popped it into my mouth.

"What can I tell you? River people *are* different."

It was when we were having coffee that he reminded me of something that I had forgotten about. It was something that I had hoped that he had forgotten about, too.

"I need to tell you something," Jack said, turning his coffee cup around in his large hands.

"OK," I said slowly. There was another paddle wheeler going upriver, but I turned my attention away from the window.

"I don't want you to take this the wrong way, and . . ." Jack paused. It was strange to see him searching for words. He seemed nervous, which was not like Jack at all. "And I don't want you to feel self-conscious, but I think I need to clear the air."

Clear the air. Uh-oh. A phrase that always spells trouble.

Now I was getting nervous.

Jack paused again and then plunged ahead.

"I saw you one night in the crisis center. I volunteer my services there as a handyman of sorts. LaDonna, Nancy, or whoever's on duty leaves a list on my fax machine, and I follow up. That night, they had a broken pipe."

I clutched the coffee cup so tightly that I could have crushed it. I felt a stone settle in my stomach. Its name was "shame."

"You were sitting in a corner. You looked . . . so . . . sad. I asked you if you wanted the light on, and you said, 'No, thank you.' And then, I left."

"I remember," I murmured. I studied the swirls of cream in my coffee as I stirred. I busied myself with the sugar packets even though I don't take sugar in my coffee. "I was hoping that you wouldn't."

Jack's warm hand settled onto mine.

"Opal."

Very unwilingly, I looked up. I was so humiliated, so embarrassed. All these months, I'd thought that he hadn't recognized me. I was sitting in the shadows, wasn't I? He probably thought I was a deadbeat, an idiot. Who the hell else would stay in a marriage like mine for almost a quarter of a century? If I'd been younger, I probably would have cried. But I was too old. And most of my tears had dried up years ago. I managed to look him in the eye, but my throat was tight and dry and I couldn't say anything.

"Opal, none of what happened to you has anything to do with us. And I hope . . . that there will be an 'us.' "

"Why . . . why do you volunteer for the crisis center?" I asked finally.

His answer was simple, but it wasn't what I was expecting.

"It's because of my sister," he said.

I knew that he had a sister a little older than he was. But when I said so, he shook his head.

"No, not Theresa. Linda. My twin. She married a sick bastard who abused her. But there wasn't a place like the Center where she lived, and every time she tried to leave he followed her and forced her to come back. The police . . ." Jack paused for a moment before he continued. "She went to the police, but they said that they couldn't do anything until *he* did something."

I felt the tears welling up in my eyes. I knew this story by heart, even the ending.

"They kept their promise. They arrested him after he shot and killed her."

"I'm sorry." It was all I could think to say.

Jack shrugged his shoulders and picked up his glass.

"I couldn't save my sister," he said simply. "So, I offer my services to the crisis center. Maybe, in some way, it will help another woman and her family."

I looked out the window again.

"What you did took a lot of courage, Opal," Jack continued. "That's why I haven't said anything. Until now. I didn't want you to think that I felt . . ." He paused as if he was looking for the right words. "I didn't want you to think I felt sorry for you or thought you were weak or anything like that. You're a brave woman; you have no idea how brave you are. My sister was brave, too. But her luck ran out."

Our conversation had a sobering effect on the rest of dinner. That was to be expected. But it wasn't a negative thing. I was quiet but not sad, and I wasn't embarrassed anymore. And Jack seemed to be relieved that he had gotten something off his chest. In the twilight, we walked back to the yellow house. The birds chirped, but they were saying good night as they headed for nests and sleep. The lightning bugs sparkled here and there, announcing the transition from day to night. And Jack and I walked hand in hand down Burning Church Road in the warm, familiar silence of an old couple.

Chapter Eleven

Is there a quotation in the Bible that says, to paraphrase, "There's no rest for the wicked"? Or is it "no rest for the weary"? I should know this from over twelve years of Baptist Sunday school. But I can't remember everything, plus I like the second version best. There is, absolutely, no rest for the weary. The more stressed out, put upon, tired, and worn out you are, the more crap will come your way. It's a guarantee that you can get in writing.

I am trying my best to enjoy the small peaceful moments in between the chaos and catastrophe. Sitting on the front porch in the twilight and petting the dogs or painting in the sunlight of a quiet Saturday morning before the rest of the world gets up. These are the treasured times to be guarded jealously. Because it seems that since I opened the doors of the yellow house, drama has followed me in. And that's **Drama** with a capital *D* in bold letters and in neon lights.

What happened to providing a little bit of peaceful sanctuary for women who needed it? The dream was very

different from the reality. I had forgotten that I was dealing with people. And people bring problems with them in
grocery sacks, beat-up suitcases, and, sometimes, matched
sets of designer luggage. Of all people, I should have known
this, considering all of the baggage that I lug around.

The days came and went, some better than others. And,
as can be expected, on the day that was the absolute worst
of the week, the floodgates burst open.

It was one of *those* days.

The human spirit is tremendously resilient. It can with-
stand the most horrific of circumstances, whether of human
or divine creation. Floods, famine, cancer, death, severe ill-
ness, financial decline, the human spirit comes through
these with the light of survival and hope every single time.
It is not these larger-than-life situations that beat us.

It's the little things.

It was a Tuesday. Of course. A day from hell is never on
a Friday so that you can rest up and recover on Saturday.
It is always on a Tuesday, Wednesday, or Thursday, leaving you in a nasty mood for the rest of the week.

First off, I overslept. Then, I realized that I hadn't laid
out my clothes the night before, so I spent ten minutes
rummaging around my closet trying to find something to
wear. I had an 8:30 meeting with a new client, so I wore a
skirt. Unfortunately, my last pair of panty hose had a run
in them. The shower I took wasn't as warm as I liked it, so
I made a mental note to check the water heater. Wells had
eaten something that disagreed with him and thrown up
on the carpet next to my bed. And, the crowning glory of
the day, I started my period. I was so mad that I was
yelling at the Menopause Goddess.

"Hey, bitch! I'm forty-eight; I thought I wasn't going to
have to deal with this anymore!"

She laughed and threw me a tampon.

So, it was one of those days.

I barely made the meeting on time and then returned to my desk to find fifty E-mails and that charming little message that pops up on your voice mail: "Your mailbox is more than 85% full! Please delete unwanted messages or greetings."

I was growling at the computer screen when Bonnie at work popped her head over the top of the divider separating my office from hers.

"Opal! Have you heard the latest?"

I picked up the receiver of my phone that hadn't rung and shook my head at Bonnie.

"This is Opal Sullivan."

Bonnie moved on to the next victim.

Another coworker called about an issue that he thought I should know about. I growled at him, too.

"Tom, that's nice, but you need to tell someone who cares." I hung up.

Then, the new up-and-coming executive strolled by. He was the boss's golden boy and too cocky and too cute for words. I can't stand him. He is one of those MBA wonders who are a fountain of the latest business lingo and not much else. I am not cut out for that kind of business acumen. I don't care about "value added," I am not a "team player," and the only time I sing off the same page is in church. He intimidates most of the other people around here, but as I am the only old black broad with an attitude in the office, most of his barbs bounced off me like a Wilson basketball on the court.

We traded a few insults when he finally turned to leave, with a smirk on his face that said, *I'm going to talk with Kellner about you.*

His parting words were, "What's the matter with you? You on your period or something?"

I grinned at him like the Grinch did just before he stole Christmas.

"Yes, I am, but that's my excuse. Is it yours, too?"

He turned red and left.

Most of the office were walking a wide berth around me by lunchtime.

And then, the crowning event of the day was a telephone call from Ted.

"Opal Sullivan, may I help you?"

"Yeah, bitch, you can help me."

The anger seeped through my shoes again and started up my legs. The cramps in my back disappeared and I felt my eyes narrow and my mouth pull back, baring my teeth. Standing at the copier, Bonnie glanced my way. Her eyes widened as if she had seen Godzilla.

I let him rant for almost a minute as I continued to sift through my E-mails. That DELETE button works really well; did you know that?

Ted paused in his rant for a moment, realizing that I had not said anything to him. Silence always drives Ted crazy.

"Opal! Are you listening to me?"

I deleted the last E-mail with a flourish and turned my attention back to the telephone.

"You know what, Ted?" I said, the hostility and anger dripping from my voice. "If you don't like the damn agreement, don't sign it. If you don't want to pay the money, don't pay it. And since you want to be an asshole about paying for your only child's education, then I'll make sure that she stops in to see you so that you can tell her that to her face. But, as far as I am concerned, you aren't doing me any favors and I don't owe you a damn thing. You can do what you want to do; just leave me the hell alone."

"You know what? I just might come over there and—"
I was seeing red again.

"Ted, today is not the day," I told him. And I hung up the phone.

Of course, I knew that it was just a matter of time before another shoe dropped.

I drove home like a crazy woman, ready to shut myself up in my third-floor sanctuary, sit in a bathtub of water, and soak for about six years, until the world came to its senses. I was sick and tired of being on edge. Tired of fighting and being afraid all of the time. Hating Ted and his threats. I almost wished that he would come over so that we could have a showdown. And then it really *would* be over, one way or another. That's an awful thing to say, but I was tired and crampy and my back hurt. And I was feeling real sorry for myself. How did I ever think that I could have some peace in my life? How stupid was I?

I passed through the dining room and yelled at Rodney, who was cleaning up for the day. He was working on the plaster repair and doing a decent job. But I wasn't an appreciative client that day.

"Will you be finished in this century, Rodney?" I asked him curtly. "My daughter will be home in a few weeks."

Rodney, bless his heart, took no offense.

"Absolutely," he replied cheerfully, dipping his brush into a bucket. "Almost wrapped up here!" Then he added, "Hey, Opal? There's something I need to show you—"

"Not today, Rodney," I snapped, my heels clicking on the shiny wood floor. I felt like a Victorian schoolteacher. I was not in the mood for any shit today. *Probably wants more money,"* I grumbled to myself.

"Right," said Rodney. He'd noticed my bared teeth. "It can wait. Maybe tomorrow?"

Troy was coming in through the back door.

"Wipe your feet, Troy," I snapped at him as I got a glass of water.

"I did," he said.

"No, you didn't," I snapped back. "Wipe 'em."

Troy took one look at my face (which resembled an alien monster from a sci-fi movie) and decided not to give me another smart answer. He wiped his feet and headed up the back stairs to the room he shared with his mother.

I heard Rodney's truck pull out of the driveway and looked out the back window. Dana's curtains were open. That was different. Then I looked out toward the rose garden.

Gloria was home early. Some days she worked 6:30 until 2:00; other days she worked later. She was standing in the rose garden, but she wasn't working. She was talking to a man I hadn't seen before. A tall, thin man with collar-length blond hair, who wore a baseball hat, work shirt, and jeans. He was smoking a cigarette and looking down at his feet as he talked to Gloria. She stood about six feet away from him, her legs planted in the ground, her arms folded across her chest. I couldn't see the expression on her face.

I am not usually nosy.

OK, I am nosy, but when it comes to the women who share the yellow house with me, I try to give them enough room to work out their own problems. My job is not to act as a counselor. My job is to provide a place.

But I was curious. Since she'd been here, the only person I'd seen in Gloria's family, besides Troy, was her brother, who was still nameless.

The man talked for a while, chain-smoking. I saw him raise his head once, then look down again as if looking

Gloria in the eye was hard for him to do. I guess it would be after he'd almost burned her to death.

When Gloria said something, she backed up a step, a movement that troubled me. She kept her arms folded and she wasn't smoking. She even turned down a cigarette when he offered her one. That action worried me, too. Gloria would not turn down a cigarette from the Devil.

Finally, the man threw his cigarette down and moved toward Gloria, his arms open and outstretched. I started to open the back door.

But Gloria must not have felt his movements were threatening, because she didn't move, and the man, after talking earnestly for a moment, finally shrugged his shoulders and turned away. He moved briskly down the garden path and disappeared around the other side of the house. I didn't remember seeing an unfamiliar car or truck parked near the house, so I assumed that he had walked here.

I set aside my plans for a bubble bath and decided that it was time to think about dinner. I was still thinking about it when I heard the back door open behind me.

"Saw you looking through the curtains," Gloria said. She headed toward the sink to wash her hands. I was rummaging around the pantry looking for another jar of mayonnaise for the tuna salad that I was making.

"Sorry. I was trying not to be obvious," I said. "And I don't mean to be dipping in your business."

Gloria smiled weakly.

"Opal, that doesn't matter much. If it weren't for you, the only business I'd have would be me and Troy out on the streets somewhere."

I shook my head.

"Nope, Gloria. You've got too much goin' on for that to happen." I rinsed off the celery and started chopping.

She sat down wearily in a chair.

"That was Butch, in case you hadn't guessed. My brother told him I was here. Sorry." I shrugged. "He wants me to come back with him. Says Troy needs his daddy. Says I need a man. Says he's found Jesus."

I didn't look up from my chopping. Didn't want to lose a finger.

"Jesus must get lost a lot," I said. "Someone should give him a map from Triple A."

"I don't know what I'm gonna do." Gloria sounded more tired than I felt. I turned around. Her voice was rough and hoarse. "I want a good life for Troy. I know he needs his daddy. Every kid needs a daddy. And Butch is workin' again; he got his old job back at the dealership. It pays good." She stopped for a moment and looked at me. I bit my tongue. Sometimes, I talk too much. And sometimes, I interrupt. This was not the time for either of those. Gloria needed for me to listen.

Without thinking, she lit a cigarette, took a deep drag on it, then rolled it over and over in her fingers.

"But I been married to him for twelve years and he's punched me around for most o' those. The only time he didn't slap me was when I was carryin' Troy. I think he was afraid I'd lose the baby or somethin'. He says he's stopped drinkin'. Says this new preacher at the Pool of Bethesda has helped him . . . see the error of his ways and find Jesus." At this turn of a phrase, Gloria laughed bitterly and looked up at me. There were tears in her eyes. I felt a lump form in my throat. "As if the man were wanderin' around the country trying to find the interstate or somethin'. I felt like sayin' the same thing you did: 'Butch, Jesus isn't lost. You're the one that was lost'."

She blew a cloud of smoke into the air.

"He's pounding on me, Opal. Not literally, I mean; he

keeps talking at me. He needs me. He needs us to be together. He needs Troy. Troy needs him. . . ."

I took a deep breath and broke my silence.

"What do *you* need?" I asked. It was the one question
that LaDonna had forced me to answer aloud.

Gloria looked up at me with tears streaming down
her face.

"I don't know," she said, choking. "I just don't know."

I drained the tuna.

"Nobody can answer that question for you," I said, remembering how agonized I was standing at the same
crossroads. "You have to do it for yourself."

Gloria didn't say anything. She just sat there smoking
her cigarette in the kitchen against my house rules. I
chopped a little onion and some hard-boiled egg and
mixed up a bowl of tuna salad. And it was quiet for a few
seconds.

Then Beni Douglas burst into the kitchen like a carny
flying out of a cannon.

"Hey!"

Her exuberance was exhausting. I glanced at her while
she leaned on the counter watching me as I mixed the
salad greens together. Her pupils were like pinpoints. She
was flyin'. She bounced around the room chattering excit-
edly about the new play she had auditioned for, the manager at the bistro where she worked, and P-Bo's newest
portfolio. My ears perked up at the mention of P-Bo's name.
Out of the corner of my eye, I noticed that Gloria was
watching Beni, too, instead of staring out the screen door.

"He has four pieces on the short list for the show at
the Marble Smith Gallery!" Beni exclaimed breathlessly.
"If he gets even one piece in, he's launched. Completely
launched. Any snapper who gets their pics in the M-Smith
goes sky-high. It's inked."

"Snapper?" Gloria asked.

Beni grabbed a stalk of celery and started munching. "Photographer. You know, snapping pictures. Snapper!" She chewed and talked at the same time. It was a wonder that she didn't choke.

"Are you staying here tonight?" I asked, not looking up.

Beni wiped her hands on her jeans. "Nope. Just stopped by to get stuff that I left here. P-Bo and I are back together."

I looked at Gloria, who closed her eyes as she exhaled a huge cloud of smoke.

"Hey! We can smoke in the house now?" Beni asked hopefully.

"You're back with P-Bo?" I asked.

Beni's shoulders tensed and her bright smile dimmed a bit in its wattage. "Yeah. We worked everything out. He's talking to someone, a counselor at school, about taking an anger management seminar. We're cool."

Gloria turned away. I looked at Beni.

"Beni, why don't you stay here for a few more days? Or stay here until P-Bo finishes his 'anger management' course? Maybe you two need some time apart."

Beni's eyes flashed. "Forget that. P-Bo needs me. He's going through some real dramatic shit right now and I need to be with him. He needs me to support him emotionally."

"Maybe he needs more emotional support than you are equipped to give him," I said softly. Why was I trying to reason with someone who was high?

Beni's face hardened. "Please. I know what you want. You, LaDonna, even my best friend. You just want me to walk away. Just walk away and leave him." Her words were coming so fast now that I could barely keep up. "I can't do that. I can't just walk away. Maybe that's OK for *you*. You can just run away and be bitter and talk about how you've saved yourself and how independent you are.

What a bunch of bullshit. I know what commitment is. I know what real love is. P-Bo loves me; he's just going through a rough time right now. And he needs me. *He needs me.*"

Gloria's cigarette had burned low and the smoke filling the room had become thick and strong. She looked at Beni with an unreadable expression on her face, but she didn't say anything.

"I'm getting out of here. You don't understand what the hell I'm talking about," Beni said, pulling her backpack up on her shoulder. We listened to her clump up the back-stairs and down the hall.

"She'll be back," Gloria said. There was no hope in her voice or in her eyes when she looked at me.

Despite the afternoon heat that had settled in the kitchen, I felt cold.

I stirred the tuna salad around and around until it almost turned to mush.

"Yes. She'll be back," I said. But I knew that both of us were wrong.

The wind rustled the miniblinds in the open window. I glanced outside and noticed the steel gray color of the sky. I wiped my hands on a kitchen towel.

"I'd better make sure my windows are closed up on the third floor," I told Gloria. "It looks like it's going to rain."

The storm rolled in from the west a little after midnight, bringing brilliant lightning and earth-shaking thunder. I was still awake when the telephone call I had been dreading came at about 3:00 A.M.

"Ms. Sullivan? This is Amy at the emergency room at St. Catherine's. Do you know Benetia Douglas?"

I closed my eyes and said a prayer. I had only one question.

"Is she alive?" I whispered.

"Just barely," the nurse replied grimly. "I haven't been able to reach her parents. Can you come down here?"

The emergency room on a busy night is like a three-ring circus without the laughter. It is loud, colorful, and crowded. There is something going on in every corner. No one does anything in unison. The sirens pierce your eardrums and the doors slam open and closed. Gurneys fly by at forty miles an hour. The doctors are the ring-masters; the nurses and aides are the performers. They move quickly past in blurs of white, blue, pink, and green. Patients are only the props. The deep red of blood is the accent color. The chatter is constant; the phones are always ringing. But unlike a circus, the audience does not clap with appreciation or smile with delight. The waiting room is filled with sad, silent faces. Hands that form clenched fists or wring tissues into shredded, wrinkled pieces of paper. Eyes that fill with tears or are red with sleep denied. Seating is general admission. There aren't any luxury boxes.

The nurse walked me toward a door where a policeman was standing.

"You can go in."

I glanced at the police officer.

"Have they picked him up yet?" I asked, referring to P-Bo.

The nurse shook her head. She didn't ask how I knew what had happened.

"Not yet. That's why he's here." She motioned toward the police officer.

"How—how badly is she hurt?"

The nurse's face was solemn. This was her business, but I could tell that it never got easy.

"She's nearly comatose. Stabbed ten times; one wound missed her heart by inches. I can tell by her driver's license that she is a pretty girl. . . ." She paused as if searching for the right thing to say. I read between the pauses. "She'll need a lot of reconstructive surgery. And . . ." The nurse looked down at her white shoes. "She had some internal bleeding. Dr. Rau is waiting for her condition to stabilize before he takes her to surgery. I . . . She may need a hysterectomy."

I squeezed the tears out of my eyes.

"Is she conscious?" was all I could manage to croak out.

"She's in and out. But she needs a hand to hold and soft voice of encouragement in her ear," the nurse replied, her brown eyes holding mine. "It would help a lot."

"I can do that," I said.

Nothing could have prepared me for what I saw. I tried to keep the horror and pity out of my face in case, miracle of miracles, Beni could see anything from beneath her swollen eyelids. Her face was a red-and-black pulpy mess wrapped in gauze, with braces encircling her forehead and neck. One arm was in a cast; the other was, remarkably, unmarked and resting limply on her stomach. My chest filled up and I did everything I could to stifle a gasp. It was horrible. I wanted to curl up in the corner and cry.

I sank into the chair next to the gurney and put her hand into mine. It was so small and cold. I hadn't expected it to be cold. I glanced at the monitor. The *blip-blip* sound was still there. She was alive. I looked at Beni. Her eyes were closed.

"Beni, it's me; it's Opal. I'm here, sweetie. You'll be fine. I'll stay here with you." I took a deep breath. It was so hard to keep from crying.

"Beni, can you hear me? You're safe now," I put her hand up to my cheek. *Oh, God, I hope that she can hear me.*

She squeezed my hand.

Startled, I looked up. Her swollen eyelids were still closed.

"Beni, can you hear my voice? Squeeze my hand if you can."

She squeezed it again. She tried to move her lips but grimaced.

"Don't try to talk. Just rest. You're safe now."

"Thank you." It was a whisper that sounded like tissue paper floating on the wind.

I laughed and rubbed my hands over her ice-cold fingers.

"Don't talk. I want you to rest. I want you to listen to the sound of my voice. I'm going to try to bore you with a story so that you'll go to sleep. And you're going to be fine. You are." I had to say that as if I believed it with all my heart and soul. Because if I could believe it, then she could believe it. And maybe she'd come through this.

I stroked the small section of her forehead that wasn't bandaged. And I saw a small tear roll down her cheek.

A dark cloud settled over the yellow house for the next few days. Beni's condition stabilized enough for her to have surgery. I spent a lot of time at the hospital. Beni's parents had finally been contacted and were driving in. When I was home, the only thing we could talk about was Beni. Every telephone call I got was about Beni. By Sunday night, we were all exhausted and depressed.

"Why don't you let me take you all out for dinner?" Jack suggested. He had stopped by to check on me, he said, because my telephone line was constantly busy. "You need to get out of the house."

I shook my head.

"I wouldn't be good company. All I can think about is Beni and how I'd like to get my hands on P-Bo." Just the thought of P-Bo sent me into a homicidal rage.

"You're too late. P-Bo's been picked up. My boy called me. He'll be arraigned tomorrow. The charges are heavy and plentiful. He made the mistake of beating her up with other people around. There are a lot of witnesses."

I held up my hand.

"Please. I can't hear this. I was at the hospital. I saw her. Jack, he practically beat her to clay."

"I wouldn't think he'll have much of a chance of bond. He pulled Judge Stevens. My friend tells me she doesn't have much of a sense of humor when it comes to domestic violence."

I shook my head.

"I can't talk about this anymore. I'm done. I need something to laugh at. A little bit of nonsense to take my mind off things. I need—"

"I'm offering to take you out to dinner!" Jack said, exasperated.

I smiled at him. He really was a nice man. If only . . .

"I know. But I look like that mouse that CW dragged around for a week. And . . . I'm too lazy to get dressed and go anywhere. Tell you what. I'll call Dominic's and order pizza. You up for that?"

Jack grinned. "With onions, green peppers, and black olives."

I scrunched up my face.

"OK. I'll order two pizzas. I can't stand green peppers." I stood up. "Let me see if Gloria and Troy want anything. I think Tia went out." Tia was a respite "guest."

I didn't have to move an inch. Troy came barreling out of the front door like the Devil was chasing him.

"Opal! I found a hidden secret picture! " He was jumping up and down and screaming at the top of his voice. "I found it in the dining room! " He waved his hands around. They looked as if they'd been dipped in flour.

Gloria came out of the house behind him.

"I didn't know you were out here," she said. "I thought

you were still at the hospital. Hi, Jack." She sounded as if she was out of breath. "Troy, stop jumping!"

"What's going on? What's he talking about?" I asked.

Troy answered.

"There's a picture! And I found it!"

I looked from Troy to Gloria. Her expression was solemn.

"I think you need to see this," she said.

The chandelier in the dining room was lit and Jack clicked on Rodney's work lamps. The plastic sheeting had been pulled away from the wall and lay in a heap on the floor.

I gasped. Jack's eyes widened.

"I don't believe it!"

"See! I told you there was a picture!"

It was not just a picture. It looked like a mural, and only the middle third of it was visible behind the dark brownish-greenish sludge color that I had thought was mildew. It was a landscape that depicted hills, valleys, two riverbanks, and a wide, dark river. The colors were muted earth tones, with a myriad of shades of green, brown, burnt orange, and gold. The sky was, as Troy tried to describe it (much to Gloria's chagrin), a pinkish orange like his mother's salmon cakes, with blue highlights and thin white clouds. The sun peeked out from midway down the horizon.

The mural depicted a river scene, but when I got closer I realized that there was more going on here than just a serene landscape. Three men on the left stood on the banks with rifles in their hands, their tan and black hats nearly covering their creamy-colored, expressionless faces. And on the right side, a man sat in a tiny boat that had just washed up on the shore. Five people stood looking back across the river. Two men, one woman holding a baby, and a small child. They weren't waving at the men with the guns. They weren't running, either. They merely stood there with their faces raised up toward the sun. Beautiful.

I touched the edge of the exposed painting. The wall was sticky and dirty in places where the old layers of wallpaper had been attached. But the paint on the mural was still intact, the colors rich.

I peered at a little boat settled in the murky water where "Duncanson, 1847" was scrawled.

"Rodney said that he had something to show me," I murmured, trying to remember why the artist's name was familiar.

"Oh, you knew this was here?" Gloria asked.

"Um, no. Well, yes. I was kinda in a bad mood the last time I saw him," I confessed sheepishly. "I told Rodney that we'd talk another time." Actually, I think I barely answered poor Rodney. I went to the telephone.

Jack was still frowning and talking to himself. "Who was Duncanson?"

"Good question," I said, going into the kitchen to get my notebook with Rodney's card in it. "The first thing I'm going to do is track down Rodney. *Then* we'll find out about Mr. Duncanson."

Chapter Twelve

The house was in an uproar for the rest of the afternoon and evening. Pam dropped in with her boys and was enthralled by the mural and the mystery behind it. The ruckus even attracted Dana Drew's curiosity. Once again, I was surprised to see her in the daylight. She was returning the WD-40 and a rope that she had borrowed from me a while ago.

Her dark eyebrows raised above her sunglasses as she looked at the mural. She pulled up the glasses for a split second when she read the artist's name scribbled beneath the little boat that floated on the dark water.

"Duncanson . . . hmmm . . ."

I tried to get a peek at her eyes, but she was too quick for me. The sunglasses were replaced in a split second. Darn!

"Are you familiar with the artist?" I asked.

Dana's shiny black brows knit together.

"No . . . yes. Yes, I've heard the name before, but I can't remember where I heard it. You could check with the art department at the university." She paused for a moment, then looked at me.

Do you know how hard it is to look someone in the eye when she is looking at you through smoky black lenses?

I watched her float back across the cobblestones in her black six-inch stilettos. She didn't wobble once. Aside from Bette, Dana is the only person I know who can walk like a fashion model in high heels.

I walked back into the dining room to cover up the mural. With all the people running around the house, not to mention Pam's little ones, the mural would be too much of a temptation to leave uncovered. I could just see the fingerprints and hand marks all over the house from curious little ones and big ones alike.

"Opal, the pizza man's here!" Jack's voice carried in from the porch. "Bear! No!"

Uh-oh. As I headed quickly toward the front door, I thought about what Dana had said. Her suggestion about calling the university was one I had thought of myself. I also intended to hit the Internet, but I wouldn't get the chance to do that until everyone left and the house settled down.

Then something occurred to me. Something about Dana was different. It wasn't the clothes; they were still black and expensive. It wasn't the hair; she still wore it long like Morticia Adams. Today the sunglasses were Versace instead of Chanel, but who's quibbling about logos?

The moment I opened the front door, I remembered. But I only had a quarter second to record the thought, because I had to rescue the pizza deliveryman from Bear, who loves pizza crust. Jack held the huge barking ball of fur while I paid for the pizzas and apologized. I'll probably have to find another pizza place. My intuition tells me that Dominic's won't deliver to 1010 Burning Church Road anymore.

Dana's voice was different. The Garboesque Transylvanian accent was completely gone. In its place, for a few

sentences anyway, was the voice of a midwesterner, probably from Ohio or Indiana. Interesting.

"Bear! Quit!"

The mystery of the mural was the only topic of conversation over pizza, salad, and sodas that night.

"I think Rodney was going to steal it!" exclaimed Troy,
talking and chewing at the same time. His eyes gleamed
with excitement. "And sell it to art pirates!" The tomato
sauce that now circled his mouth made him look like a little clown with his wide bright blue eyes and freckles.

"Too many mystery stories before bed," Gloria said under her breath as she handed her son a paper towel. "Troy,
wipe your mouth."

I shook my head. "Good theory, Sherlock, but it doesn't
hold up. Rodney told me there was something to show
me, remember? He wouldn't do that if he was going to
steal anything."

Troy was undeterred. He had another idea.

"Then, I'll bet—"

"Troy! Wipe your mouth!"

Pam daintily pulled the mushrooms off her pizza and
stacked them neatly on the side of her plate.

"Obviously the mural was here all the time. It might
be valuable. Or at least it may have historical signifi-
cance. Maybe Miss Caroline's great-grandparents commissioned it in the early eighteen-hundreds. Decorative
styles changed and she had it covered up." Tré reached for
a piece of pizza, and a can of Coke was in his way. "Tré!
Don't!" Skillfully Pam moved it out of the way just in time.

"I agree with Pam," Jack said just before he stuffed a
tomato-covered piece of crust into his mouth. He was as
bad as Troy. "You'll probably want to call the university
and get the name of an art historian or restoration expert.

Somebody who'll know whether you have a decorative mural or a historic treasure."

A historic treasure? In my house? Was that Miss Caroline's secret?

There wasn't time to consider the possibility, however. Tyler knocked over Pam's glass and pop went everywhere and over everyone.

"It's probably worth five hundred dollars!" said Troy, who does his best thinking in the midst of chaos and confusion. He snatched a piece of sausage off the pizza while his mother wasn't looking. "And I found it," he added proudly. "Is there a reward?"

I had grabbed some kitchen towels and handed one to Troy.

"Wipe up the pop, Troy. I'll give you ten dollars; how's that?"

"Cool!" he said.

I was rewarded with a huge open-mouth grin that revealed a nicely chewed wad of pepperoni, sausage, and pizza dough. Yum.

Things quieted down after dinner and even Troy, who was wired up after all the excitement and all of the Coca-Cola, went to bed early. The hospital called—Beni's operation was successful. As much as I enjoyed being with Jack, I was glad that he, Pam, and the boys left, too. I hadn't slept more than five hours since Beni's run-in with P-Bo and I was tired. But I couldn't sleep. I kept thinking about the mystery painting on my dining room wall.

I had finally gotten hold of Rodney, but he wasn't any help.

"I *told* you that I wanted to show you something!" he said earnestly. "You said another time. . . ."

Details, details, I said to myself.

"I come across murals once in a while," he continued.

"In my line of work, you never know what's on those old walls. There's a professor at the university that I call in when I find 'em. She might be able to help you. Now, what did I do with her card?"

Rodney hadn't found it by the time we ended our conversation but promised to call me back. I let the dogs back in, checked the doors and windows, and headed up to the computer. I came across an entry on the Internet:

> Duncanson, Robert S., 1821–1872, Landscape
> painter, United States; African-American painter . . .

I fell asleep that night amazed, and embarrassed, that I, who had studied what I thought was American history and art, did not recognize the name of this painter.

I caught up with Rodney's "art expert" the following afternoon.

Dr. Eva Innis, who smiled indulgently at me from behind owl-sized eyeglasses, was not surprised that Duncanson's name was unknown to me. She pulled a book off her shelf and laid it flat on the desk. The paintings were glorious and had intriguing names to go with them:

> Land of the Lotus Eaters
>
> Minnenopa Falls
>
> Cliff Mine, Lake Superior

"During his lifetime," she commented, "Robert Duncanson was hailed by some critics as 'the best landscape painter in the West,' " she said. "And yet, within fifty years of his death, he was virtually unknown. Times change;

tastes change. The style that made him an icon in the mid–nineteenth century fell out of favor."

The more Dr. Innis talked, the more fascinated I became. It was also serendipitous. Duncanson had lived and set up a studio in Cincinnati just west downriver. He had studied in Europe and had influenced a Canadian school of art technique. He made his living accepting commissions from the wealthy citizens in the region, painting their portraits and painting murals on their walls, a decorating touch popular at the time. And, in the summers, he traveled around the river valley, sketching and painting.

Dr. Innis filled me in, briefly, on the details of his life.

"Robert Duncanson was born, a free man of color, in Monroe, Michigan, and grew up there. He came from a family of housepainters, if you can believe that," she said, her pixieish face beaming. I could tell that Duncanson was a favorite of hers. "It's a sad footnote to a remarkable life that the same profession that started him on his art career also killed him."

"What do you mean?" I asked, turning the pages of the book until I came across a photograph of Duncanson, proud and elegant-looking and wearing a fur hat.

The explanation was poignant. Lead was a primary ingredient in paint. Duncanson, who began his career as a housepainter and ended it as an experienced artist who mixed his own paints, had prolonged exposure to high levels of lead. The effect was deadly. By the end of his life, he was unable to paint or even to function and eventually died in a home for the mentally ill in Michigan in 1872 at the age of fifty-one.

I shook my head at the irony of it as I flipped through the plates of his landscapes. They were incredible. Some of them were mystical and dreamlike. What could he have accomplished had he lived ten more years? Twenty more years?

"He doesn't put a lot of people in his paintings," I said to Dr. Innis. "And I don't see many African-American faces in his work. Why not?"

Dr. Innis pulled another volume from her shelf and leafed through it.

"The painting of African-American subjects would have been considered provocative," she said simply. "He painted before, during, and after the Civil War and may have felt that he had to be particularly careful in that regard. Fortunately for Duncanson, however, many of his commissions were from wealthy citizens who had abolitionist sentiments."

She found the page that she was looking for and turned the book toward me.

"But it's not true that he didn't paint African-American subjects. Here is a piece painted for a commission from Reverend James Francis Conover, an abolitionist. It's entitled *Uncle Tom and Little Eva*. It was painted in 1853 in response to the book by Harriet Beecher Stowe." She flipped the page and there was another plate, this one in black and white. It was entitled *View of Cincinnati, Ohio, from Covington, Kentucky*, and was painted in 1851.

I glanced at the plate and then asked Dr. Innis a question.

"Are all of his works accounted for? Did he keep a record of every painting that he did?"

"Yes and no," Dr. Innis replied. She flipped through another large book and showed me several color plates of landscapes that were unsigned. "Duncanson had a fairly large body of work," she said in an attempt to footnote what I was seeing, "and, frankly, most of them are unsigned."

"What if there was an uncataloged Duncanson mural,

signed and dated? A mural that depicts the crossing of the Ohio River by fugitive slaves? Would that be a valuable discovery?"

Dr. Innis nearly jumped out of her underwear.

"Assuming that it could be authenticated," she said sharply.

I nodded.

"Yes, assuming that it could."

Her huge glasses shifted to one side.

"I would say," she answered breathlessly, "that if such a mural was to be found and authenticated, and if it had African-American subjects, which Duncanson rarely, if ever, used, it would be an unprecedented find."

The yellow house was turning out to be a lot more than I had bargained for.

The full moon came in the second week of August. Every screwy thing that could happen did happen that week. It was enough to drive me to drink. If I'd been so inclined.

So far, there had been no word from Imani. I was on needles and pins. I had cleaned her room so many times that I was getting sick of myself. I arranged the furniture one way, then changed my mind and moved it around again.

Jack grumbled.

"I am not accepting calls from you anymore," he warned me. "I don't want to move that damn armoire again." Not to mention my studio, which was housed, temporarily, in the front parlor. The light was better in there.

Gloria's apartment would be ready in three weeks, so she and Troy had been packing. I would miss Gloria's dry wit and, despite my allergies to children, I would miss Troy, too. Thank God, Gloria had agreed to continue working the rose garden. I was petrified that if she left and the roses got wind of it, they would commit suicide rather than let me take care of them.

I had a new "guest" coming at the end of the week, a writer, who was staying through the end of the summer and early fall to finish a manuscript. And Beni was released from the hospital and went home to Illinois with her parents for the rest of her recuperation.

I'd called an art historian to evaluate the mural, and Troy had taken to disappearing again looking for pirate's treasure. But even those adventures couldn't keep his mind off what was really bothering him. His father.

As I climbed the stairs to the second floor, I heard Troy's voice.

"I don't see why we can't go home!" Troy's whine carried out into the hall.

I was carrying up a stack of towels to put into the chest. I heard Gloria say, ". . . burned down, Troy! We can't go back there!"

"But Dad says that we can move into *his* new house! He's got a bedroom for me and I can get a dog."

Gloria's voice faded out. Troy's response, however, was crystal clear.

"I can't have a dog at that apartment. I can't even have a cat!"

"Troy, you will have your own room and you'll go to the new elementary school on Rockwell. They have a computer lab and you can join the science club that the principal was telling us about."

"But I won't have Dad!" was Troy's response.

I put the towels away and headed up to the third floor. Bear lumbered up after me.

How do you explain to a ten-year-old that having Dad might mean physical damage to Mom? Again, I didn't hear Gloria's response, but I could guess what it was because

Troy said, "But he said he was sorry. He didn't mean to do it."

Imani was older, but I didn't think that I would have an easier time explaining things to her. She had wanted me to leave Ted. But Ted was still her father. She knew that he beat me and slapped me and locked me in closets. But when he was with Imani, he was kind, charming, and generous. It was like living with Dr. Jekyll and Mr. Hyde. I was married to Mr. Hyde. Imani and most everyone else in the world saw Dr. Jekyll.

Imani finally called.

"Momma, I'm flying standby, so I don't know when I'm coming exactly." Imani's words came across a telephone line that was, as usual, popping with static.

"What day?" I yelled into the receiver.

She gave me the tentative date and flight number. I marked my calendar in red: "Imani! Home!" Something wonderful to look forward to.

The date coincided with another appointment on my calendar. I hadn't told Imani that on the day she was coming home I was hoping to finalize my divorce from her father.

The hearing was held bright and early on Wednesday morning. Judge Paul Perry was about seventy years old (mandatory retirement hasn't reached River County yet) and liked to take a nip after lunch to help him "deal with the insane and the ugly." He was reputed to be a ladies' man and had been the subject of more than a few juicy rumors and "situations" over the years. He had also been on the domestic relations bench for almost thirty years and had heard it all. He was not sympathetic to situations that involved abuse or violence. Ted's attorney knew this, so he tried to move the case to another court. Unfortunately,

Judge Perry caught wind of this and it made him mad. My case stayed in Courtroom 14A.

I wore my best and most boring business suit with pearls and tried to pull my unruly corkscrews up into a semblance of a French twist. I brought along my own file, which had grown to be as thick as a stack of Bibles. Georgy just stared at it.

"Opal, what on earth?"

What can I tell you? I am a paralegal, and note taking and paper saving are second nature. I am an incurable pack rat and cannot throw any piece of paper out, no matter how small or insignificant it appears to be. My file landed on the table with a loud thump.

"What do you have in there?" He tapped the file with his hand. "*Your* file is thicker than mine! And I'm the lawyer!"

"I just want to be prepared," I told him, taking a deep breath. My stomach was jumpy and I was getting a head-ache. "I don't want anything to go wrong, George. I don't want to come back here."

He patted my hand.

"You won't."

Judge Perry, tall, slim, and distinguished-looking, with nearly black hair that was graying at the temples, peered over the top of his reading glasses at Ted's attorney.

"Is your client running late, Mr. Schwartz?" Amazingly, Ted wasn't there.

I had never seen a person squirm standing up, but Mr. Schwartz managed it.

"Ah, yes, Judge. He is."

Judge Perry swung his arm around in a rather dramatic gesture as he looked at his watch. Then he cleared his throat and opened his file.

"We will begin. If Mr. Hearn comes in, fine. If he doesn't,

then the court will assume that he is willing to accept the outcome of this hearing."

"Your Honor, I would like to formally request a continuance," Mr. Schwartz responded.

"Request denied, Mr. Schwartz." The judge turned his attention to his notes.

"The file contains an Agreed Entry prepared by Mr. Cox with a notation that the terms have been agreed to by, by verbal consent, Mr. Schwartz and his client, Mr. Hearn. Is that correct?"

"Yes, Your Honor," Georgy replied.

"Yes." Mr. Schwartz's voice was subdued.

Judge Perry reviewed the terms of the agreement, including the payment of Imani's college tuition and a cash settlement for me, which was a surprise. Mr. Schwartz looked more and more unhappy and kept glancing at his watch.

Judge Perry didn't miss much.

"Are we holding you up, Mr. Schwartz?" he asked.

"No, Your Honor," the attorney replied with a sigh.

"Good. Now, Mr. Schwartz, I do not see your client's signature on this document. However, I note for the record that this hearing has been rescheduled twice at Mr. Hearn's request. I note also that on the last two occasions Mr. Hearn did not appear before this court. Further, I note that there is a restraining order in place. I see, from a report included in the file, that Mr. Hearn, after agreeing to pay the college tuition of the couple's daughter, Imani Michele Hearn, has failed to do so and that Ms. Sullivan has paid this obligation. Is that a correct statement of the facts as they pertain to this case, Mr. Schwartz?"

Mr. Schwartz looked unhappy.

"Yes, Your Honor."

"Mr. Cox? Is that correct from your standpoint?"

"Yes, Judge." Georgy was trying very hard not to look smug.

"All right, let's get this wrapped up, gentlemen and Ms. Sullivan. As Mr. Theodore J. Hearn has repeatedly decided not to participate in these proceedings, he has signed agreements that he has not fulfilled, and the parties have not lived together for one hundred and twenty days, I hereby grant a divorce to Ms. Opal R. Sullivan, pursuant to the terms outlined in the Entry in this file. I hereby amend the order adding that Mr. Hearn will reimburse Ms. Sullivan for the tuition payment made by her within thirty days. Further, I will leave the restraining order in place for the next six months."

The judge took off his eyeglasses and looked straight at me.

"Ms. Sullivan?"

The judge's voice startled me. His tone was soft and personal and he didn't look stern anymore.

"Yes, sir?"

"I left that restraining order in place for a reason," he told me. "I suspect that Mr. Hearn will be none too pleased when he finds out that this divorce has taken place without him." The judge glanced over at Mr. Schwartz, who looked away. "I have read your file thoroughly," he added. "Please be careful. And good luck to you."

I wanted to smile and I wanted to cry. Instead, I took a deep breath and nodded.

"Thank you."

I was a free woman.

Now what?

Everyone had a suggestion. Bette sent over champagne. Jack wanted to take me to dinner. Gloria suggested a night on the town, and Pam wanted to treat me to a visit to a day spa. I liked Troy's suggestion best of all: an ice-cream cone, two scoops, purchased with his allowance money. My hips didn't need even half a scoop, but the idea was a good one.

I turned them all down and took a solitary walk instead. Excuse me, I didn't walk; I strolled. It was way too hot to march around like you were actually going somewhere.

The humidity had settled gently on Prestonn like a flannel blanket on a sleeping child. I walked down the street, being nosy as usual, looking to see who had up a FOR SALE sign and who hadn't brought in the paper. So many contrasts: a brand-new Saab convertible in one driveway, a 1980 Cadillac with its hood up in another. The house on the corner still had its Christmas decorations up. Well, it was August now, so I wouldn't bother to take them down, either. You'd only have to put them up again after Halloween.

The old Rebel was at his post, sitting in a lawn chair with a six-pack at his side. A piece of fur with legs stood on the sidewalk along the house.

"Hey!" he yelled at me, grinning from ear to ear. "How you this evening?"

I waved as I passed but didn't stop.

"Fine! How are you?"

"Doin' all right for a museum piece," he replied. "I like what you done to Caroline's house," he added.

"Thanks!" I told him. This was the second time that he had mentioned Miss Xavier to me. Somehow, though, I just couldn't see the old coot and stately Miss Caroline Xavier sipping mint juleps together on the porch.

The Stars and Bars fluttered in a brief hot summer breeze.

"You want a beer?" He held a can up high in the air.

"No, thanks!" I yelled back.

"All righty!" he said amiably, popping the top. "You change your mind, you know where to come!"

"Yes, I do," I said to myself. Friendliest Confederate I ever knew. *Only* Confederate I ever knew.

The Colonel passed me as I turned the corner. He smiled politely and tipped his white ten-gallon hat, but he didn't say anything. He was too busy surveying the back forty.

I kept moving, letting my mind wander as my feet moved one in front of the other. Sometimes I drop into a time warp on these walks. The homes are so old that it is easy to imagine that you have stepped across a dimension and back to days of horse-drawn wagons, derby hats, and long skirts. So many things in Prestonn are out of time, like the Colonel, like the old Rebel, and the ancient river keeps its own time. But sometimes, I'm jerked forward, not to the present day, but into the 1960s, when I pass a man whom I call Woodstock.

He wears flared jeans, a denim jacket, heeled boots, and a hat pulled down onto his head like the top of a toadstool. He looks like a time traveler from the sixties snatched up from the muddy mess of Woodstock right after Richie Havens finished singing. He is one character in the layers of this river town and, aside from me, no one else around here ever gives him a second look.

As Jack would say, "River people are different."

Finally, I reach the old bridge that has spanned the river for seventy-five years or more. It doesn't take much traffic anymore, since it only has two lanes across and the newer bridges carry the freeway headed north. I stand there at the entrance and look out at the boats and the barges, some of them city blocks long, watching them until they round the bend either downriver to the Mississippi or east to the coalfields of West Virginia. I stand on the top of the levee and watch and think.

Over six months ago, I was Opal Hearn, wife of Ted, mother of Imani, contracts supervisor, and living in Shadeside Heights on the east side of town. I had a car payment, half of a mortgage payment, impatiens in my flower beds, and a Sears charge card. Oh, and a library card. I had my period once a month, went to church twice a month, and got beaten up, punched, slapped, hit, kicked, or cussed out once a week or so whether I needed it or not.

Things were different now.

I am Opal Sullivan, mother of Imani, still working as a contracts supervisor. But now I live in Prestonn in a house that is over one hundred years old. I have two dogs, a few cats, an alleged vampire in my coach house. I have a historic mural in my dining room. I have a car payment, a mortgage payment, and roses in my yard. And a library card. The Sears bill went with Ted. I paint. I still had my period once a month, but, lately, I had noticed that it is beginning to slip away.

Both my period and Ted are making an exit. I don't think that I'll miss either of them. But I was going to miss that Sears charge card.

Chapter Thirteen

I walked home by way of downtown Prestonn, going the back way, as I call it, down the alley and through the back gate. The cobblestone path took me through the rose garden that had flourished under Gloria's loving care. I caught a flash of calico out of the corner of my eye, and CW strolled by giving me her usual "Oh, it's you" glance. I walked up the steps and opened the screen door. Becca was fixing dinner. Her cat, a sleek Siamese named Cayenne, was curled up at her feet. Becca was a writer and my newest guest.

"Hi, Becca! Did Imani call?" I still hadn't heard from my daughter and I was starting to get worried.

Becca stopped chopping for a moment and looked at me, a solemn expression on her face.

"Nope, no calls. But some guy stopped by to see you. He wouldn't give his name, so I didn't let him in the house. The dogs and Cayenne don't like him, though, whoever he is. The dogs wouldn't stop barking. I almost broke my arm trying to hold Bear back!"

I frowned. I wasn't expecting anyone, and Becca knew

Jack and even knew about Rodney. But Rodney would have said who he was.

"What did he say?" I asked, picking up a carrot stick from the vegetable medley that she was making.

"He asked if you lived here, then if you were home. I didn't like all of the questions, so I asked for his name. Which he refused to give. Then the dogs started barking. I got tangled up with Bear, and he left."

"What time was this? I've only been gone an hour."

She shrugged her shoulders.

"About a half hour, forty-five minutes ago."

"Did he say anything else?" I asked.

Becca handed me a celery stick. Her dark eyes were serious behind the lenses of her wire-rimmed eyeglasses.

"Only that he would be back."

I chewed on the carrot stick and on what Becca had told me as I walked toward the front of the house. It was hot out and I was sweaty and smelly from my walk, but I just didn't feel like scaling the stairs yet to the third floor to take a shower, so I strolled out onto the front porch. I told CW to scram and unfolded the morning newspaper that we had all forgotten to bring in. I was getting settled on the settee when I heard the dogs barking in the house and Bear galloping toward the front door, with the yaps of Wells behind him. Darn! Just when I was getting comfortable.

"Bear! Wells! What is the matter with y'all?"

I stood up and went to the door, looking through the screen at the dogs approaching, Becca following on their heels. Wells stopped just short of the door and continued barking, his tail rigid. Behind him, Bear loomed like a mountain of fur, his deep *woofs* almost drowning out the barks of the pug.

"What set them off?" I asked Becca, reaching for the

doorknob to let the dogs out. She had reached for Bear's collar to pull him back before he tore up the screen when I noticed that she was looking past me.

"You have company," Becca said in a low voice.

I looked over my shoulder.

Ted stood on the sidewalk just beyond the front gate.

"Is that your ex-husband?" she asked.

I nodded.

"I thought so. Do you want me to call the police?" she asked.

"No." I looked down at Bear, whom Becca was holding by the collar. Then I smiled. "But I'll take the dogs with me."

She grinned back and opened the door.

"I'll be in the kitchen. If you need me, just yell."

I took a deep breath and turned around.

"What do you want, Ted?" I asked.

He watched as I tied up both dogs on the porch. Neither of them stopped barking until I shushed them, which I took my time doing. Wells continued to stand at attention with his tail rigid. His little smushed-in nose sniffed the air. Bear growled every few moments just to put the interloper on notice. Ted didn't open the gate until the animals were tied up.

"Somebody might call Animal Control on you about those dogs, Opal," Ted said, trying to sound calm. Ted doesn't like dogs. Just the sound of Bear's bark had probably cleaned out his bowels. "They're vicious."

"Did you come here to lecture me on pet control?" I asked.

Ted started to move up the front walk, but Bear let out such a loud *woof* that he stopped in his tracks. I smiled.

"My attorney tells me that we're divorced," he said.

I patted Bear's huge head.

"You came over here to tell me that?"

"He went over the divorce decree with me and I don't agree with any of it. That cocksucker of a judge must be insane."

At the sound of agitation in Ted's voice, both dogs started barking again. Ted took a half step back.

"Then you should have been there. You knew when the hearing was," I told him.

"It's not final. I'm having my attorney file a motion to throw it out. I'm not paying you a goddamn dime. And I'm not paying back the money to the university, either. You paid it. Tough shit."

I looked at the man I used to be married to. In that split second, I decided not to refer to him as "my" anything ever again, not "my ex-husband," not "my former husband." I did not want to have any possession, past or present, of this hateful person. How in the world had I let myself stay tied up to such a piece of manure for so long?

"Whatever, Ted. There's a restraining order on you, and right now you're in violation. So why don't you get the hell out of here?"

His eyes narrowed. I could tell that a tongue-lashing was imminent.

"I don't give a shit about that goddamn restraining order! If I want to get to you, I can."

"Yes, you can," I admitted to myself as well as to him. "But not today."

Bear growled and lunged. Good thing for Ted that the leash held.

Ted stopped, his eyes widening for a second.

"It's a good thing you have those dogs."

"Don't play hard-ass with me, Ted. I just plain don't give a rat's behind. I don't care if you pay the money, I don't even care if you try to get the divorce decree thrown out," I said, dragging Bear back from the edge of the porch. "I am never coming back to you. *Never.*"

"I was a good husband to you," he said soberly, changing direction. Dr. Jekyll, Mr. Hyde. "I was trying to make you a good wife." *Make me a good wife. By God, he believed that garbage, too.*

I was starting to "see red" again.

"How? By blacking out my eyes? Kicking me? You're full of shit, Ted."

His eyes widened. I am not usually so explicit. And I think that Ted expected me to be more demure if he accosted me in person. He was wrong.

"You always overreact—"

Whenever someone tells me that I am "overreacting," he is trying to push me off course.

I was not fooled and I was tired of this conversation. It wasn't going anywhere and I had an iced tea to drink.

"Get the hell out of here, Ted. Before I turn the dogs loose on you."

I let out Bear's leash a little more so that he could gallop down the front steps.

"Someone should call Animal Control on you!" Ted yelled over his shoulder. "I'll be back!"

I watched him walk quickly down the sidewalk and sprint to his car. The tires squealed as he raced away. I am ashamed to say that my knees were shaking. My palms were sweaty and it had nothing to do with the heat.

"I'll be back!" Ted had said. "I'll be back!" He meant it, too. He would be back. Again and again, he would be back. Over and over like rewinding tape, we would play out this scene, using the same words, filled with the same emotions and motivations: Power, fear, control, resistance, manipulation. Rage. I knew that, just as surely as I was standing there, one day Ted would catch me alone, without other people around, without the dogs. And I might get a twisted arm, bruised neck, or black eye.

Or I might get killed.

For just a flash of a moment, I doubted myself. Why did I leave Ted again? Look at the mess I had created! Look at the risks I'd taken! Was I any better off? I was still looking over my shoulder. It would never be over.

How do you move forward when you are always looking *back?*

Ted's visit put me in a "blue" mood that spilled over into my date with Jack. I was so down that I tried to cancel it. Jack wouldn't let me. I am grateful for that.

He wouldn't tell me where we were going, only that it was a surprise. I was a nervous wreck. I didn't know what to wear, whether to wear perfume or not wear perfume, heels or no heels. Bette, of course, was filled with advice.

"Poison perfume and a lace thong," she'd said, her voice dripping with exasperation. "Opal, do I have to teach you how to get in touch with your sensual side?"

"Noooo," I told her, laughing.

Yes, I said to myself soberly as I looked in the mirror for the last time before Jack picked me up. *Yes.*

When had I last been sensual?

As far back as I could remember, I had not had an experience with Ted that could be classified as "sensual." I was berated. Then we had sex. He twisted my arm. Then we had sex. I remember one notable occasion when we had sex first and then I went to the hospital to have my broken ribs taped.

It would have been comical if it hadn't been so tragic. I had rarely ever had sex with my husband without being hit first. The violence aroused him. And sedated me.

How could such a broken woman have a normal relationship with a man?

What *was* normal, anyway?

I came out of my reverie long enough to notice that none of the scenery looked familiar.

"Jack, where are you taking me?"

Jack beamed with a huge Kool-Aid grin from beneath reflective sunglasses on a head as round as a basketball. It was comical.

"To dinner."

I rolled my eyes.

"We have been driving for twenty minutes. There aren't any restaurants out here. Are there?" I looked around me at the river on my left and the rolling hills on my right. I hadn't been this far east on Route 10 before.

"This place is new," Jack replied turning his attention back to the road, which had two lanes and curved around the steep foothills. "It just opened up."

Oh, great, I said to myself. I love food. My hips will attest to that. But I am a wimp when it comes to trying new things. And I don't like to be a guinea pig for a new restaurant. I wait until they've trained the waiters and the chef before I try out a place. I said a little prayer and hoped for the best.

I shouldn't have worried.

Jack stopped at a secluded spot off River Road. It looked like an abandoned rest stop, but the grass had been cut and there were stone picnic tables and a beautiful view of the river through the cluster of willow trees on the bank. The river was wide here and the opposite bank seemed really far away. There were fields on the other side, and in the distance I saw a farmhouse and a barn and what looked like people moving around. It reminded me of the mural on my dining room wall.

Jack unfolded a chaise lounge and sat me down under a tree as he set the table. I was charmed.

It was like dining in a French café, with checkered tablecloth, fine wine, crusty bread, and wonderful cheese. He unpacked cloth napkins, silverware, and a bud vase. The roses were compliments of Gloria. We ate Steak Diane (it didn't matter where it came from; it was delicious), green beans with almonds, and new potatoes. Dessert was fruit and cheese and strawberries dipped in chocolate. Jack fed me the strawberries one by one. Talk about sensual.

"Congratulations, Opal," he said, wiping my mouth with a napkin. "Now you are really a free woman."

I smiled at him.

"Thank you, but I know that it's not over. I still have a few mountains to climb."

His expression was solemn for a moment. We had talked briefly about Ted's threats on the drive over. Jack's response had been curt.

"Put the dogs on him. That will make him think twice about coming around."

The picture of Ted running for his life with Bear lumbering after him was a pleasant thought.

But it reminded me of something else.

"I'm not really a free woman, Jack," I said, looking out across the river. "I won't ever be rid of Ted. Ever. Despite the divorce, the restraining order, where I live, you . . ." My nerve was giving out. I hadn't wanted to get serious. Hadn't wanted to drop rain on such a lovely evening and a lovely man. But Jack had to understand what I was up against. Call it truth in advertising.

A future with me was a future with Ted. What man would want to live with *that?*

Jack was quiet as I stammered through my tale of woe. He poured me a glass of water; he passed me a napkin to wipe away the melted chocolate. I finished my rant and waited for him to say, "Too much drama, Opal. I'll catch you later."

Instead, he was silent. That was worse.

"Aren't you going to say anything?" I asked. Now I was frustrated out of nervousness.

"What do you want me to say, Opal? Adios? See ya? Later? No chance, lady; you won't get rid of me that easily—"

"But Ted will always be there. He's like the Terminator. He won't stop—"

"I've heard this story before. I've seen this story before. Maybe Ted won't stop. But what are you going to do? Live like a hermit? Locked up in your spooky old house? What kind of life is that? Besides." He passed me another chocolate-covered strawberry to distract me. It worked. "Moving targets are harder to catch. Keep moving through your life. Don't stand still for him. Don't do that."

"Don't do what?" I was happily slurping chocolate off my fingers.

His dark eyes danced with merriment and he smiled slightly.

"Don't lick the chocolate off your fingers like that." He leaned over and kissed me gently on the back of my neck. I felt that kiss on the bottom of my feet. "Unless you want to do something that will frighten the squirrels."

"Quit it," I threatened him. "We are too old for that stuff."

Jack shrugged.

"OK, not on the picnic table then." He grinned at me. "How about the backseat of the car?"

I started laughing and almost couldn't stop.

For work, Jack drives the biggest gas-hogging SUV on the road. It is large enough to house a family of four plus a dog. It is black, has tinted windows, and uses diesel fuel, I think, because the air stinks whenever he starts that monster up.

For pleasure and for tooling around town, Jack drives a vintage fire engine red Corvette. There is barely enough room in it for me to put my purse on the floor.

"*What* backseat?" I coughed out, tears coming out of my eyes.

Jack's grin only got bigger.

"I was reading the other day in a magazine that the stick shift of a sports car can be used as a marital aid. Do you want me to show you how?"

I laughed until my stomach hurt.

And for those few precious moments I forgot all about my bills and my divorce and the man I had been married to and his threats. Jack and I sat on the picnic table, watched the red-gold sunset, listened to the birds chirping as they flew home, and watched the river roll by.

Then we took the long way home. I think we drove through three states. Jack had taken the top off of his car, so I just leaned back into the seat and smiled as the summer air hit my face. I caught the faint smell of honeysuckle and the rich, dank aroma of the dark bottomland that bordered the river. I watched the stars come into focus. The full moon rose and reflected enough sunlight to light the winding roads and the gentle waves in the water.

By the time we pulled up to 1010 Burning Church Road, it was ten o'clock.

Jack turned off the roaring engine and we both looked at the house. The lights were on from the third floor to the basement. It looked like a Christmas tree.

"Are you planning to pay the salaries of the utility executives all by yourself?" Jack asked. "Or are you having a party?"

I sighed. Obviously, there was a crisis in progress. Never a dull moment.

"Maybe Imani's home," I said hopefully. "And she's . . . taking a tour of the house."

Jack gave me "nice try but no cigar" look. I shrugged my shoulders. Well, it was a pleasant thought, anyway. Together we trudged up the walk to the front porch and braced ourselves for whatever drama was waiting.

Gloria's face was ravaged by tears, her hair was all over her head, and she was wringing her hands and chain-smoking in the house. Becca was doing her best to comfort her.

"Troy's disappeared again," Gloria said flatly. " I can't find him anywhere. I tucked him into bed. And now he's gone! I-I went to check on him, and he wasn't there!"

"Gone?" I barely had the words out before Jack took the stairs two at a time, reaching for the cell phone clipped to his waist as he ran.

Gloria had dissolved into sobs, so Becca finished the story.

"We were on the porch, talking, and the phone rang. Gloria went to answer it. While she was in the house, she went to check on Troy and—"

"And he wasn't there!" wailed Gloria.

I frowned. Was he off on another one of his adventures? Or had he run away? Troy was not happy about his parents' separation, especially now that Butch was out of the hospital.

"Do . . . do you think that Butch would . . ." I hated to finish the thought.

Gloria raised her red, swollen eyes to meet mine.

"I thought about that. No. Butch wouldn't do something like this. It—it just doesn't make sense!" She sniffled. Becca continued to hand her tissues.

"Have you called the police?" A missing child was nothing to fool around with.

"Have you looked everywhere?" Jack's voice boomed from behind me.

Gloria blew her nose and Becca shook her head.

"No, not everywhere. We were just heading outside when you two showed up. Why?"

Jack shrugged his shoulders.

"Both of the bedroom windows are securely shut and one of 'em has the air conditioner in it. It hasn't been moved. So, I'm willing to bet that he didn't climb out of the window. He must have sneaked out the back door while you two were on the front porch. His Spiderman shoes are gone."

Gloria stopped dabbing her eyes.

"Troy never goes anywhere without his Spiderman shoes," she said.

Jack's lips began to curl up.

"And a kidnapper wouldn't take the time to gather up a kid *and* his favorite sneakers."

"Let's check outside and go to the end of the block. Isn't there a little boy on Park Street that Troy likes to play with?"

Jack took Bear and went down the street, Becca and Gloria combed the churchyard across the way (Troy liked to go "ghost hunting" over there), and I took Wells and went back over the house and through the yard.

"Come on, Wellington," I said to the pug trotting obediently by my side. "Let's go check the rose garden." Wells sniffed in agreement.

The moonlight was so bright that I didn't need the industrial-sized flashlight that I was carrying. We walked down the cobblestone paths through the rows of Gloria's well-tended roses and I could see the colors of the blooms.

The toolshed wasn't wired for electricity, so I shone the flashlight's wide beam in every corner. I disturbed a few sleeping field mice that would now have to run for their lives, because CW and Ice Tray were patrolling the grounds. A couple bags of peat moss were stacked against the back wall, and mulch, several bags of fertilizer that stank to high heaven, and the rest of the gardening and yard tools were neatly arranged in the shed. But no Troy.

Wells and I came out and I replaced the padlock. Now what?

I glanced over at the coach house. Dana's blinds were drawn, as usual, and there was no light escaping from the windows, plus the Mercedes was nowhere to be seen, so I assumed that she wasn't there. Her apartment would be locked and there was no way that Troy could get the key, so I wasn't worried about that space, but I figured I'd better check the garage below.

As we headed toward the coach house, Wells started to bark and ran ahead. I tightened my grip on the flashlight. Except for Wells's barking, everything was silent. I walked as quietly as I could toward the coach house.

The dog ran around to the back of the coach house and stood beneath the old maple tree that had stood in the yard for four hundred years. He kept barking and jumping. But he wasn't growling and he didn't sound angry. He sounded happy.

"Wells?"

I turned the flashlight's beam across the patch of grass next to the tree. There were pieces of wood scattered around on the ground. They looked suspiciously like the wooden stakes that Troy had fashioned for his vampire-hunting escapade. The light bulb clicked on.

I looked over my shoulder. I thought I heard a noise.

And then I heard it again.

"Opal! Opal! Up here!"

I looked up.

Troy was perched on a branch in the old tree. His backpack was overflowing with wooden stakes.

"Troy! What are you doing up *there*? We've been looking for you everywhere! Your mom's worried sick!"

"Shhhhhh!" He put his finger to his lips. "Looking for the vampire! They come out when the moon is full," he said breathlessly in a loud whisper.

I started to smile and then I started to giggle.

"Troy, Miss Drew isn't here tonight," I told him. Wells would not stop barking. "Shush, Wells! Troy, get down from there right now."

"I can't!" came the loudly whispered response. "I'm stuck!" he wailed.

"What do you mean you're stuck?" I asked. A really stupid question.

"My foot is stuck! Can you come up and get me?"

I shined the light down his leg and saw the red, blue, and black Spiderman sneaker wedged between two branches.

Thank you, Lord. I have not yet had enough challenges today. And when was the last time that I climbed a tree? Forty years ago when my brother and I were playing pirates and the oak tree in the backyard served as the crow's nest. Climbing a tree is like riding a bicycle, isn't it? You never really forget how. Do you?

"Wonderful," I said, shedding the jacket of my brand-new cappuccino-colored knit outfit, and hiking up the dress to my thighs. I kicked off the sexy little snakeskin mules that Bette had forced me at gunpoint to buy and looked up.

"I didn't have anything else to do tonight anyway," I mumbled as I began to scale the tree. "Anyway, how hard can it be? I only did this four decades ago. It's just like it was yesterday."

Well, it wasn't yesterday. Climbing a tree is a bit more challenging than riding a bike, and it's a real ordeal if you're wearing a knit dress and a lace thong. I dropped the flashlight. Why was I trying to carry a flashlight and climb a tree at the same time anyway? My dress ripped, which was wonderful. The check hadn't even cleared the bank yet. And Wells wouldn't stop barking.

Thank God for moonlight.

I fumbled around in the heavy foliage until I reached Troy, perched on a thick sucker branch, his little face contorted.

"You OK?"

He sniffled.

"Yeah, but my foot really hurts."

I balanced myself on the branch and reached down for his sneakered foot.

"You have it squeezed in here pretty tight," I said, trying to gently move it around.

"Ouch!" he yelped.

"Sorry, Troy, this might not be easy. I can't believe that you climbed up here!" I said, trying to distract him. I was afraid that he might have a sprained ankle.

"I thought if the vampire woke up, I could put a stake through her heart . . . and . . ."

I was untying the shoelaces. My best bet in getting Troy off his perch was to free his foot and come back for the sneaker later.

"Put a stake through her heart? Your momma told you to give up on that idea. Vampires aren't real! There! Got it!" I jerked his little foot free from the sneaker.

"Owwww. . . ." Troy howled, and Wells started barking again.

At that very moment, the window shades in Dana Drew's apartment flew up and a blaze of light fell across our faces. The window opened and Dana Drew leaned out. I was so startled that I almost fell out of the tree.

"Hi! It's you guys! I wondered what all the racket was about! Great! You're just in time! I could use some help!"

Troy and I would have answered, but we were busy picking up our jaws from the ground.

Dana Drew was wearing a black leather corset with a row of small silver buckles going down the front, a leather miniskirt, and thigh-high four-inch-heeled leather boots. She was holding a riding crop in her hand. I tried not to speculate on its purpose. In the background of the sparsely decorated apartment the chauffeur, dressed in a golf shirt and khakis, sat in a straight-backed chair. That in itself was not remarkable. The fact that his feet were tied up with ropes and his chest was wrapped in chains was. His hands were free, however, and he was reading what looked like the *Wall Street Journal*. He smiled at us from behind his gold wire-rimmed glasses and gave us a half-hearted wave.

They were magicians. That's it, magicians.

"Ah, some help?" I asked with a forced smile. I felt a little awkward sitting in a tree talking to a, er, vampire standing in an open window. She, on the other hand, acted as if it were the most ordinary thing in the world.

"Yes," she said in the unfamiliar midwestern voice that she had revealed briefly once before. "I've got Tim, that's my husband, tied up in the chair, and I can't get the ropes untied. Could you lend me a hand?"

Well, this sure seemed to be an evening of getting people out of tight spots.

"Uh, oh, sure," I said as if this were a routine request. "I . . . uh, we'll be right down." Then I realized that there was a child present. And Troy's eyes were as big as dinner plates. What we had just seen in Dana Drew's apartment looked like a lot of things, but vampires it wasn't. I decided that I would send Troy off to the house with Wells before I went upstairs to help Dana.

"But I wanna go," whined Troy. "I want to see the vampire!"

I handed him his backpack and his twisted-up sneaker and pointed in the direction of the house.

"Take Wells and go," I said.

"But—"

I glared at Troy.

"No buts."

"Oh, all right," he said as he scuffled off, Wells following at his heels. "I never get to have any fun."

Once on the ground, I used my cell phone to call Jack and call off the body search.

"She's a . . . what?" Jack's voice was breaking up.

"I'll explain later."

I thought I heard laughter, but maybe it was just static.

Chapter Fourteen

"Tim, you've met Opal Sullivan. Opal, this is my husband, Tim Jablonski."

"Nice to meet you, Tim." I tried to keep my expression pleasant and my voice neutral. How do you exchange social pleasantries with someone who is, er, restrained? Plus, I was having a little trouble unlocking the chains that Dana had wrapped around his abdomen. I glanced around the room. There was an interesting array of paraphernalia neatly displayed on tables and shelves, including a selection of chains and feathers. *Eclectic* is the word, I think. Not a kiln or a potter's wheel in sight.

"I guess you're not a sculptor," I told Dana as I helped her untie the cords at Tim's ankles.

She smiled sheepishly.

"It was the only thing I could think of at the time. Actually, I'm a—"

"That's OK," I said quickly, handing her the cord. I wasn't sure that I wanted to hear this story. Facetiously I added, "As long as you aren't a serial killer or a vampire."

"A vampire!" Dana's Transylvanian accent was long gone. She looked at her husband, who shrugged his shoulders.

I nodded. "Yes. Troy was vampire hunting."

"Really! He thinks there's a vampire in your house?" She was genuinely intrigued by the prospect and not at all aware that it had anything to do with her.

"Well, not in my house, exactly. Here, in the coach house," I said slowly.

Dana gasped.

"Oh, my goodness!" Unconsciously she put her hand over her heart. It was all I could do to keep from laughing. This woman was standing in front of me dressed in the most provocative black leather clothing that I had ever seen. (OK, I lead a sheltered life.) Of course, she had taken off the spike heels and was now wearing yellow Tweety Bird house slippers, but there was a riding crop tucked in her belt.

"I've never noticed anything unusual in the coach house. It's as quiet as a church when we're here," she said sincerely. She leaned closer to me and lowered her voice. "Has he ever seen the vampire?"

"Dana, he thinks that *you're* the vampire."

"Me, why . . ." She stopped and frowned. But only for half a second.

"Oh," she said, looking down at the polished buckles on her Merry Widow. "I can see where he's coming from."

Then she started laughing. We all started laughing.

Troy couldn't believe that vampires really ate pizza, hamburgers, and ice cream and drank soda. We convinced him that, over the centuries, they had broadened their diets beyond the usual blood-based foods. He also tried to argue a case for staying up. But by now, it was obvious that Dana wasn't a vampire and that whatever she really was would not be an appropriate bedtime story for a ten-year-old boy regardless of how hard he pleaded.

"To bed, Troy!" his mother ordered, pushing him toward the stairs.

"Mom," Troy wailed in protest. "I never get to have any fun!"

"No, you don't," his mother said. "Now, go!"

"Don't start until I get Troy settled in bed," yelled Gloria as she took the stairs two at a time. "I want to hear *this* from the beginning!"

I poured iced tea, Becca grabbed a soda, and Jack served up giant-sized scoops of chocolate chip ice cream. Whips and chains go better with sweets.

"La Dana Drew" was gone in an instant.

In her place was Dana Drew Jablonski, wife, mother of three, PTA vice president, and second soprano in the choir of First Presbyterian. The Junior League meetings didn't start until Ms. Jablonski arrived. If they only knew.

Without the sunglasses and the long Cher-style black wig, Dana Drew was an average-looking woman with brown eyes and short highlighted blond hair. She looked like a million women that I had seen on the street or at the mall.

She laughed when I told her that.

"You are absolutely right."

"And the accent?" Gloria asked.

"Greta Garbo."

I snapped my fingers in triumph. "I knew it!"

"I thought it was Marlene Dietrich," Becca murmured.

Dana shook her head. "My maternal grandparents are Swedish. It was easier. With the research I'm doing . . ." She stopped and raised her eyes toward the ceiling. "I just find it hilarious that you thought that I was a vampire!"

Dana grinned and laughed. "That never occurred to me. I figured that you would make me for a Goth extraordinaire."

"The vampire theory was Troy's. Just be glad I came along when I did. He had a whole backpack full of wooden stakes!"

"And garlic necklaces," added Jack, handing Tim a mixing bowl of ice cream. I looked at Jack, surprised. He shrugged his shoulders. "All of your garlic bulbs are gone."

"Troy . . . ," I growled.

Gloria landed at the bottom of the stairs with a thump. "OK, I'm back. And I want to hear everything. From the beginning. Then I'll have to figure out how to tell Troy the G-rated version!"

"I don't think there is one," said Jack under his breath. I elbowed him.

"I don't know where to begin really," Dana said, fiddling with one of the buckles on her bustier.

"Start at the beginning, honey," Tim urged as he lapped up a soupspoonful of ice cream.

"About fourteen, fifteen years ago, I was a grad student. Three-quarters through the MBA program, I realized that I hated every minute of it. I was at my wits' end! With every day that passed, I was more and more bored. And more and more panic-stricken. What was I going to do with this degree? And how was I going to pay back my student loans? I hated international finance! Tim and I met in the securities law class—"

"It was love at first sight," Tim interjected, with his mouth full again.

"We got to talking and he suggested that I keep a journal—"

"I was a grad student in psychology," Tim interrupted. "We're big on journal writing."

Dana shook her head with a wry smile.

"Oh, sure," she commented sarcastically. "Anyway, he suggested that I record my feelings in the journal."

"I had no idea what I was asking," Tim interrupted again. "I just thought that she would put her frustrations down in writing and that would help her get through the rest of the term."

Dana grinned. "And it did."

"I started writing stories, little pieces and parts of things that had happened to me. Observations mostly. I remembered a roommate I'd had," Dana rolled her eyes. "Sarah was a little different. She was into spanking her boyfriend with a paddle. And he liked it! One night, the rest of us girls came home early from a bar and . . ." Dana giggled. "Sarah was dressed from head to toe in black leather."

Becca chuckled. "You just never know."

Gloria's eyes were as big as dinner plates. I was trying to be cool and sophisticated, so mine were only as big as saucers. Jack leaned over and whispered in my ear.

"Maybe we could try that sometime?" he said hopefully.

I pushed him away. Silly man.

"It gave me an idea. I am a mystery fiend and I love Agatha Christie. I started writing about an absentminded dominatrix who sometimes forgets how to untie her clients. She also solves mysteries."

"I read one of her stories and thought it was great," Tim offered. "Maisie is dominant and scatterbrained all wrapped up in a leather—"

"Or latex," Dana interrupted.

Tim smiled and nodded.

"Yes. A leather *or* latex package. She gives spankings in the morning, discipline training in the evenings, and tracks down mysteries in the hours in between."

"Latex," repeated Jack with a huge grin. He turned to me with his eyes wide and winked. "Latex."

"Quit it," I said under my breath.

"The story was funny and erotic at the same time. I sent it off to an old buddy of mine who was an editor at a publishing house."

"The *Maisie Beatme* mystery series was born," Dana said proudly.

"Maisie . . . who?" asked Becca, almost choking on her iced herbal tea.

"Maisie . . . Beatme?" Jack repeated.

Dana and Tim grinned.

"Cute, isn't it?" Tim said.

"They are sort of tongue-in-cheek. You can't take Maisie seriously. Except that the books really caught on and the next thing I knew, I was writing two books a year!"

Jack's grin was so wide that I thought it would bust out his cheeks. Gloria was turning red.

Tim nodded, wiping his mouth. It had been a long time since I'd seen anyone but Troy put away so much ice cream in so short a period of time. Thank God I had another gallon in the refrigerator.

"Sometimes," Tim offered, "I help Dana come up with titles for the books. They have to be catchy, but they also have to have a double meaning. Like *All Tied Up, Never Let Me Go, Cuffs and Saucers*—"

"And my personal favorite, *Planes, Chains, and Automobiles*," Dana added with a smile.

"*Planes, Chains* . . ." Gloria dissolved into a fit of giggles.

"I know," Dana commented. "They're campy as hell, but for some reason, the books work. I've written twenty of the darn things. They've made us rich! I have a fan club, we have conventions, and, well, in order to make the books authentic . . ." At this, Dana started turning a little red. Now *that* was interesting. Modesty in a woman wearing leather, silver buckles, and chains as accessories. Not to mention the fuzzy yellow house slippers.

"I take on the persona of my main character. That helps make the writing more authentic. I dress like her, speak as she would, live as I imagine she would live."

"Really?" was all I could think of to say.

"We have a home over off River Road just across the county line," Dana went on to explain. "We also have three small and very curious children. And Tim and I didn't feel comfortable exploring . . . er . . . doing the research at the house. We're building a studio, but it won't be ready until March. So Tim got the bright idea of renting a place until it was finished."

"Jared, that's our oldest," Tim continued, "he is about Troy's age and just like Curious George. We didn't think it was time yet to explain to him that Mommy dresses up in black latex and ties up Daddy with chains and rope."

Gloria glanced over at me and said, "How am I going to explain this to Troy?"

"We'd just better stick to the vampire story," I told her.

"Yes, that's probably best," Jack agreed. "You'll just have to keep him from using all of Opal's garlic bulbs and tell him not to drive a stake through Dana's heart."

We all had a good laugh at the thought of Troy, with a garland of garlic bulbs hanging around his neck, creeping around the coach house after dark in Spiderman sneakers carrying a backpack filled with wooden stakes.

"Tell him I'm a *good* vampire," Dana added. "Good vampires eat regular food like everybody else."

"*Vampires?*"

The screen door slammed. My daughter, Imani, stood in the open doorway carrying a duffel bag the size of Alaska. Her eyes were wide and she looked as if she wasn't sure that she was in the right place. I can only imagine what she was thinking as she stood in my kitchen and saw her mother with a group of strangers that included a woman dressed in a black leather miniskirt, bustier, and psychedelic yellow house slippers.

"Imani! Why didn't you call me from the airport?" I jumped up, almost knocking over my ice cream and several cans of soda. Ice Tray slipped in the open door and was immediately followed by CW, and Bear and Wells, who tolerate the cats when they are outside but don't tolerate their presence inside. The dogs barked as they flew through the kitchen after the cats, and Troy, hearing all the racket (we knew that he wasn't asleep), came running down the back stairs to find out what all the excitement was about. So much for a quiet, uneventful homecoming.

It took almost fifteen minutes for things to settle down, for Troy to catch the cats and send them back outside, for Jack to drag Imani's body bag–sized duffel bag up the stairs, and for Gloria to set out a sandwich and a soft drink for my daughter. Sometime during the melee, introductions were made.

"I'm Troy." A slightly grubby hand was offered.

Imani smiled and shook it anyway. "Hello, Troy," she said.

"Do you believe in vampires?" Troy was not letting go of that idea.

"Troy . . ." Gloria sighed.

Imani glanced at me for a second. "I don't know if I do or not. Do you?"

"Yes," Troy whispered, and he would have said more except that his mother was maneuvering him back toward the stairs.

"Say good night, Troy."

"Mom. . . ." Troy wailed.

"Hi. I'm Dana Jablonski and this is my husband, Tim,"
Dana said, extending her hand. "I rent the apartment over
the coach house."

Imani's eyes dropped to the leather corset that Dana
was wearing.

"Oh, this. I almost forgot that I was wearing it! I use the
apartment to do the research for my books."

"What kind of books do you write?" Imani asked. She
loves to read.

"I write the *Maisie Beatme* mystery series. They are light
erotic mysteries," Dana said. After a pause, she added,
"You've probably never heard of them—"

"You are kidding me!" my daughter exclaimed, "I *love*
Maisie Beatme! I have every single book you've written!
My girlfriends and I pass your books around until we've
all read them! Wait until I tell Toya—"

My daughter reads about Maisie Beatme? My precious
child reads books about a riding crop–toting crime solver
who traps criminals with the spikes on her high-heeled
boots?

Where did I go wrong?

"I have them all in a box in the dorm," my daughter
said. "I want you to autograph each one. Toya will be so
jealous!"

"I would be happy to," Dana said graciously. "And, if
you're interested, my new book comes out next month.
I'll make sure that you get a copy, 'fresh off the press,' as
they say."

Imani was ecstatic.

"Thanks! What is it called?"

After titles like *Cuffs and Saucers*, I didn't think I was
ready.

"*Double Buckles, Chains and Trouble,*" was the reply.

Nope, I wasn't ready.

Later when everyone went home and everyone in the house disappeared behind closed doors, I sat on Imani's bed and helped her get settled. I just wanted to sit there and look at her.

Imani is tiny, about the size of a minute, so she doesn't take after me, with her father's reddish-brown skin, black hair, and dark eyes. She keeps her curly hair cut short and now, I noticed, she had pierced her ears again and another set of silver hoops swung back and forth. She is the most beautiful creature I've ever seen in the world. But then, I am biased.

"This is quite a place you're running here, Mom," she said, stuffing jeans into a drawer. "Talk about a melting pot! Gloria and her son, Jack Neal—I like him, Mom. Dana, she practically has a cult following; I can't believe that you didn't know that! And Dr. Rebecca Levine, I had to read her in my world religions class."

"Becca? World religion? I thought she wrote short stories."

Imani sighed and rolled her eyes.

"*Doctor* Levine, Mom," my daughter corrected me. "Becca to you, Dr. Levine to the millions of people who've read her books on religion and women. You've never heard of her?"

"I guess I lead a sheltered life," I said frowning. "I spend a fortune at bookstores. How did I miss Dr. Levine and the absentminded dominatrix series?"

Imani laughed.

"They aren't in the general fiction section, Momma," my worldly daughter informed me. "You'll find Dana's books under 'Erotica.' "

I just looked at her. We had discussed birds and bees, hadn't we?

She laughed when I asked her.

"Mom, you told me all of that stuff when I was eight, remember? Don't worry; I know what I need to know to take care of myself—"

I held up my hand to stop her from continuing.

"OK, Mom," Imani said calmly. "I'll spare you the gory details."

"Thank you," I said, somewhat relieved.

She closed the last drawer and sat down on the bed next to me. "This is an interesting room."

I followed her gaze as it took in the three nightstands, peg-leg table, and dinosaur-sized armoire, not to mention the four paintings I'd hung on the remaining wall space and a stack of unhung ones leaning against the wall. Poor Imani. Her room looked like an antique furniture shop.

"I wanted to make sure that you had enough drawer space," I said innocently.

Imani made a face.

"And you're painting again," she commented, nodding toward a colorful experiment that hung opposite her bed. I had been in a purple funk mood when I painted it.

"Do you like it?" I asked. I try not to sound too eager, but like most artists, I am desperate for compliments on my work.

Imani bit her lip, but her dimples were showing.

"Um, it's . . ." She paused as she searched for a word that wouldn't hurt my feelings. I smiled to myself. I knew it was awful. "It's bright . . . and daring."

And Gloria said it looked like blueberry yogurt that had gone bad.

"Everything is so . . . different now," Imani murmured. She looked around the room. "This place, this town, you."

"Me! I'm your same old momma," I said modestly. But I wasn't. Not even close.

"You're different, Mom. You look different; you talk

different." She pulled a corkscrew strand of my multi-colored hair. "Act different . . ." She sounded thoughtful.

I looked down at my hands.

"Some things had to change, sweetie," I said. "I wanted my life back. And if I didn't do something soon, I wouldn't have a life at all."

Imani heard that and looked at me a long time without saying anything. She had an odd expression on her face, a mixture of sadness, wonder, and something else. Anger?

"What is it?" I asked. Suddenly I felt defensive and guilty, like a fugitive. What had I stolen?

"Have you divorced him?" she asked. "Daddy, I mean."

"It was final on Wednesday." I had wanted to tell her since she stepped through the back door, but it just didn't seem right to hug her, kiss her, and say, "Imani, I'm so happy to see you, baby. By the way, I've just divorced your father," before she had a chance to set down her luggage.

"I see," she answered in a very quiet voice. Her eyes were pensive. "How did he take it? Was he mad?"

I told her as best I could about the hearing and about Ted's visit to Prestonn. I left out a lot. His comments about not paying her college tuition. His pet names for me. She smiled when I told her about Bear's and Wells's reaction to Ted. They had taken an instant liking to her. Even now, Wells had made himself at home in Imani's lap and was snoring.

"I'm supposed to see him next week," she said slowly. She sounded as if she was talking to herself. "I don't know if I should."

"Of course you should," I told her because it was the right thing to say. "He is your father." *And I can't change that even though he is a mean, violent, shape-shifting sonofabitch.* Despite his treatment of me (or because of it?) Ted had never been violent or mean to Imani. He was gentle, indulgent, patient, and just plain nice. To my knowledge, he never even spanked her when she was small. As far as I knew, Ted was an exemplary father.

My daughter looked at me with another unreadable expression; then she yawned.

"Mom, if you're OK with it."

I stood up.

"I'm OK with it and you need to go to bed. How long since you slept?"

She stretched. "Since six A.M. yesterday," she replied. Her eyelids were drooping.

"To bed, kid," I said, patting the pillow. "Come on, Wells." I reached for the snoring pug.

"No, let him stay." Imani cuddled the imperious smushed-face tyrant. "He's cute."

Pugs are a lot of things, but cute is not one of them.

"If you don't mind the snoring."

"I don't mind."

As if to say, "I told you so," Wells opened one eye, blinked it a couple of times, and turned over.

I closed the bedroom door.

Chapter Fifteen

"Momma, it looks as if you've been renovating more than this house. You're renovating yourself."

Imani's words echoed in my mind. They were true, but I hadn't thought about it in terms of renovation. That sounded too much like a construction project. But she was right. I had been renovated, inside and out. To "renovate" is to restore to a better state, to life and vigor. Yes, that's what I had been doing all right. And I was making discoveries about myself—and about the yellow house—that I could never have imagined. Both of us were turning out to be more valuable than anyone thought.

What Troy had described as looking like "cat puke" with a salmon cake–colored sky would turn out to be a nearly priceless historical treasure. A week later, Dr. Innis and a colleague and art restoration expert, Dr. Kuenning, arrived at lunchtime to examine my north dining room wall. They were still there at six o'clock when I got home from work. Dr. Innis's eyes were shining with excitement behind her horn-rimmed eyeglasses. She could barely contain herself. Dr. Kuenning was more subdued, although at one point I thought he might wet his pants. In those few hours, with a little help from Rodney, who was repairing the plasterwork on my other walls, they managed to clear away some of the old paste, wallpaper, and dirt from a section of the mural so that its true beauty and message could come through. Imani, Gloria, Troy, and Becca were already admiring their handiwork when I came in.

"I guess you won't want me to do any plasterwork on this wall, Opal," Rodney teased, giving me a smile of satisfaction as he wiped his hands on his coveralls.

"Not a chance, Rodney," I told him.

Dr. Innis told me what she and Dr. Kuenning had discovered.

"Ten years ago, we found correspondence from a Methodist minister describing a Duncanson painting of an escape by fugitives landing their boat on the Ohio side of the river, with slave catchers in pursuit on the Kentucky banks. But the correspondence trail went cold and we presumed the picture had been lost."

Dr. Kuenning chuckled. "The entire affair was taking on the aura of a myth, like looking for Atlantis or the Seven Lost Cities of Gold. We had so little to go on. The only thing we knew about the painting was its title, *Over the River*, and it was circa 1847."

"Now, of course, I know what happened," Dr. Innis said, smiling as she waved her hand over the mural. "The letters left out the most important clue. *Over the River* isn't a portable piece that you can track down at a flea market or in your great-aunt's basement. It's a mural and was part of a permanent structure."

"But if it was commissioned by an abolitionist minister, what was it doing on the walls of this house?" I asked. "I thought that I was the first person outside of the Xavier family to own the house."

Dr. Kuenning agreed.

"You are. Apparently Lorene Xavier was the driving force behind the commission. But the contact for the mural was made through the clergyman who had befriended Robert Duncanson earlier. We may never be sure what really happened."

"Piecing together a historical record is like a putting a jigsaw puzzle together with only half of the pieces. You may get part of the picture, but you'll never get all of it," Dr. Innis added.

Dr. Kuenning gently brushed away a fleck of paste. The colors emerging from the wall were muted and rich. Amazing. And I had thought it was mildew.

"I grew up here," the doctor commented. "I remember hearing my granddad say that Prestonn was a hotbed of abolitionist activity and that there were lots of 'stations' here in town." His eyes twinkled from behind his glasses. "You haven't come across any trapdoors, false walls, or secret passages, have you?"

I thought about Troy's continuing expeditions in search of buried pirate's treasure. Gloria and I smiled at each other.

"Not yet," I said. *But that's not from the lack of trying.*

We all crowded around the portion of the painting where the fugitive family had disembarked on the riverbank and turned to face their pursuers. At least, that's the way it first appeared. On closer inspection, I realized that the little woman, who held an infant in her arms, was looking toward the sky. It would be her first sunrise as a free woman.

"Miss Caroline was the last of the Xaviers," Dr. Kuenning mused.

"She was probably the only person who knew that the

mural was there," I murmured, still looking at the woman with the baby. Miss Caroline was right when she told Bette that there was a "treasure" in the house. It just wasn't the kind of treasure anyone expected.

"It's a masterpiece," Dr. Kuenning told me. "But it will need to be cleaned, restored, and appraised. Ms. Sullivan, we can help you with this if you want. In fact, it would be a privilege."

Appraised?

"You'll have to figure out what you're going to do next," Dr. Innis added. "This mural sort of transforms your home into an art museum."

My home? An art museum?

Everyone turned to look at me as if I were the goose that had laid the golden egg.

What was I going to do with that egg? All I ever wanted was a simple, quiet life.

What happened? Now I needed an appraiser and a special insurance policy and an art restoration expert and . . .

Thank God that Bette arrived to distract me from thinking about these serious propositions. She stopped by to drop off a new homeowner's welcome kit ("Lots of good coupons, hon") just as everyone was leaving. Her eyes widened with interest as I told her about the mural and its legacy. But the historic mural wasn't what had gotten her lace thong in a knot.

The tips of her tangerine-colored nails went back and forth so fast that I got dizzy looking at them.

"*You* didn't tell me that Dana Drew is Maisie Beatme!" she said sternly, her eyes blazing with the accusation.

I waved her off and acted nonchalant.

"It didn't come up," I said, shrugging my shoulders. Then I looked at her. "Who told you?"

"Never mind that. What do you mean, it didn't come up?" she screeched.

My shoulders rose in pain.

"Yikes! Bette! You don't have to shout! What's the big deal? Dana Drew is Maisie Beatme. There. I've said it. That's what the limo, the black-on-black clothes, the Cher wig, and the spike heels are all about. She dresses up as Maisie in order to make the characterization more . . . authentic," I explained as if it were the most normal thing in the world. I figured that if I kept repeating this over and over, then I might come to accept it as normal myself.

Bette was way beyond that.

"I am a Maisie fan from way back," she said, rummaging through her huge purse and pulling out a business card. "Give her this and ask her to call me."

Another Maisie fan? I was still getting over the shock of hearing that my daughter was one.

"Why, my third husband . . ." She paused and frowned. "Or was it my fourth? Anyway, we went to one of her conventions in Reno." Bette's eyes twinkled and she smiled like the cat that had swallowed the canary. "It was *unbelievable.*" Her voice was husky.

I held up one hand.

"Bette, stop right there. If you want an introduction, fine. Dana's usually here Tuesdays, Wednesdays, and Thursdays."

"Wonderful!" She stuffed the card into the pocket of my blouse. "You just give her this and tell her I'm a true fan. Why, before our divorce was final, Templeton and I tried that triple knot maneuver with the chocolate syrup—"

"Give me a break here!" I screeched. I hadn't had enough coffee this morning to listen to this!

Bette rolled her eyes at me.

"Darlin', you need to get out more."

I laughed.

Get out more? Why? When I had all of this right here on my doorstep?

I added the Duncanson mural dilemma to my "to do" list. It was a multifaceted problem. What about the cleaning and restoration of the mural? Whom would I get to do that? Dr. Innis? Dr. Kuenning? And how would that be paid for? Did I need a special security system for the house now? A guard? How much was that going to cost me? I rubbed my temples. I was starting to get a headache.

I did call my insurance broker, however, a nice gentleman fondly known as "Arnold Agent." He drove over a few evenings later in his 1970 Impala wearing his trademark fire engine red jacket. After I'd explained the situation to him, Arnold ran his hands through his coal black hair. Bless his heart. Arnold is four hundred years old if he is a day, but I have more gray hair in my head than he does in his. He has sold insurance around these parts since Jesus Christ wore short pants.

"Well, golly," Arnold said, peering at the mural through the smudged lenses of his glasses. "I don't think I've seen anything that looks like that anywhere 'cept in a museum."

"I don't doubt it," I said. "But I have a preliminary appraisal on this beauty and I need to have my homeowner's policy amended." I handed Arnold the quote that Dr. Kuenning had prepared.

Arnold's eyes popped out of his head. "That's really something!"

That was the understatement of the year. The mural was worth nearly as much as the house.

Arnold put on his best "I'll have to call this in" expression.

"I'll have to talk to Underwriting about this," he said. "We may need to have a meeting."

"Of course," I told him. I could only imagine what Underwriting was going to say, and it wouldn't be, "Golly!"

As I went inside, the telephone rang. I stopped for a moment and waited. Gloria and Troy were shopping for furnishings for their new place, Becca was working upstairs, but she used her cell phone, and Imani had gone shopping. The phone was probably not for any of them anyway. Ted had started calling again. Calling and hanging up. Calling and cursing at me. Calling at three in the morning. Caller ID was a wonderful thing, except that it didn't always work.

I took a deep breath and picked up the receiver.

"Opal? Opal, it's me, Beni Douglas."

I hadn't seen Beni since her parents took her to Illinois after she got out of the hospital.

"Beni, how are you? You OK?"

The voice that came over the telephone was so small, so young.

"I'm fine. I'm only in town for a minute. My father brought me over to pack up my stuff. I'm moving back to Illinois. I just wanted to thank you for helping me a-and letting me stay awhile."

The snap and enthusiasm of the old Beni was gone and that made me sad. I hoped that P-Bo hadn't robbed her of it forever.

I hated to hear her say that she was giving up on the theater program that she enjoyed so much, leaving all of her friends and moving away. But, as she explained it, the experience with P-Bo had left so many bad memories that she needed to make a fresh start.

"I don't want to see anything that reminds me of him," she told me. "I don't want to see anyone who remembers . . . what I went through. I want everything new."

I wished her luck. But as I walked out onto the porch I thought about what she said and how subdued and quiet she had sounded and wondered. For women like Beni, Gloria, LaDonna, and me, can life, or anything else for that matter, ever be "new" again? Different, yes. But new?

I heard the back door slam. I put my pen down and took off my glasses.

"Mom? Mom, where are you?"

"Out here!" I yelled back. "On the front porch!"

The screen door opened behind me.

"This house is so big," Imani commented. "You need to get an intercom system or walkie-talkies or something." She flopped onto one of the chairs and reached over to stroke CW, who didn't move.

"Is it alive?" she asked facetiously.

"Oh, yes," I said, grinning. "She just doesn't let anyone interrupt her siesta, that's all."

"I see," Imani replied, still stroking the cat.

"What did you buy?" I asked, snuggling into the cushions.

Imani shrugged her shoulders. "Two sets of sheets; the ones I have got those little beady things on them. I picked up some towels and another frying pan. Somebody walked off with the other one."

I remembered those days. I am still looking for the felon who stole my Sly and the Family Stone album.

"Did you stop at the designer discount store I told you about? The one off the interstate?"

Imani nodded. "Yes, I did. I picked up two pairs of jeans and a nice shirt. Where'd you find that place?"

I smiled triumphantly. "I'm not telling you. You think your momma's out of touch and doesn't know what's up. I have my sources for stylish shopping bargains."

Imani chuckled. "OK, Mom," she said.

I raised my eyebrows. "I'll have you know that I bought

a pair of Fred jeans there for twenty-nine fifty," I said
smugly, referring to a brand of jeans made from the same
denim as Levi's but costing five times as much at retail
price. "And they fit, too," I added proudly.

"I guess I'll have to start getting up earlier so that I can
keep up with you."

"Believe that," I testified. I closed my eyes against
the bright red sun and leaned my head back against the
cushion.

"I saw Dad," Imani said abruptly. "He took me to dinner."

I opened my eyes and looked at her. Then I reached for
my iced tea glass and almost dropped it. Good thing I'd
grabbed an el-cheapo plastic tumbler.

It didn't make me happy to realize that the mention of
Ted whether by name or by the title Dad still had an effect on me.

"Oh," was all I managed to say.

"Mom, he's a real asshole," Imani said without emotion.

Of course, I knew that Ted was an asshole, but it was a
revelation hearing it from Imani. She was usually ambiva-
lent in her feelings about her father. But there was no am-
bivalence in what she just said.

"Imani, he is still your father, asshole or not." Not the
most adult thing to say to your daughter about her father.
But it was all that I could think of.

"Whatever. I mean, he takes me to dinner and says he
wants to hear about what I'm doing. Then, he let me go on
and on about India and Bombay and Delhi and wanted to
hear about Kashmir. But that's not what he really wanted
to talk about. He started asking me a lot of questions
about you, what you are doing, where you go, if you're
seeing someone." At this, Imani stopped and looked at me.
Her pretty features had settled into a serious and angry
expression.

"About me," I said, thinking aloud.

"Yes, about you," Imani repeated. "And then the dinner went to hell because Dad started on a rant. He went on and on about all this money you had taken from him. *Robbed* was the word he used. And how you never earned a damn penny in all the years that you were married. And that now he was going to have to sell the house and work more hours and that was your fault for being . . ." Imani sniffed and looked away. "Momma, he called you a lazy, stupid bitch." She bit her lip.

If I could have gotten my hands on Ted at this moment, I probably would have choked him to death. The thought gave me a lot of satisfaction.

In the divorce from Ted, I promised myself that I would not trash his sorry ass in front of his daughter. I figured because he was really a lowlife bottom dweller I might get a bid for sainthood if I did that. I wouldn't call him a violent, mean, drunk son of a bitch (which was actually true, because his mother, God rest her soul, was a bitch). I wouldn't talk about him beating me up; that was between him and me. And I would try, even if it meant biting a hole in my tongue, not to resort to name-calling or try to come between him and Imani.

Some wounds are self-inflicted. Ted was destroying his relationship with his daughter on his own.

Imani wasn't finished.

"Then he—he said that I didn't need all that expensive university education. That . . . I was just like you, trying . . . to be something I'm not. He said that the court has ordered him to help pay for my college, but that he'll be damned if he does it. He says that if you want me to go, you can pay for it."

She stopped for a moment and looked at me. There was so much pain in her dark eyes.

"Mom, I'm not a leech. I'm willing to take on another job to pay for school."

I closed my eyes. I tried to call on my Baptist Sunday school upbringing to get me through this. I tried to think of a Psalm that would calm me down. I remembered lessons from the Scriptures. But turning the other cheek didn't work for me this evening.

She was angry when she spoke again.

"Why didn't you divorce him years ago? Why did you stick around and let him treat you like that?"

The accusation stung and kicked the air out of my lungs. My mouth was open, but nothing came out.

"Momma, I don't understand you!"

My first reaction was to lash out at her and put her squarely back in her place as my daughter. Where was the respect?

"*I don't understand you!*" What was she talking about?

"*You* don't understand me?" I snapped back at her. I could feel my face splitting open in anger, my eyes bulging. My skin felt as if it were stretched drum-tight over my cheekbones. "What are you talking about? You don't even *know* me!"

I sent the words out like knives in the soft, unseasonably cool evening air. And Imani, whose dark eyes were flashing with anger, had opened her mouth to send back a sharp retort. She changed her mind. Instead she sat there on the edge of the settee, her hand resting on the cushion where the cat had been. CW had long ago given up on taking a quiet evening snooze and vacated the porch.

"No, I don't know you at all. You were always quiet and . . . and sad when I was little. My pretty, quiet momma, I called you. You painted in the dark and in secret. 'Don't tell Daddy, OK?' "

I took a breath and closed my eyes. I had sent these

memories deep inside. I had hoped that my child, only four or five years old then, would have forgotten. I was wrong.

"You were a good momma, but you were never really there. You were like a ghost. You gave me what I needed, fed me, took me to school, helped me with homework, but . . ." Imani paused and looked down at her feet. "But, Momma, I never knew what you were. *Who* you were. Daddy did that to you, didn't he?"

The easy answer would have been yes, it was all Ted's fault. But I don't believe in easy answers anymore. Nothing is black-and-white, not even newspapers.

"Why didn't you fight back, Momma?"

Why didn't I? My retaliation had been retreat. Withdrawal. Survival.

"How do I say this?" I fidgeted. Squirmed in my seat, scratched my head, and grabbed up Wells, who was strolling by. When I'm nervous, I can't keep still. I turn myself into a ball of energy. "I buried myself, Imani. Sent my personality, my dreams, my self into a cave, put her on cold storage. I kept quiet to survive. Until I thought it would be safe to bring me out." I paused. "Only it was never safe. And, for a long time, I—I was afraid to walk out of the door and leave. Your dad . . . threatened to take you away from me. He threatened to have me locked up for being mentally unbalanced. He . . . I . . . ."

I didn't want to make excuses. And I didn't want to tell it all; no daughter should hear the things I could have said. Obviously, Imani had absorbed enough in her eighteen years living with me and her father.

"He said that he would kill you, didn't he?" Imani said quietly.

I looked at her and thought about my answer. *No, Imani. He said that he would kill you.*

"Yes, he did," I said aloud.

She looked away. I decided to move in a different direction. Something that I had been doing a lot of these past months. Something the "new" Opal was prone to do. I stood up and extended my hand to my daughter.

"Hello," I said. "I'm your mother, Opal Sullivan. I don't think we've been introduced. Let me tell you something about myself. I like to paint. Very badly, so everyone tells me. I love to eat, so I'm taking Italian cooking lessons. I like jazz, the color blue, roses (but I have a purple thumb), and buttered popcorn with lots of salt on it."

Imani took my hand and gave me a huge hug.

"I'm Imani, your daughter," she said, smiling. "And I'm really proud of you, Mom."

I smiled and gave her a long hug. She was proud of me. That alone was worth millions.

"I love you, Mommy, a bunch," murmured my daughter.

"I love you, too, Imani. A bunch."

Chapter Sixteen

"You're just using me for my body."

These words came from Jack, whose face was hidden behind a tower of boxes. We were thumping down the back stairs to the kitchen, where I was moving my studio.

"I *am* using you for your body; now quit whining. Will you set those boxes over there in the corner?"

I turned my attention back to the easel that I had set up. *Yes. Absolutely. Just about perfect.* I had completely rearranged the kitchen so that I would have enough room for my art studio. After trying the third floor (ceilings too low), the second-floor sleeping porch (cluttered because of the furniture that didn't fit up the third-floor stairwell), Imani's room (cluttered because of the furniture that didn't fit up the third-floor stairwell *and* not enough natural light), the back parlor (too small), and the dining room (too large), I was disappointed that I couldn't find a decent painting space in such a large house. Following the dining room fiasco, I was ready to give up and paint in the toolshed. That night, when I went upstairs to bed, I left my sketch pad on the kitchen table. In the morning, when

I came down to make coffee, I noticed it lying there. The sunlight filled the room and cast a warm golden glow on the paper. I stepped back and looked around the room. It was as if I was seeing at it for the first time. The kitchen faces north, with windows on both the east and west sides, and it gets great natural light at all times of day.

Of course! I thought. *Why not? Great light, plenty of room, lots of storage space in the pantry.* I made up my mind right then.

That evening, Jack came over to pick me up for our Italian cooking class and ended up helping me take my painting supplies downstairs.

"What kind of nut uses a kitchen as an art studio?" Jack exclaimed, shaking his head. I handed him a box of pastels and pointed to their destination. He groaned. "Opal, this is strange."

"I don't see anything wrong with it. The room is empty eighty percent of the time. I've set up my stuff in one area, away from the cooking, cutting, cleaning, and eating. The light is perfect. You know what's the matter with you? You don't have any imagination."

Jack gave me a baleful look. "You're getting to be a little peculiar, you know that?"

I smiled at him and started unpacking my pads and reference books. "You're the one who said it: 'River people are different.' "

Dana floated through looking for duct tape. Since we all knew what she was doing (except for Troy, who still believed that she was a vampire), she had decided to dispense with some of the more flamboyant trappings of Maisie Beatme unless she was out in public. Without the Morticia Adams wig and thigh-high boots, she looked like any other suburban mom wearing a latex minidress and Tweety Bird house slippers. She approved of my new studio location and promised to buy me another roll of duct tape.

"I keep using it up," she said. I didn't even ask. "Say, Opal," Dana added as she floated back through the dining room. "You really ought to let me show you how to rag roll this wall. I think that would be a great decorative touch. Plus, you could add a paisley border at the top."

"Get out of here, Martha Stewart," I growled. Dana will not be happy until I let her redo the dining room, mural and all, in a neo-modern Early American design.

"Just trying to help!" she yelled back.

Gloria called down the stairs.

"Opal? Is Troy down there?"

"Nope!" I yelled back. "Haven't seen him!"

"Where did that boy get to?" I heard Gloria mutter as she moved back down the hall.

Jack helped himself to a soda.

"His bike is around back, so he's got to be here somewhere."

"Gloria!" I yelled upstairs. "He's probably outside somewhere; do you want me to send him in?"

"Yeah. I need some help with the packing!"

"OK!" I yelled back. Imani was right about needing walkie-talkies.

I stepped back from the easel that Jack had set up. My newest piece (I was calling it *Enchanted Indigo*) was in progress. It was a rich mélange of navy, deep purples, and merlots. I was having a blast experimenting. So far, it was my favorite painting. But no one else shared my good opinion.

Imani made a face and then giggled.

"Mom, it's really awful."

Becca shook her head and refused to comment.

Gloria laughed until her eyes watered.

Fortunately, Jack and I had reached the point in our soon-to-be-more-than friendship where he felt that he could be completely honest and open in voicing his opinions of my artistic endeavors.

"Opal," he said, shaking his head. His expression was stern. "It looks like shit."

So what? I'm only painting for fun. I can take the honesty.

"I still like it," I said primly.

Jack shook his head.

"River people . . . ," he mumbled.

Then I remembered something.

"Oh, hold this," I pushed a box of painting supplies into Jack's arms and grabbed a towel. "Speaking of rivers, the washer has been acting up lately. Getting stuck on the rinse cycle." I sped to the basement door and opened it. "I'll be back. I think I still hear it running. I don't want a river in the basement."

Jack headed out the back door.

"Go ahead; I'll see if I can track down Troy."

This time I was lucky. The rinse cycle had finished up properly. I was setting the dryer when I heard a rustling behind the washer. My hand froze on the dial. The rustling started again. The wall behind the washer was boarded up, but that was definitely where the sound was coming from. And it wasn't the rustling of a little field mouse or a squirrel. It was big rustling. I was so scared my jaw froze. All I could think about was those furry five-legged things that I'd seen down here when Bette first showed me the house. I leaned over the top of the washer and looked down.

"Boo!" Troy jumped out at me. If I hadn't been so glad to see him, I would have wrung his neck.

"What the . . ." I glared at the little monster and caught him by the ear. "Don't you ever do that to me again! What were you doing back there?" I did give him a good shake.

It was lost on Troy, though. He grinned like Howdy Doody and wouldn't stop talking.

"Playing in the tunnel with Wells. I play in there all the time. But Wells ran off. I was just about to look for him when you came down." Troy was breathing hard with the excitement of his fright tactic. "You were scared, weren't you?" he asked, thrilled to death.

"Your mom is looking for you—what tunnel?" It just dawned on me what Troy had said.

"The tunnel, back there." He slipped behind the washer and pulled open the wooden panel that I had thought was nailed and secure. It wasn't. It had hinges and swung open like a door, but only far enough to let Troy in.

Together we scooted the washing machine over, and I peeked inside. Troy accommodated me by switching on his flashlight.

"It gets kinda dark sometimes," he said. "So I need a flashlight when I dig for the treasure."

It *was* a tunnel.

I couldn't believe it. It was about five feet wide and nearly that tall, so I had to scrunch down and practically walk on my knees. The floor was earthen, but the sides were stone. It was damp and dank but empty, no debris, no litter or evidence that anyone had used it recently. It was also quiet, although at one point I thought I could hear street noises.

Troy had found the tunnel that was used on the Underground Railroad. The yellow house really was a station. Amazing. Now I not only had a historic mural, I had a historic landmark. And I thought I was only buying a fixer-upper. It just goes to show you how wrong you can be.

We reached a dead end and there was still no evidence of Wells. No barking, no dog poop, nothing. Where could he have gone? Just as we decided to go back I heard some noise, rustling, scratching, and then the sound of

rusty hinges. We looked up. A trapdoor that neither Troy
nor I had seen creaked open above our heads.

Looking down on us was Wells, who was barking and
jumping around. Standing next to him was the Confederate, gray cap and all.

"Howdy do! I was wonderin' how long it'd take you to
find my little secret. I guess this little piece of dog is yours
then? Hold on a minute; I'll get the ladder."

The Confederate settled both me and Troy in lawn
chairs that had seen better days and offered us orange sodas. He apologized to me. Said his great-grandnephew
hadn't gotten back from the carryout with the beer yet.

"Yessiree, that tunnel there starts in Caroline's basement and runs all the way t'here!" He pointed to the ram-
shackle shed that covered the trapdoor that we had
climbed through.

"Back before the war, the Xavier brothers brought colored slaves up from Tennessee and from around these
parts, in the false bottom of a wagon. Let 'em off after dark
at the house and they hid in the tunnel. When the coast
was clear, my granddaddy fetched 'em up and hauled 'em
over to Swanson's Landing. A colored minister that he
knew carried them across the river." The Confederate spit
out a plug of tobacco the size of Troy's head. "Me and
Caroline used to play hide-'n'-seek in that tunnel when
we were kids. She'd visit me; I'd visit her." He took off his
hat at the mention of her name.

"We grew up together," he continued, his voice somber.
"I woulda courted her, but her daddy didn't like me. But
she never married, and neither did I. So when her daddy
died, we just kept on being friends." He looked down for
a moment. "Till she moved on."

I glanced up at the Stars and Bars flapping in the breeze.
The old man caught my look and gave me a wily grin.

"Fooled ya, didn't I? My grandpappy did the same thing. Flew that flag and hauled as many colored folks as he could down to the landing to send them to Ohio. Didn't believe in slavery. He grew up poor as a skunk in Wales, didn't have nothing. Said if he could work his own land and make do by hiring help and letting another man's family eat, why couldn't them slave owners? His folks back in Wales weren't more'n slaves themselves."

Troy couldn't sit still. I could tell that he would like nothing better than to get back into the tunnel.

"Is there any buried pirate's treasure in there?" he asked hopefully.

" 'Fraid not, son," the old relic replied with a shake of his head. "Might be some down by the landing, though. That's where the bootleggers loaded up."

Bootleggers?

I stood up quickly. It was time to go.

Troy was enthralled.

"What's a bootlegger?"

"Troy, let's go," I reached for his hand. "Thank you for helping us, Mr.—"

"Jones," the Confederate volunteered. He tipped his gray cap. "My pleasure, ma'am." He tapped Troy on his head. "Come back sometime, boy. And I'll tell you about them bootleggers and the revenuers and—"

"Thanks so much, Mr. Jones. Troy, come on. Your mother is looking for you. She's probably wondering what happened to us."

Troy's face scrunched into a frown as he grabbed Wells's leash.

"I want to hear about the bootleggers. What's a revenuer, Opal?"

Gloria and Jack were standing in the front yard when Troy and I returned. Gloria could not believe our story.

"I didn't know what to think! First Troy disappears; then you disappear. And now you tell me there's a tunnel in the basement and buried treasure—"

"No, Mom," Troy interrupted. "Bootleggers," he said, pronouncing the word carefully. "And revenuers." This was added with solemn authority.

Gloria coughed and took Troy by the shoulders.

"Enough of this. Your grandma is picking us up in ten minutes and you haven't packed up the rest of your stuff. Get going."

"Mom, what's a bootlegger?"

Gloria gave Jack and me a look that said, *Help me!* as she escorted her son to the house.

Jack and I shook our heads and made our escape.

"Uh-uh, I'm not in this, Gloria," I said, retreating quickly. "You're on your own."

There are just some things that parents have to do for themselves.

Gloria and Troy were moving at the end of August and I would miss them. Gloria had not only helped my garden grow, but she had given me the inspiration to follow my passion, too. Even if everybody said my paintings looked like digestive upsets. And despite my allergic reactions to children, Troy had helped distract me from my problems. It was hard to worry about Ted when you were yelling at Troy or wiping off his fingerprints from freshly painted woodwork or picking up the trail of towels that he had left in the hall. Not to mention his many capers, adventures, and discoveries. I had to set my fear aside while I climbed a tree. Even Ted's threats faded in importance for a moment in the light of one of Troy's bizarre vampire-hunting treks. Troy reminded me that you need a little nonsense in your life to keep from going completely crazy.

Beni's dramas took me out of myself in a different way. She pushed me to open my mouth and give advice, forced me to face the worst of these kinds of situations from the outside looking in. It is hard enough to live this nightmare. Watching it visited on someone else, especially someone as young as Beni, is like having ice water thrown on your head. Beni's run-ins with P-Bo opened a window on my own circumstances—and made me realize how critical it was to live my own advice. You have to end it. You have to leave. You can't go back. And it won't be easy.

But there aren't any tidy endings.

Wal-Mart has a huge parking lot. It was a hot day and I was in a hurry. I was planning something selfish, decadent, and sinful. The house would be empty tonight. Gloria was working late and Troy was at a sleepover. Becca was in Michigan for a long weekend, it wasn't one of Dana's regular days, and Imani was visiting high school buddies in our old hometown. Bette had a new "beau." Jack was out of town on business. I was planning a "spa" night for myself: a self-inflicted manicure and pedicure, shampoo and air dry, shave whatever needed shaving, and soak in the tub night. And there was a book I had been dying to read. Add to that hot buttered popcorn, sweetened iced tea, and I was going to be in heaven.

I was distracted with my evening's plans and just plain not paying attention when I pulled into what I thought was a lucky parking space. I didn't do my usual drive-around that night. I was only running in to pick up a few things, right? It would take only ten minutes.

Ten minutes is long enough for a lot of things: to listen

to a couple of songs on a CD, brush your teeth, or tap out a telephone number and have a brief conversation. It was more than long enough for Ted, who had followed me from work, to park his car in the space in front of mine.

I came out of the store with my arms full of bags and my head full of how much I was going to relax when I got home. I wasn't paying attention. I barely noticed what should have been the familiar charcoal-colored sedan parked in front of my Ford. I popped my trunk and unloaded my packages.

"Your lover boy's not around to help with those?"

I slammed the trunk closed and saw him standing alongside my car. His body was tensed and, even though he was smiling, his eyes held the malevolent glint that usually meant that I was about to be assaulted. I pulled my keys from my purse and headed toward my door.

In the old days, the glint in Ted's eye was enough to freeze me in my tracks. It turned my blood cold and left me shaking. But not today.

Today, I was angry with myself for not being watchful. I was aggravated that I hadn't recognized his car and walked away. I scolded myself for letting my guard down. But not once was I afraid. He moved quickly around the car and I opened the door.

"I bet you're going to call the police, aren't you? Tell them I've violated that goddamn restraining order. Well, I'll tell you something, bitch: It's not worth the paper it's printed on. I can get to you whenever I want and however I want. I don't care how far you move away. I'll kick your ass." He leaned closer, but I pushed the car door between us. He glared at me. I just looked at him.

"I don't care about your lover boy, either. I'll kick his ass, too—"

"Ted, you know what? I just don't give a shit," I yelled back at him. "About you. About your threats. None of it."

"I'm tired of this," he shot back. "Don't you know I can kill you?"

"Then just do it, Ted!" I heard myself say. "Just make sure that you don't miss."

He grabbed me by the arm and twisted it hard. Just like the old days. But he had grabbed the wrong arm. I had my purse in my other hand and took a swing. It caught him clean on the side of his face.

The blow surprised him and he let me go and fell against the car next to mine, grimacing with pain. I took the opportunity to get into my car, lock the door, and start the engine.

He was still leaning against the car when I pulled out of the parking space.

"Don't you know I can kill you?" he had said.

Yes, I know it. But as bad as it sounds, as scary as it is, I can't let the reality of his hatred be the centerpiece of my life. I cannot live every day thinking about the fact that Ted can kill me today. Because the truth is, he can kill me today, tomorrow, next week, or next year. But he didn't kill me that day at the Wal-Mart. And he hasn't killed me so far.

He sent me roses on my birthday. And cut off all the blooms. He caught Ice Tray unawares and nipped off the tip of her tail, but she got away before he did any more damage and she's fine, thank God. I've had my tires slit at work, and every once in a while he'll get drunk and call at three in the morning. I have my restraining order renewed every three months. Judge Perry has been very accommodating. Ted even sent out Animal Control on me because Bear ran him off.

"Good evening, ma'am," the officer had said politely. "I'm sorry to bother you, but we've had a report of a vicious and uncontrolled dog on your property."

I was sitting on the porch, as usual. I gestured toward the two canines snoozing at the other end of the porch. "I don't know what to tell you. Those are my two dogs. And, as you can see, they are anything but vicious."

The man walked over to the furry doormats. Bear, who was lying in his usual spot, directly in front of the door, looked like a shag rug. Oblivious to the officer's presence, he snored loudly. Wells had taken over the welcome mat. He opened his eyes, gave an imperious sniff, and went back to his nap.

The Animal Control officer went away. Said he must have been given the wrong address.

And on what would have been our twenty-third wedding anniversary, Ted sent me a card and drove by the house. "Just to let you know I'm not going away," the card read.

I have warned Jack that getting involved with me means getting involved with Ted.

"You can bow out now if you want," I told him. "I won't think any less of you."

He gave me a sly smile and pulled me into his arms.

"Don't think you can get rid of me that easily. I can stand it if you can."

And as for me, I have decided to put Ted in his proper place. It's like having a chronic health condition that you control with medication. The condition will always be there and you take your pill, but you can't make a life around it. You can't be defined as a person because of it. You can't limit your dreams because of it.

You accept it and go on. Life is too short to do otherwise.

"Mom, you're a lot different than I thought you'd be,"

Imani told me as we packed up her suitcases before she left for school.

I stopped in the middle of what I was doing.

"What do you mean, 'different'?" I asked, surprised.

"The momma that I knew was quiet and scared all the time. You hardly ever said two words without looking to see what Dad would say or do. You didn't paint. You didn't go anywhere. You didn't even talk on the phone unless you were talking to Grandmother or Grandpa."

I stood quietly listening. The description sounded like someone I'd known in high school but barely remembered.

"Now . . ." Imani opened her arms.

"Now?" I repeated.

She beamed at me.

"Now, you live in this huge house that creaks. You paint. You take in boarders. Boarders! People who need help, people who don't, interesting people either way. You have Jack. . . ."

Yes. I have Jack.

"You take . . . cooking lessons! And Spanish lessons! You're in a yoga class for God's sake! Momma, you're turning into a hippie!"

I sniffed.

"I *was* a hippie before I had you and had to be respectable."

"You go to church again and see your friends again. Momma, you're a lot different from the woman I grew up with."

I sighed.

"Better than she was, I hope."

Imani shook her head.

"She wasn't bad, but . . . you're not afraid anymore, are you?"

This time it was my turn to smile.

"Nope. The things that scare me in this life are a whole lot different than they used to be."

"And Dad's not one of them," Imani concluded.

"No. Your dad is not one of them."

"You are sitting under the shade of your own tree," my daughter said, pulling the zipper around the side of her suitcase.

"The shade of what?"

"It's a line from a poem. I heard it in a monastery that we visited. It was written a zillion years ago by a Buddhist nun."

I was impressed. I didn't know there were Buddhist nuns. When I said so, Imani shrugged and gave me an impish grin.

"Part of that expensive college education that you're paying for," she said.

"It's worth every penny," I said. "Now, let me hear the poem."

> " 'At last I am a woman free!
> No more tied to the kitchen,
> Stained amid the stained pots,
> No more bound to the husband
> Who thought me less
> Than the shade he wove with his hands.
> No more anger, no more hunger
> I sit now in the shade of my own tree.
> Meditating thus, I am happy, I am serene.' "

About the Author

Sheila Williams was born and raised in Columbus, Ohio. She attended Ohio Wesleyan University and is a graduate of the University of Louisville. Her most recent book was *Dancing on the Edge of the Roof*. Sheila lives with her family in Newport, Kentucky, and is working on her next book.

Printed in the United States
by Baker & Taylor Publisher Services